THE NEIGHBORHOOD

THE NEIGHBORHOOD

ANTHONY PELLICANO

The Neighborhood is a work of fiction. Names, characters, places, and incidents are the product of the author's imagination or are used fictitiously. Any resemblance to actual events, locales, or persons, living or dead, is entirely coincidental.

Published in the United States by Phoenix Books, Inc.

For licensing information, please contact:

Phoenix Books, Inc.
11201 N. Tatum Blvd, Suite 300
Phoenix, AZ 85028
info@pbiaudio.com

ISBN: 978-1-59777-900-5 (Audiobook)
ISBN: 978-1-59777-901-2 (Paperback)
ISBN: 978-1-59777-902-9 (Ebook)

For My Loving Brother,
Ron Meyer,
My Truest and Most Loyal Friend

ACKNOWLEDGEMENTS

I would like to acknowledge and most graciously thank Julie Opperman and Robert Newlen without whom this book would have never existed. Without their undying guidance, expertise, and sincere and positive faith in my abilities, *The Neighborhood* would have remained in my mind and would never have been written.

THE NEIGHBORHOOD

1

THE BOYS OF TAYLOR STREET

It's the summer of 1960—a hot, humid day—and a group of young men are gathered in front of a small restaurant on the west side of Chicago. All the guys are dressed pretty much the same: dark pants, black shoes, and black socks. Some wear wife-beater T-shirts, known as "Italian Ts." Without exception, their pants are pulled high up to their waists, sometimes even with suspenders, for the gangster look. They do not wear white socks *ever*, except in gym class at the high school, but sometimes not even then.

The momentary focus of the wannabe gangsters is on a light pole where the corpse of a blond, long-haired, bearded man hangs by his right ankle at the end of a long rope. His pants are urine soaked, and a swarm of flies circle his body.

This motorcycle gang member was hung up there, because he sexually molested a fifteen-year-old girl—one from the Neighborhood—who foolishly accepted a ride on his bike. The police won't take him down, nor will anybody else until they get the word, so his body will hang there for a day or two. Late one night, some members of the fire department will take him down, and he will go to the morgue. The Neighborhood has its own law, and its message has been dramatically delivered.

Out on the streets, the fire hydrants have been wrenched open, and gallons of water pour out of the open spigots. Wooden boards have been fastened against the openings, so that huge fountains of water spray upward and outward. The local children frolic in the water. When reluctant firemen eventually come to shut off the hydrants, the Neighborhood will patiently wait for them to leave, then immediately open them back up again. This means free car washes for those who wish to drive through the spray, but mostly fun for the street kids who may never see a swimming pool. Along pot-holed streets, wading pools are everywhere for kids to splash in. This is their very own theme park.

The "guys" are gathered on the patio of a restaurant called "The Patio," owned by Johnny "The Bug" Varenzano, boss of the Taylor Street crew. Across from The Patio, slightly to the east, is the single block of Garibaldi Street. It's named in honor of the Italian General Giuseppe Garibaldi, called the "Father of the Fatherland" for uniting Italy in the mid-1800s—the first time since the fall of the Roman Empire. Chicago's "Little Italy" was already united.

One of the young men in the group is seventeen-year-old Vincent Joseph Scalise, an up-and-comer and wannabe contender. Wiry and tough, he has dark curly hair, stands five foot ten, and is 135 pounds soaking wet. His gait is always measured as if he anticipates an interruption—his alert hazel eyes miss nothing around him, always prepared for any eventuality. His demeanor is intense. A distant relative to one of the Valentine's Day massacre shooters, he is, for the most part, a loner. Besides his mother, he trusts only one person, his best childhood friend, Paulie Andriano.

At The Patio, the conversations vary, but mostly the guys talk about how to earn—the term for making a buck. They don't talk sports, unless it relates to making money, in whatever way possible. They never talk about movies, either. No one mentions the biker hanging from the light pole. The Neighborhood kids playing around the hydrant pay little attention to the upside-down guy—they also understand the message or were told as much by their parents.

The Neighborhood is one of the Little Italy areas of Chicago. It is a fourteen-block long area, centralized around the main drag, Taylor Street, surrounded by other ethnic areas, ghettos, and the Chicago business district known as "The Loop."

The Neighborhood has spawned many Organized Crime leaders and soldiers in Chicago's mafia contingent—the "Outfit," as it's known locally. Part of the First Ward, the Neighborhood is the powerhouse of the ruling political machine in Chicago, where the Outfit and the politicians have an understanding that dates back to the Capone era. The Outfit is as strong and influential as ever. So the police, for the most part, leave Neighborhood residents alone—who cares what they do for a living? Live and let live, right? But that's only for the locals. For outsiders, it's another story.

One of the Outfit's hangouts is St. Anthony's Social Club, which is "members only," located on Taylor Street across from the Italian beef stand called Al's for non-locals and Baba's by Neighborhood residents. It's short for Ali Baba from *Ali Baba and the Forty Thieves.*

That's because Baba's also serves forty thieves if not more—it's the depository and fence for the Neighborhood. Every day you can go in the back and sell or buy stolen items—shoes, suits, dresses, toasters, or whatever you want—then go up front and buy an Italian beef or sausage sandwich. That is, every day but Fridays, when no meat is served in deference to the Catholic Church—only peppers and egg sandwiches.

Once you're in the Neighborhood, there's no crime. That is to say that there are no robberies, no muggings, no vandalism, and no women get harassed—none of those everyday crimes that plague most of Chicago. Everyone in the Neighborhood enjoys these circumstances and understands the rules. If a conflict arises between residents, there is a "sit down" where decisions are obeyed without question. The dynamics of the Neighborhood are instilled in everyone, especially the youth. It is a way of life that becomes deeply ingrained.

There are no calls to the police. Not here. Everything is handled locally—like the biker. In fact, except for the locals who actually serve on the police force, cops are rarely seen in the Neighborhood—except to pick up their envelopes at the Sunday dice game. It's the biggest dice game in the country and is always held outdoors next to the bocce courts.

But Vincent, bored, has had enough chitchat for one afternoon. "I'll catch you guys later. I'm going to meet Paulie," he says.

"Why do you hang with that guy?" asks loudmouth Sonny Caruso. "He wants to be a fucking FBI agent, for Christ's sake. You will never be able to trust him, Vincent, believe me."

Vincent rolls his eyes and shakes his head in annoyance. They all watch as Vincent walks down Taylor Street toward Tony's grocery store.

"One of these days Paulie's going to turn on him," Sonny says.

The others, except for Angelo Ragatta and Mikey Solanotti—two of Vincent's closest buddies and crime partners—slowly nod their heads in agreement.

Vincent Scalise is a tough kid who gets into trouble from time to time, but his best friend does not. Paul Anthony Andriano is an anomaly in the Neighborhood. The guys call him "Paulie the G," as in G-Man, but that does not bother Paulie—he's flattered, even. As strait-laced as they come, Paulie's sole ambition is to become an FBI agent. He even tried sporting a crew cut for a time, because that's how G-Men wear their hair—well, at least on the TV shows.

But no one harasses Paulie about his career goals, mostly because of his grandfather, Antonio "Tuff Tony" Andriano, the owner of the local grocery store.

Vincent walks into the store and sees Paulie's mother, Catarina, sitting by the cash register. Everyone in the Neighborhood loves "Rina." For Vincent, Rina is like a second mother. He greets her with a kiss on the cheek while she asks about his mother, as she always does.

"Where's the boy wonder?" he asks Rina.

"Out back unloading a truck, honey."

Catarina Andriano is a quiet, stately woman. Although quite naturally beautiful, she shies away from attention, dresses modestly, and wears almost no makeup. She does not need to. She rarely wears down her beautiful, long, light brown hair. It's almost always in a ponytail or pinned up. Her kind, hazel eyes reflect an underlying sadness. Like most Catholic girls—including Vincent's mother, Teresa—Catarina was spoon fed guilt.

Teresa Scalise and Rina were Neighborhood girls who shared an almost identical ordeal, even if they did have two different and complex personalities. They attended Catholic school together but never really got close. Their friends traveled in very different social circles.

Like Paulie, Vincent was raised by a single mother. Teresa is a tough, dominating, stern woman for the most part, at least outwardly. Constantly on the move, she knows everything that goes on in the Neighborhood and functions as the listening post for the women, and very often, some of the men. But under that veneer of hardness is a warm and kind heart, one that is rarely seen except by those she respects and cares about, especially her son, Vincent. Only eighteen years older than her son, Teresa—"Teri"—is more like Vincent's trusted big sister than his mother.

Like so many other girls in the Neighborhood, Teri dropped out of high school to attend beauty school. She still works at the local beauty salon. Her bleached, blonde hair is always styled and her makeup heavy.

She harbors many resentments.

Like Catarina, "Teri" never married. They both got pregnant about one month apart. Paulie was born two weeks after Vincent. That was the bond the two women had, and they were always consoling each other after their sons were born. Neither of them asked each other about who the father was—it just wasn't done. They shared the shame of being pregnant teenagers in silence. Their sons became best friends, more like brothers.

Teri once was a very beautiful young woman, standing five foot one with a busty hourglass shape. Her life changed when she turned seventeen. When Vincent's father left, she thought her life had ended. After Vincent's birth, she became hardened, to cope as best she could.

Teri told her son that his father disappeared shortly before Vincent's birth, without ever knowing of Vincent's existence, and had not been heard from since. Although Vincent knows his father's name, the rest remains a mystery, the details of which Teri never shares with him. He has learned to accept this, because his mother is as secretive as they come. He only knows that his father's entire family resides in Sicily, and Vincent hopes to meet them one day. They send presents and write from time to time, but they speak no English.

As for Rina, she has never spoken of Paulie's father to anyone. Tuff Tony's wife—Rina's mother—Angela, died shortly before Paulie's birth. Angela was a loving mother who embraced and supported her daughter no matter what the circumstance. She did all she could to stay alive long enough to see her grandchild but died after a long and painful fight with ovarian cancer the week before his birth. Catarina thought to call Paulie "Angelo" after her mother, but Tuff Tony rejected the idea. So, they called him Paul. He looked to his grandfather—whose middle name was Paolo—as his dad since he was a small boy, so "Paul" fit. Tony had deeply loved his wife, and he became distant and withdrawn after her death.

Paulie asked about his father as he grew up, but that information was kept from him. He slowly learned not to ask—or rather, his grandfather forbade him to pry. Catarina saw the pain her son suffered without a father, and she suffered because of that. Paulie would see his mother weep from time to time and he decided that there must be a reason to keep his father's identity from him. Older now, Paulie acts like he does not want to know so as not embarrass his beloved mother. But he vowed that one day he would learn the truth somehow, and hopefully not hurt his mother by doing so.

As for Rina, these days her life is mostly spent in solitude. She goes to church and chats with residents of the Neighborhood. Although friendly and caring to everyone, she remains distant.

Though Vincent and Paulie are different in so many ways, they are dead loyal to each other, and their bond is strong. They argue constantly and banter incessantly, but their friendship never wavers. It was born of the same fatherless hardships.

Rina watches as Vincent walks to the back of the store. Even if she and Teri are not social friends, they care about each other and are there for each other if needed. Teri is not at all jealous of Catarina's love and caring for Vincent. She welcomes it. On the other hand, Teri is caring, but distant to Paulie. She has her reasons, which she keeps to herself.

Vincent walks past the customers. At the back of the store, he takes in the aromas of the Italian meats, fresh breads, and other scents, and exits the door to the loading area. He sees Paulie unloading a truck with his grandfather, Tony.

Tony is an old-school Sicilian-American who has obtained what is most important: absolute respect. He gets it from everyone, including all of the Outfit members, without exception. Rumors abound about his real status, but no one asks. Tuff Tony—although no one dares to call him that to his face—is a respected leader in the Neighborhood and is often visited by many "made" men. From time to time, he functions as a consigliere to the Outfit and others.

Tony's grocery business flourishes. So does the barbershop next door. At the barbershop, the main source of revenue comes from the large back room where Gaetano "Shoes" Aiello runs his bookmaking operation. There are those who seek haircuts and some who function as lookouts. Tony's building is protected. Everything in the Neighborhood is protected.

Tony cares about Vincent in tough-love fashion, knowing what Vincent needs for a father figure and direction in life. But Tony is wary of Vincent's desires to join or be associated with the Neighborhood's Organized Crime contingent. Paulie and Vincent are best friends, and he encourages that.

Tony never shies away from giving Vincent a punch in the arm, just to make him aware that he is keeping an eye on the young man. Now, Tony gives Vincent another requisite punch. Tony's hands are callused and strong—they hit like steel. Vincent winces internally when struck but says and shows nothing. Paulie smiles broadly at the encounter and waves Vincent over.

Paulie is sweating from his exertion. His light brown hair has turned almost blond in the summer sun, and his dark blue eyes turn to Vincent with a twinkle of amusement.

"Come here, help me, and actually do some work for a change."

Tony hides his smirk and walks away, leaving the two.

Once Tony is out of sight, Vincent rubs his sore arm and says, "Fuck you, Paulie."

They unload the truck, playfully insulting each other. Paulie is five foot eleven, wide-shouldered, about195 pounds, and strong. He was chubby as a child, mostly from being overfed, but he has thinned out and his baby fat has been replaced with hard, youthful muscle. Paulie loves to box and is always ready to do anything athletic. He's a friendly guy but never backs down from a challenge and wins most of his fights decisively. That fact gives him respect even though the guys still hate that he wants to be an FBI agent.

When finished with the boxes, Vincent and Paulie grab a soda, stopping at the counter to talk to Catarina on the way out.

"I'm done, Ma, and we're going to meet up with some friends."

She smiles as she gets cheek kisses from the two of them.

After they leave, Tony walks up to her, points to Vincent, and says in his thick Sicilian accent, "What am I going to do with him? Vincent is a good kid, but he's nothing but trouble. Someday, and I hope that day never comes, those two may be at odds." Tony shakes his head, "Vincent loves the life way too much."

Paulie and Vincent stride down Taylor Street, enjoying the summer evening and each other. The Neighborhood may only be a small town, but it's theirs.

2

UNSTANDARDIZED TESTING

It's a Friday morning in early fall. On school days, Teri puts a plate of breakfast in front of Vincent with some toasted Italian bread and a glass of milk with Ovaltine. He has drunk milk with Ovaltine since he was very young. After he has finished eating, he looks out the window and sees Paulie waiting outside. He grabs his stuff and goes out to meet him.

"If you don't show up for school, you're not going graduate, Vin," says Paulie—who has been trying his best to get Vincent to finish his senior year of high school—as they walk toward school. "You never do homework and don't seem to give a shit."

Their morning walks, once a daily ritual, have become less frequent. While Vincent occasionally attends his senior year of high school, Paulie is an A student, excels in every subject, and is well liked by the faculty.

"Yeah, so what?"

"So what? It's your life!"

"You're going to graduate, go to college, and then become the enemy, you fuck, so why bother me?"

"I just wish you would get wise."

"Yeah, yeah, G-Man."

True to form, during first period, Vincent is called out of his math class to his homeroom teacher's office and is told to sit down at a desk.

"Vincent, you refuse to do homework," his home room teacher, Miss Hudson, says. You're going to flunk out and not graduate. You barely made it this far."

Vincent says nothing but fidgets in his chair.

"Those As you get on your tests are not going to save you." Beatrice Hudson, kind to a fault, smiles. She likes Vincent but is powerless to help him unless he toes the line. "Dean Miller thinks you are cheating and is just looking for a reason to expel you, you know that. I don't know what to do."

"I am not cheating, Miss Hudson. When the teachers tell us to read a chapter and that the next test will be based on that chapter, I read the chapter. Mostly, though, I'm bored stiff."

She stands, walks around, and leans on the other side of her desk.

"So, you read the chapter and know the answers, huh?"

"The teachers, even you Miss Hudson, say that the answers to the tests are contained in the chapters, so yeah. What's the big deal? I'm actually learning, ain't I?"

"*Aren't* I?" She corrects him. "Okay, let us see. Dean Miller says to give you a chapter to read for the next test and to see how you do. So, read chapter thirteen and let me know when you've finished. Then I will give you the test I just mimeographed. There is no way to cheat, because this is a new test and has never been seen by any student."

She hands Vincent an English textbook and leaves him alone to read. He watches her cross the hall to Dean Miller's office, then turns to the textbook. Paging through, he finds chapter thirteen and begins to read. Though bored, he goes along just for the challenge. He loves challenges, especially when they come from that fuck, Dean Miller.

Vincent finishes the chapter, reads it again, and continues to be bored. As he waits for Miss Hudson to come back, he turns to the next chapter and reads that, too, just for something to do. He's on the last paragraph when Miss Hudson enters the room, carrying a manila folder. She looks over his shoulder.

"I told you chapter thirteen, not fourteen, Vincent."

"Yeah, I read it, but I got tired waiting for you, so I read the next chapter."

She places a sheet of paper before him.

"Okay, here you go, fresh off the mimeograph. Complete this test, and I will grade it after you're done."

"I need a pencil, Miss Hudson."

She rolls her eyes, but not unpleasantly. She goes to her desk and, bending slightly, retrieves two newly sharpened pencils with pink erasers. She hands them to him and pats his arm for encouragement. She then retakes her seat.

Vincent reads the entire test first, then smiles, and circles the answers to the multiple-choice questions. When he's done, he looks over his work, makes one adjustment, scoffs at the test, and calls out to her.

"You're finished? You should review your answers, because I have to give Dean Miller the results."

"I'm done. Can I go now?"

Miss Hudson looks at Vincent sternly.

"No. Wait until after I grade this, then Dean Miller wants to speak with you."

Vincent grimaces and thinks, *Of course, he does. The dean is always harassing me—why should this time be any different?* Vincent puts his hands behind his neck and leans back.

Though Miss Hudson knows the book by heart—she has been teaching from it for many years—she looks over the test intensely. She finishes quickly. She frowns as she looks up to Vincent, who now is smiling. He's seen that he did well.

"You got one answer wrong, Vincent, and you probably would have gotten it right if you had taken your time."

Vincent sits up and glares at Miss Hudson. "What did I get wrong?"

"Question twenty-two. You checked off the wrong answer." Miss Hudson then pauses. "Wait, my mistake—you *did* get it right!"

"So, I read the chapter and got all the answers correct, right? Can I go now?"

"Sit tight, Vincent. I will be right back."

With a look of dismay, Miss Hudson gets up and walks across the hall to Dean Miller's office. Vincent can see her hand over the test to him. Dean Clarence Miller, a former football player, is about six foot two and weighs well over 200 pounds. A bully, he roughs up male students on a regular basis. Miller glances at the test and then gets up, angrily throwing it in the trash can.

They both walk back across the hallway, Miss Hudson behind, wringing her hands.

"Scalise, this doesn't matter," the dean snarls. "I am flunking you out, wise ass. You're nothing but trouble, and I don't want you here any longer. You refuse to do homework, you hardly ever show up to most of your classes, and I believe that you are a cheat, just like the rest of your goombah buddies. I don't even want to see your face. Get up. I'm expelling you today."

Eyes glazed with fury, Dean Miller grabs Vincent by the arm and pulls him out of the chair. Miss Hudson tries to intervene, but the dean pushes past her, and she retreats meekly to her office. Miller walks Vincent down the hall and toward the top of the stairs that lead to the exit.

Vincent has had enough. As they reach the top step, he quickly glances around to see if anyone is looking, turns toward the dean, cocks his fist, and punches him squarely in the nose. The dean pitches backward before falling down the stairs. Vincent trots down to the dean's crumpled body, kicks him in the back, and heads to the exit. *He had it coming*, thinks Vincent, as he sprints out the door.

Vincent spends the rest of the day and early evening walking around the outskirts of the Neighborhood, avoiding everyone. For a while, he hangs out at Peanut Park, east of The Patio, where he sits under a tree, the same tree where members of the Black Hand—extortionists from decades before—hung up signs to threaten their victims. That evening, he grudgingly goes home. Now he will have to face the music. When he arrives home, two patrol cars are waiting outside his house. From the street, Vincent can hear his mother yelling. He knows what's coming.

He walks in the door and is immediately grabbed by the neck by 200-pound Sergeant Nick Locero, a cop who lives next door. He's one of the only cops from the Neighborhood. Vincent shrugs him off.

Locero grabs him again and says, "Come'ere, tough guy. Are you stupid, crazy, or what? Did you think that Dean Miller would never call the cops? He says you sucker punched him in the nose! He has a broken arm from falling down the stairs."

When Vincent smirks, Locero cuffs him on the back of his head. Locero leads him to a chair in the kitchen where his mother is looming. She has tears in her eyes and is livid. They stare at each other. Neither one says a word.

"Look, Teri, we went to school together and I take no pleasure in locking this punk up."

"So, what now?" she asks Locero.

Locero slowly nods to Teri, then looks pointedly at Vincent.

"Vincent, you have two choices. You join the Army or you go to jail. I got the word from you-know-who. Your mother will go with you tomorrow to the recruiting office, and you will join. If not, I will arrest you and throw your punk ass in jail. You understand, tough guy?"

His arms crossed, Vincent says nothing.

"You avoid jail but join the Army," Locero continues. "We'll have to deal with the dean who will not be happy with this decision. Someone will handle that, but you will owe him a big favor when you get out, believe me."

Vincent remains mute. His mother walks Sergeant Locero to the front door. She says goodbye to the sergeant and waves to the patrolmen in their cars. She comes back in to confront Vincent.

"You realize you have no choice? I had to make a call to you-know-who, and if not for his loyalty to this neighborhood, Locero would have locked you up. Tomorrow we go to the recruiter, you join up, and then you're out of here. Do you hear me?"

She starts to cry and walks away.

Vincent realizes he has no real choice in the matter. Better the Army than go to the joint. But he is concerned about the favor. There is only one thing left to say.

"Fuck!"

3

LEMONY FRESH

When Vincent is tested by the Army recruiter staff, everyone is surprised by his high IQ. He possesses a sharp mind that no one suspects because of his disdain for school, and he's street wise to beat the band.

Impressed with his test scores, the recruiters ask him what he would like to do. Unsure and confused, he looks around the recruiter's office, grasping for something to say. His eyes land on a magazine about electronics. So he says, "electronics," not knowing a thing about them. He's a street kid and only knows what the street has taught him.

Vincent arrives at boot camp in Fort Leonard Wood, Missouri, having absolutely no idea what lies ahead. When he gets there, it's like another world. With their pronounced accents, the people seem to speak another language. This is the South, and he's never gone farther south than South Chicago.

He enjoys very little about boot camp, especially the food, but gets into great physical shape. He puts on over twenty pounds, mostly muscle. He pushes himself through the obstacle courses and weapons training. They are just more challenges, the kinds of challenges he loves to meet. He even obtains a merit badge for expert marksmanship without ever having fired a weapon before—well, at least not a rifle.

But he does, as usual, manage to get himself in trouble from time to time. One such occasion occurs during a physical training session. Vincent is called out by the drill instructor, a strict master sergeant whose smile masks a sadistic nature. Master Sergeant Melvin L. Watkins stands over six foot five, with dark leathery skin and a shaved head. He looks like the textbook version of a hard-ass. His fatigues are starched and creased to perfection. He slaps his leg with his swagger stick as he yells out instructions that radiate "no nonsense." Vincent is in the back row, having a good time and joking with others during the drill.

"Ssscccaaaliiooowse, front and center!"

Vincent smugly guffaws at the blatant mispronunciation of his name and steps forward with bravado. Big mistake. The drill instructor slaps his leg with his swagger stick and looks out at the group.

"You people wanna play fuck around, we gonna play fuck around. Scaaaliiooowse, get down and give me thirty."

Vincent gets down, does thirty pushups with ease, and looks up at Watkins. "That it?"

Another big mistake.

The drill sergeant eerily regards the squad and then dismisses them—all but Vincent. Watkins slowly takes a knee in front of Vincent, who is still in a prone position, looks him directly in the eye, and speaks in a scary calm manner.

"No, that's not it, boot, not by a long shot. You stand up and follow me. We gonna get better acquainted and have some fun."

Vincent thinks to himself, *Oh boy.*

Master Sergeant Watkins leads Vincent to the mess hall and points to the doorway.

"You go in there and get you a sack of lemons and come back out here. You EYEtalians know what a lemon is, right?"

Vincent, angry, confused, knowing that he's fucked up, enters the mess hall. He tells the staff sergeant inside what the drill instructor told him to do and receives a stack of halved lemons. He has no idea what to expect, but apparently the staff sergeant knows, considering the shit-eating grin he gives Vincent.

Outside, Master Sergeant Watkins points to three galvanized, highly corroded, and blackened trash cans.

"You gonna take them lemons and rub them onto those trash cans until they shine, you hear me? I mean SHINE, boot. When I come back, I wanna see my ugly ass face reflected in that shine!"

The sergeant executes a sharp about-face and walks off, slapping the side of his leg with his swagger stick. Vincent kneels down in front of the cans, picks up a lemon half, and begins to rub it against the blackened trash can. The effort produces little effect on the corrosion, and Vincent sits down. *"This is going to be a bitch."*

As he works, an open-top half-ton truck pulls up. The driver gets out and walks directly into the doorway of the mess hall. Vincent stands and peers into the bed of the truck. Like a vision from heaven, inside are brand new, glistening trash cans. He immediately climbs onto the back of the truck and unloads three of the cans. Working quickly, he hides the cans behind the mess hall. Then he waits. The driver comes out of the mess hall with some forms and a clipboard, looks up and sees Vincent standing by the truck, glaring at him. The soldier is about to ask what Vincent is doing, but merely shrugs and gets back into the truck.

After the truck pulls away, Vincent hurriedly retrieves the new cans. He transfers the trash from the three corroded containers into the new ones. He then rubs the arms and legs of his fatigues against the corrosion and slathers some of the grime on his face. He wants to look a mess, and he succeeds. He smells of lemons and trash, just the effect he wants to present. After hiding the old cans behind the mess hall, he squeezes out the remaining lemons and tosses them onto the top of the trash pile.

A couple of hours go by before Vincent sees Sergeant Watkins approach the mess hall, flashing that grotesque grin. As the sergeant nears, Vincent blocks the trash cans from view. Master Sergeant Watkins smiles victoriously as he takes in Vincent's grimy appearance and filthy fatigues.

"Where my cans, boot?"

Vincent steps aside and points to the new shiny cans heaped with trash.

"There you go, Sarge. You can step up and see your reflection." He wants to add, *of your ugly-ass face.* But, in a rare show of prudence, he keeps that to himself.

The drill instructor angrily slaps the swagger stick against his hand, visibly confused. He looks back and forth from one can to another, inspecting them closely, and then back again at Vincent, who stands grinning—filthy and reeking with the smell of garbage and lemons.

For a moment, Sergeant Watkins is at a loss for words. Then he smiles that insidious smile.

"You fuck with me, you gonna be sorry, boot. Get outta my face, get cleaned up and rested, because tomorrow we got us the obstacle course and you gonna shine for me tomorrow, just like them cans, ain't you?"

Vincent grimaces, nods his head, turns, and goes off to get cleaned up.

4

THE HAM HOCK AND INDIANA

After successfully completing boot camp, Vincent is sent to Fort Gordon, Georgia. Once there, he meets a few guys from Chicago, along with some other guys he can talk to. At the camp, he develops a camaraderie among several of the men.

One Saturday, on a rare three-day pass, they all decide to get tattoos. Vincent does not want a tattoo, but he goes along with the others, about twenty guys. *This might be interesting*, he thinks.

A big group made up of some Italians and others of various ethnic persuasions—Polish, Greek, Spanish, and who knows—arrive at a tattoo parlor. They crowd up at the entrance and watch a huge guy sitting behind the counter on a rolling stool, one with casters on the bottom of the legs. His forearm is being shaved for the tattoo. This redheaded redneck, over 250 pounds dry, eyes the group, slaps his huge ham hock of a forearm, and bellows, "I want a panther right here!"

The group looks on. Vincent is bored. When the tattoo artist begins to etch a black outline in the redneck's skin, the guy yelps in pain and slides off the stool. He stands up, his face crimson.

"Are you okay? Do you want me to go on?" the tattoo artist inquires.

The guy looks at the group with bravado, but he's clearly shaken.

"Yeah, go ahead. I just had too much to drink last night, that's all." The huge redneck sits down again.

Vincent smiles at the excuse then turns around to discover he's lost ten guys. He raises his eyebrows to those still remaining and they nod that they are going to stay. The tattoo artist, now wary, starts tattooing the redneck's massive arm. The man faints and falls off the stool, which flies across the room. Once again, Vincent looks back at the others. They are now down to three.

When the hulk comes to, he pushes his way out of the door and runs down the street, clearly embarrassed. The three remaining guys look at Vincent for some sign. Now understood as their leader, Vincent wants to leave, but sits instead. Braced for his tattoo, Vincent has no idea what his reaction will be, but there is no way he's leaving, fainting, or otherwise embarrassing himself.

After Vincent survives, the other three get their tattoos. About an hour later, they walk back to the compound feeling their oats—laughing and joking about the redneck.

Early the next morning, one of the soldiers who had braved the tattoo parlor with Vincent, awakens with horror: engraved on his bicep is a drawing of a skunk with "MOM" written below it. Vincent examines his own tattoo of a red rose—symbolizing the Omerta code of silence among made men—then back at the tall Indiana-bred fellow soldier. He has a crew cut and clear blue eyes which begin to tear.

The Indiana boy then picks up a GI brush, the one used to scour the latrine, gets a bar of GI soap, and begins scrubbing at the offensive tattoo. Vincent tries to stop him, as do others, but he screams at them and continues to scrub until his arm is a mass of blood. Indiana sits down and cries. The staff sergeant in charge of the barracks calls for medical assistance. They cart the soldier off.

Vincent has learned a lesson—but what it is, he's not exactly sure.

5

STINK PRETTY

The Army trains Vincent as a cryptographer. Without a shred of previous knowledge of electronics or cryptology whatsoever, he still manages to excel.

One afternoon, after a few months at the camp, there's a dance with lots of locals attending, along with the enlisted men from the base. The Twist is the new dance craze, and Vincent is amused by all the girls gyrating around. He spots a pretty, curly blonde-haired girl and asks her to dance. His buddies look on, grinning at him. If he gets one of the locals to dance with him, they think, maybe some of them might score as well.

All of the enlisted men, Vincent included, wear Canoe cologne, which is the rage. As they slow dance, the girl looks up at Vincent with her blue eyes shining and says in her southern country drawl, "Damn, you stink purrrdy!"

Yep, that's me, I stink pretty.

6

GOLDEN SHOWER

After training, Vincent receives his orders and is surprised to be sent off to serve in France, thus avoiding the conflict in Indochina, soon to be known as Vietnam.

Soon after boarding a troop transport ship headed to Europe, he gets seasick and is sent to medical hold three times. After the third time, the medical staff warn that he will not be put back in the hospital again—he has to buck up or be transferred to the brig. The street kid from Chicago, never having even seen an ocean, must deal with it. Vincent fights the raging seasickness best he can, hardly eating, and tries to control the nausea. He's resolved to beat this, and, after a couple of days, slowly begins to get his sea legs. Even so, he hates the boat and hates the sea.

While roaming around the deck on the eighth night, Vincent comes upon a poker game and joins in. What he learned on the streets in the Neighborhood pays off, and by the time the ship arrives at the Bremerhaven Port in Germany, he has $600 in winnings in his pocket.

When he arrives at his base in France, Vincent is informed that he has a "critical MOS"—military occupational specialty—which requires a security clearance, so he's restricted to the barracks for thirty days.

He meets a group of guys that he can kill time with, one of whom is a short Italian named Benny Milano, from the North End in Boston. Although short and non-threatening in any way, Benny has a familiar bravado that amuses Vincent. He's four years older than Vincent, but dumb. That said, he's always jovial, never ceasing to talk and tell tales.

Benny learns that Vincent has some cash and convinces him to bribe the military police at the gate to let them slip off the base. The guards are Polish nationals who will earn citizenship if they serve in the U.S. military for five years. Supervised by the U.S. Military Police, they are hardly paid attention to—especially when everyone has passes for the weekend—so they are more than willing to accept American dollars to look in the other direction. Vincent hands twenty bucks to each of the two guards who have just come on duty. He promises them that he and Benny will be back just before midnight.

In town, Vincent is awestruck, especially by the beautiful girls, and thinks he will really enjoy being stationed nearby. He wants to learn French and immerse himself in the culture. He follows Benny to a hangout for enlisted Americans. Benny's friends greet them when they arrive. When they learn that Vincent is new, they encourage him to have a glass of Pernod—a French liqueur—as some sort of initiation. Vincent sniffs the almost full glass. It reminds him of Anisette, an Italian liqueur served on special occasions. Anisette has a sweet licorice flavor but, unlike this drink, it is served in small little glasses. Never a drinker and remembering that Anisette is ninety proof, Vincent dumps the contents when no one is looking.

Benny, however, drinks the entire glass and wants more.

Around 11 p.m., Benny is wasted, and some of the guys help Vincent get their friend to his feet. They all laugh and wave as Vincent and Benny depart for their barrack. The pair must cross a bridge that spans a river. Benny drunkenly lumbers along while Vincent tries to guide him. This is no small task with Benny laughing loudly and constantly losing his footing.

"Shut the fuck up!" Vincent hisses.

As they cross the downward slope of the bridge, they see an older woman up ahead. Like many of the elderly locals, she is dressed in black. Suddenly, Benny pushes Vincent aside, runs off drunkenly, picks up speed, and yells, "Watch this!"

Vincent watches in horror as Benny runs up behind the woman, grabs her by both cheeks of her ass, and screams in her ear. Nonplussed, the old lady turns and strikes Benny on the side of his head with her large purse. He is so drunk that he loses his balance. He falls over the side of the bridge and onto the riverbank reeds, which cushion his fall and save him from real physical harm.

Vincent runs past the old lady, who is shaking her fist down at Benny. At the side of the bridge, Vincent sees Benny flailing and caterwauling among the reeds. He scurries down the bridge, rounds the river edge, and jumps in after Benny, clumsily dragging him out.

On the riverbank, Benny laughs hysterically. Vincent whacks him upside his head.

"Are you fucking crazy, you dumb shit?"

Benny, puzzled, shakes off the blow. "What?"

Vincent worries that the gendarmes—French police—will spot them. He looks around then gets Benny up and walking. The fall into the cold river seems to have sobered Benny a bit. Soaking wet, they slowly make their way back to the guard shack and, with Vincent holding Benny's mouth shut, approach the military guards.

The guards laugh at the pair. Vincent and Benny are a mess, reeds sticking to their soggy clothes. It costs Vincent fifty dollars to stow Benny back into the barracks. Vincent forcefully deposits him in a shower stall, turns on the cold water, and leaves him to get undressed.

Although most of the men are asleep, there are a couple of guys who eye Vincent, but no one says a word. Many of them are drunk as well. Vincent strips out of his clothes, grabs a couple of towels, and goes back into the shower to get Benny.

But Benny is gone.

The floor has been waxed to a high sheen, though, so Vincent follows Benny's wet footprints. He arrives just in time to see Benny stumble into the staff sergeant's room, unzip his pants, remove his formidable penis, and begin to piss onto the sergeant's sleeping body. The sergeant sleeps with the covers up to his chin, so Benny aims for the man's face.

Vincent quickly turns, runs down the hall to his assigned bunk, and jumps in just as the sergeant's enraged howl rings out. The sergeant is as mean as they come, and Benny is in a world of shit.

Vincent never sees Benny again. Benny keeps his mouth shut, though, and Vincent is never questioned.

7

BAD BILLY'S CHOICE

There's lots to do at the barracks while Vincent's background check is being processed. He enjoys learning more about electronics and telephone systems, and he becomes more proficient in the work. He figures that someday he might put this education and experience to good use.

Vincent learns that a ticket for the "flicks"—the Army's name for the movies—costs twenty-five cents. Beer costs a quarter, too. Despite his adventure with Benny, he still has some of his $600. At the end of the month everyone is flat broke, so Vincent starts loaning money at a two-to-one rate—a quarter for a half dollar.

He launches other enterprises as well, including nightly poker games. Soon he puts the first sergeant on his payroll, a necessary expense. He also brings the company commander, a heavy drinker, a case of scotch every month to look the other way.

With his increased earnings, Vincent starts to send money to his mother. She, in turn, writes him often and sends food. Though he tells her he eats pretty well in France, she doesn't listen, writing, "The stuff is from Papa Tony." He stops complaining. There is no use.

She writes about the Neighborhood and about Paulie.

Although Paulie writes occasionally, his letters are always filled with encouragement and friendship. He reports that he is doing well in college and still wants to become an FBI agent, to Vincent's chagrin. But Vincent loves Paulie, and that is that.

Vincent is approaching 19 years old, younger than most of the soldiers in his barrack. Some of the soldiers resent Vincent because of his street ways and his ability to make money. One night two soldiers, after losing heavily at poker, come after him in the shower. As he fights them off, a huge fist flies over his shoulder and slams into the face of one of the attackers, a tall red-headed guy. The soldier falls back into the shower stall, out cold. Seconds later, the other assailant is thrown in after him.

Hovering over the two stands a jet black, gold toothed behemoth—six foot three and 275 pounds of mostly muscle. He extends his large hand to Vincent.

"Billy Ray Taylor," he says.

Billy is from the south side of Chicago and he fast becomes Vincent's protector and right-hand man, collecting debts on Vincent's behalf. Vincent dubs him "Bad Billy."

Vincent and Billy's friendship continues for almost a year until they attend a briefing by one of the lieutenants about Vietnam. Vincent asks what the country is like and is told that it is tropical, rains a lot, and has centipedes and snakes. Before the lieutenant's briefing is finished, Vincent leans over and tells Bad Billy that anyone would be crazy to go there. But after the briefing, Bad Billy and a bunch of other soldiers volunteer for deployment. Vincent tries to dissuade Billy, but his protector and good friend does not listen.

To Vincent's dismay, Bad Billy dies with the entire group of volunteer soldiers when their transport plane crashes in Algiers on its way to Vietnam. Vincent misses Billy's friendship, but also misses his friend's usefulness. Shortly after Billy's death, a new first sergeant is assigned to the base, followed by a new company commander. Without Billy's protection, Vincent is out of business for good, although he still loans out money from time to time.

The Army has made a man out of Vincent. It has taught him discipline and encourages honor and loyalty—to his friends and his work, though not necessarily to the United States Armed Military Forces—traits that Vincent will cherish the rest of his life.

8

BACK IN THE OLD STYLE

In the fall of 1963, Vincent returns home from the Army. He's happy he left but he's also glad to be back. When discharged, he has a little over $2,000 in his pocket. Nothing has really changed in the Neighborhood. The same old attitudes and circumstances prevail. The Outfit continues to make lots of money and maintains its steadfast hold.

The aesthetics of the Neighborhood have changed a little, though, what with the new dress code, the drugs, and the dissent. Some of his buddies and other neighborhood guys now sport longer hair, flower-print shirts, and bell-bottoms. Not the wannabes, however. Their dress code never changes.

Back in his element, Vincent seeks out old friends. Some of them have gone off to serve, some stayed behind for one reason or another, and some, like loudmouth Sonny Caruso, sadly never returned. He was a pain, but Vincent liked him nonetheless. Before he was drafted, Sonny lived with his grandmother, after his mom and dad moved up to the northern suburbs. Sonny never wanted to leave the Neighborhood.

One of the first things Vincent does when he gets home is visits Sonny's grandmother and comforts her. He tells her if she needs anything, he still lives in the Neighborhood, and that she should contact him. She tells him that she knows his mother and thanks him for caring.

Vincent reluctantly moves back in with his mother. Since he's been gone, his mother has developed mood swings that provoke rifts between them from time to time. Vincent tolerates them because he loves his mother. He takes the bad with the good, still trusting her completely. He wants to move out at some point, but not yet. First, he needs a job.

Like so many others back from the war, Vincent looks for work in the want ads of the *Tribune*. But there are no jobs for cryptographers in the Chicagoland area—or elsewhere, for that matter. Most people do not even know what cryptography means. Scanning the want ads at his mother's kitchen table one morning, Vincent comes across a notice for "Collectors at the Catalog Organization." He applies, is invited in for an interview, and is promptly hired.

Vincent learns a lot but soon grows tired of collecting money from people who don't have it, of listening to wives and husbands complain about their lack of cash and their inability to pay.

The offices of the Collectors at the Catalog Organization are located at a building downtown, across the hall from the Skip Tracers, a company responsible for locating customers who ran off before paying their debts. One day at lunch Vincent talks with one of their best skip tracers, Valerie Franck. Vincent inquires as to how they do their job and becomes very interested. He also asks about Valerie, because he's interested in her, too.

Valerie is about five foot two, with long, wavy auburn colored hair. *It's probably a dye job,* thinks Vincent, but he loves the color. She has a great body that Vincent cannot stop fantasizing about since the minute he first met her. And he loves the way her mind works. She's tough and smart. If she were a man, she would make one good hood.

9

VINCENT'S SECOND JOB

Vincent goes to his boss, George Markham, and asks if he can be switched over to the skip tracer side. George has no problem with him doing so, but advises Vincent that he has a lot to learn.

Vincent and Valerie become friends. She teaches Vincent all she can about locating the skips—introducing him to the tools of the trade, like telephone books, cross-reference directories, maps, and the like.

She schools him on the art of "gagging" people—in other words, getting people to talk. If the job is to find people who do not want to be found, she says, you have to find the one person who can tell you where they are. Then give that person a reason to tell you what you want to know. And to do that, you must get people to believe that you are someone other than who you are.

"You can and *should* pretend you are someone else," she tells him. "It should feel close to acting," she says. *Valerie is a born actress,* Vincent thinks. He watches her use her natural gifts to her advantage, befriending women she wishes to gag with her winning, confident personality, and flirting with the men.

Vincent soaks in everything with great interest. He quickly becomes one of the better skip tracers. He seeks out contacts within the police force, the telephone company, credit bureaus, and even the DMV. His contacts are all drawn from the Neighborhood: at the credit card company, Mary Donovan, an Irish girl; Todd Billings, also Irish, his contact at AT&T; and Bill Faraday, a cop he went to school with. Bill's mother worked at the beauty salon with Vincent's mom.

Soon Vincent becomes a legend on the floor, using his connections to find the skips that the others cannot. But it's more than that. He simply has an innate ability to do so, mostly because of his skill in talking to people over the telephone. Like a gifted actor, he learns how to mimic different dialects and speech patterns. In doing so, he gets anyone to tell him what he wants to know.

But, after a few months, he becomes bored again. Once Vincent attains a proficient level of skill, the challenge dies. *There has to be more to life,* he thinks. So, he freelances for other collection agencies. He makes more money that way, but those jobs also become unsatisfying.

One day, while looking in the Yellow Pages, he comes upon a section devoted to private investigators. He cuts out all of the ads in the classifieds for investigative agencies and puts them in a file for himself. These agencies claim to be able to locate missing persons. It strikes him that is what he's doing now, but with higher stakes.

He studies the largest ad in the bunch, for Winslow, Carruthers & Associates. The fact that the firm claims to have been created by two ex-FBI agents unnerves him, but he decides to interview anyway. Even if he fails, he'll still learn something new, he figures.

He makes an appointment with one of the partners. A week later, at the interview, Vincent boldly insists that he's great at locating missing people. His bravado engenders a very amused look from Charles Winslow, the agency owner. Winslow calls in his partner, Carruthers, to listen to Vincent's presentation. Their skepticism angers Vincent.

"Look," Vincent says, finally, "just give me the hardest case you've got. I'll work on a contingency basis. But, if I find that person, then I would like to be employed and get a chance to work on all your missing person cases."

Vincent's sincerity intrigues them. After they confer, they tell Vincent that he's in. He will not be an employee, but hired as a private contractor.

On his first day, Winslow presents him with a runaway teenager case. If Vincent finds the young lady, they'll pay him a standard fee, plus any expenses he incurs. And they may consider giving him more work.

"So, if I understand you," Vincent says, "this is your toughest case."

"Well, it's a tough one," Charles Winslow responds. "We just got it."

Winslow hands Vincent a high school photograph of the young lady.

"Her name is Debra Morton, and she's from La Grange. Her parents hired us but you are prohibited from speaking to them directly."

Vincent thinks that won't be a problem. If the parents hired the agency, how much help could they possibly be? He spends the next several days gagging her friends and high school classmates and running down leads, some which turn out to be dead ends. Exactly one week from the day he's hired, though, he finds Debra walking down a street, not far from the home of one of her friends.

The agency partners are impressed by how quickly Vincent has worked, but he is once again instructed not to contact the girl's parents. As ex-FBI agents, they present a more professional presence, so they will divulge Debra's location themselves. Vincent resents this and wants to be in on the disclosure, but he relents. In any event, Vincent has succeeded, and Debra is returned home safely.

In return for his service, he's paid a flat fee of $500. Though Vincent thinks this number is low, he doesn't mind, believing that this is his entrance into the private investigator field.

However, he's wrong. He soon learns that to get a license, he must work for a detective agency for three years, take a test, and pay a fee. He also learns that the agency he works for must assess the number of hours he's worked and vouch for him. Depending on others to get what he wants does not sit well with Vincent. His already healthy ego has grown ever larger, and his confidence soars. His desire to get into this business becomes his sole obsession.

10

DEBRA MORTON REPRISE

Despite the success in the Morton case, Winslow, Carruthers & Associates give Vincent no more work. They've investigated his background, they say, and determined that he does not represent the values of the firm. Vincent believes that the real reason is that they consider him a potential competitor and want no part in helping him succeed.

One day, sick of being kept out in the cold, Vincent decides to contact the parents of Debra Morton. He's also driven by a sincere interest in finding out how the girl is doing. He knocks on the door of their home and is greeted by Patricia Morton, the young lady's mother.

"Hello, I'm Vincent Scalise, the detective that found your daughter."

"Excuse me?" Patricia replies, surprised. "Charles Winslow told me that he and his agency worked day and night to find her."

"That's not the full story, ma'am."

"Why don't you come in?"

"Thank you."

At the kitchen table, Patricia tells Vincent a sad tale. Her daughter has run away again, a few weeks after her return. She has not been heard from for a week. Patricia starts to cry. Tearfully, she asks Vincent if he'll find her again for them. She would have gone back to Winslow & Carruthers, she says, but they would not accept payment in installments.

"Will you?" she asks.

"How much did you pay them?"

"$15,000."

Vincent is astonished. He smiles at Mrs. Morton and tells her not to worry, that he will find her daughter. She hugs him. He tells her he will be in touch soon.

Because he accumulated so much information about Debra the first time, he thinks, it should be a relatively simple task to locate her again. It is. When he finds Debra in a diner several miles from her home, he approaches her and begins to introduce himself. She remembers him and becomes visibly frightened.

"Debra," he says, "Your parents hired me to find you again. I've found you before, and no matter how often you run or how far you go, I'll always find you." It sounds like a threat.

At that, Debra shrieks, and begins to weep. Vincent realizes he's stuck his foot in his mouth.

"No, I'm sorry," he pleads, "I didn't mean it like that."

She begs Vincent not to tell her parents where she is. Vincent suspects that something is very wrong.

"Why do you keep running away?" he asks sincerely.

Debra struggles to speak, but Vincent patiently coaxes her, until finally she breaks down. She tells him about her uncle Harry—her mother's bachelor brother—who lives in the same apartment building as her family. She reveals to Vincent horrifying details about her uncle—about how he visits Debra when her parents are not home, about how he gets drunk and takes advantage of her, about how he makes her bare her breasts, about how he masturbates in front of her, about how he molests her.

"He scares me so much that I just couldn't take it anymore," she says, finishing her story. "So, I ran."

Her disclosure cuts Vincent deeply. He's almost overwhelmed with guilt. *How could I not have seen this before?*

Once he's regained his composure, Vincent says, "Okay, sweetheart, calm down. I am going to fix this problem for you."

"Oh, God!" she cries, shakily. "My mom and dad don't know about any of this, and I don't know how to tell them. I thought about telling my father, but you know, he.... I don't know. I just didn't."

"Okay, trust me, your uncle will never bother you again."

Vincent then peppers Debra with questions about her uncle's habits—what does he do, who does he hang out with, where does he work. Finally, once he has enough information, he reassures her that she will be safe. He gives her some money and tells her not to worry. He promises to come back for her at the diner later that night.

Before they part, Vincent sternly warns her not to say anything about this to anyone.

Debra's uncle works nights as a warehouse watchman. He lives one flight above her parents in their three flat apartment building. Her uncle is often home during the day, drunk. He waits until her parents go to work, and then comes after Debra when she's home alone.

Vincent, now on a mission, leaves for the Neighborhood. There he contacts his buddies Angelo and Mikey and explains the situation. They set out to confront Uncle Harry. They arrive at the Morton house in the early evening and find her parents eating dinner. Chester Morton, Debra's father, invites them in. Vincent follows Mr. and Mrs. Morton to the living room and sits them down. He explains that he's found their daughter. But there's a problem.

Vincent discloses what Debra has told him. He watches their reactions, especially her father's. Chester stares out into space, impotent, while Patricia wrings her hands and cries. Vincent sees that Chester Morton is a weak man.

"Wha—wha what should we do?" Chester stammers.

The question disgusts Vincent. It clearly explains why Debra has no faith in her father to help her.

Vincent, however, is resolute.

"I'll tell you what we're going to do. We're going to take care of this right now," says Vincent, rubbing his eyes to ease the tension and anger he feels.

"Harry hasn't left for work yet, right? I need you both to stay down here. My associates and I are going upstairs right now. After we handle this, we'll bring your daughter home."

Debra's mother looks into Vincent's sincere face and nods gratefully. Her father just stands there, as if paralyzed, his small hands clasped and shaking.

Vincent, Angelo, and Mikey confer before going upstairs, then Vincent knocks on Uncle Harry's door. A 50-year-old, overweight, balding man answers. Reeking of alcohol, he staggers at the doorstep and straightens his ball cap. He holds a half empty beer bottle tightly in his left hand. He looks confused, then wipes his beer-dampened stubble with the back of his right hand.

Vincent asks, "You Harry Thompson?"

"Yeah, who wants to know?"

"You always go to work drunk, you fuck?" Vincent asks, all smiles.

"Who the fuck're you?" the fat man spits back.

With the palm of his hand, Vincent pushes on Thompson's chest, forcing him back into the apartment. He then slaps the man across the face, grabs him by the throat, slams him into the floor, and kneels on his chest. The beer bottle crashes on the floor. The contents spill out.

Angelo kicks away the glass shards and grabs Thompson by his remaining hairs, lifting him to a sitting position, though still on the ground.

"Debra told me what you did, you sick fuck!" Vincent screams.

The eyes in Thompson's face bulge in shock before he turns his head away.

"Look at me, you pervert!"

Vincent slaps him across his face twice.

"That's to get your attention," he continues. "Now, here's what's gonna happen. You're going to find another place to live—*tonight*. You are not going downstairs to see your sister. You are to leave them alone. You are not to come back here except to get your belongings, and we're going to be here when you do. If you do not do as I say, right now, we are going to throw you over the banister into the backyard and watch you bounce. You understand me?"

"Are you gonna call the cops?" Thompson asks, terrified.

"No, because the cops won't do what I will do to you, and I do not want Debra to suffer any more humiliation because of you, you sick fuck."

They pick up the uncle off the floor and watch him scuttle to get some clothes and other things. At the apartment door, Mikey kicks him in the ass, knocking him against the wall in the hallway. Then they walk him down to his car. They watch him drive drunkenly away—*off a bridge*, Vincent hopes.

Vincent returns to the Morton's apartment, brings the parents up to speed, and tells them what he told Uncle Harry. He also warns them against any further contact with Harry.

"If he comes near you or Debra or tries to reach out to any of you, get in touch with me immediately, you understand?" Vincent directs a sympathetic gaze at Mrs. Morton, a stern look at Mr. Morton.

He's bringing Debra back home later that night, he informs them. He also tells them both that they need to work to regain her trust. Patricia Morton hugs him and starts to cry. Chester Morton stands there like a stone, looking down at the floor. His weakness sickens Vincent once again. Then he leaves to get their daughter.

When he arrives at the diner, Debra is sitting at a table in the back. He tells her it's all over. Then he reassures her that this will never happen again. He gives her his telephone number and tells her to call day or night if she needs him. She sobs, and he gently guides her to the car, where Angelo and Mikey are waiting for him. He takes her home, where she cries in her mother's and father's waiting arms.

Vincent now knows his calling. But how does he get his license with so much opposition and so many obstacles?

11

UP ALL NIGHT

All night, Vincent thinks hard about his newfound passion.

Early the next morning, he walks down Taylor Street to the grocery store. Papa Tony is always there early to open up, and Vincent asks him if they can talk. Tony looks Vincent over and shrugs his shoulders. Vincent tells him about his ambition. Although very nervous, Vincent asks for advice.

"You want to be a private eye? You watch too much TV. And you're stupid," Tony says. "And you have no education."

"No, I don't," Vincent admits to this last remark, "but that's what I want to do, and I'm good at it."

Tony shakes his head. Then, exploding, he grabs Vincent forcibly by his elbow and pushes him back into the grocery store. Vincent, who is used to Tony's rough manner, doesn't resist. Tony leads Vincent back to his office and shoves him into a chair and then sits down behind his desk.

Vincent lays it all out for Tony, who just shakes his head.

"So, you need a license to make this all legal, right?"

"Yeah, I explained that to you Papa Tony, but I don't believe that I'm going to be able to do it in the normal fashion. I think I need some help from our friends."

Tony nods slowly, leans back in his chair, and looks into space. He gets up and studies Vincent's face. *Well, this at least is better than him becoming a full-time hood*, the old man thinks.

"Okay, I'll talk to some people. But in the end, this is going to cost you, Vincenzo, in more ways than one. You get help from these people and then you owe them, and then after a while, they may *own* you. Make no mistake, you understand me?"

"Yeah, I understand, but I really don't have anywhere else to go. No one else can help me get what I want, and I know that. And I don't mind owing them. I mean if they help me, maybe I can help them. Getting this license means a lot to me, and I'm willing to do anything I need to get it. I cannot get it the straight arrow way, and you know that."

Papa Tony nods his head.

"You go home to your mama and tell her I said hello. She is a good woman—don't let anybody tell you otherwise. Be respectful to her and help her when you can. I'll reach out to you when I know something. Now get outta here."

"Thank you, Papa Tony."

"I said get out of here! I don't want to see your face until I call for you."

He whacks Vincent on the arm and leads him out of the store, just as Tony's daughter comes into work. Rina looks at her father, then at Vincent and frowns. Vincent kisses her and smiles to reassure her, then leaves.

Back at home, Vincent speaks with his mother. He tells her the story of Debra. He tells her he spoke to Tony, about how he really wants to pursue detective work. He says that maybe he could do some good, thinking he could even be great at this. He explains to her that he can make a good living and not need to resort to other things, although that's always an option.

"Papa Tony is a good man and has always been good to me, Vincent," his mother replies. "There was always food when I was young and struggling, and he never asked me for anything. You listen to him and do what he says. Then go do what you need to do."

"I will, Ma, I will."

"What you did for that little girl was also good. I am proud of you for doing that and I am sure her parents appreciate it."

She tousles his hair, kisses his cheek, and hugs him. He feels very good and much closer to his mother.

Vincent has not been to work, so he calls Valerie at home and tells her to make up some excuse for him. Then he goes out to meet his buddies. Angelo and Mikey wait for him at Baba's beef stand. After he thanks them for helping him, they tell him he's needed on a score. One favor in return for another.

Vincent nods. He's in.

12

THE FAT LAWYER

Two days later, Vincent comes home from work and his mother tells him to go see Tony at the grocery store. He doesn't know what to expect, but puts on a smile and walks down the street to the store.

He goes inside, kisses Paulie's mother on the cheek, then asks where the old man is. Rina brushes back his hair in a motherly fashion and points toward the loading dock. Vincent finds Tony talking to a truck driver. Tony points to the truck and tells Vincent to unload it. Without another word, Tony walks off.

Vincent does what he's told without comment or argument, because he knows that means he's about to get some news. After an hour, the truck is empty. Sore and sweat-laden, Vincent seeks out Tony.

"Okay, Papa Tony, it's unloaded. You need me to do anything else?"

"Yeah, I don't write so good, so you need to write down what I tell you."

Tony hands Vincent a pencil and a piece of paper. Vincent waits patiently while Tony collects his thoughts.

"I was told that you need to go to the First Ward office downtown and speak to James D'Amico. Do you know who that is?"

Vincent nods as he writes on the piece of paper. Tony recites a phone number and an address.

"You go down there tomorrow at three o'clock and explain everything to Jimmy D. You don't say anything else, just give him the information. Do you understand me?"

Vincent nods. Tony continues, pacing now.

"He's going to explain to us, not you, what needs to be done. You keep your mouth shut and sit back and wait. In the meantime, you go about your business and leave it to us. You may have to talk to a lawyer friend of ours, and he may need more information from you. I don't want you to tell anybody what's going on. Do you understand?"

Once again, Vincent nods.

"I don't want you to *nod*!" bellows Tony. With his iron-strong hands, his grabs Vincent's face, clenches his cheeks together, and forces his lips to protrude. "I want you to *acknowledge* what I say!"

Vincent pulls away.

"Jeez, yes, I understand, and I will do exactly what you tell me to do. Don't worry!"

"Go on, get outta here. And quit your job. You're gonna work here for a while, so I can keep my eye on you during all of this. You show up here tomorrow morning at six to unload trucks. Understand?"

Vincent leaves with a smile on his face. The process has started. He's going to get what he wants. It's going to cost, but he doesn't care. Maybe he gets closer to the street boss, and maybe that ain't such a bad thing.

Vincent calls Valerie, "Tell the boss I quit." She argues with him, but he says he'll see her later that evening to explain.

Vincent shows up at the grocery store at six in the morning. He unloads trucks until noon. It doesn't matter—he's happy. In his own way, the old man seems like he's warming up to him.

Vincent is eating a sausage sandwich that Rina made for him when Tony shows up. Tony tells him to go home and get cleaned up.

"Dress nicely, not like the punk you are. I want you to go downtown to see Jimmy D at three sharp. Be presentable. You're just gonna explain what you want and need. Then you are gonna listen and keep your mouth shut. Now go home and get dressed."

Vincent does what he's told. When he gets home, his mother is ironing a shirt for him. She looks up at him, a smile in her eyes, but doesn't say a word.

He showers, puts on a pair of shined shoes, some dress slacks, and the ironed shirt. He calls his friend Angelo and tells him he's needed.

"You're gonna drive me downtown."

His next call is to his former boss, Mr. Markham. Vincent tells him that he's sorry to leave, but he has some real good opportunities coming up. Though George is a sad-sack, he is also likable and fair and he wishes Vincent well.

"I want to thank you for all you did for me, Mr. Markham. Maybe one day I'll be in a position to help you, sir. You have been good to me and I will not forget that."

He then goes downstairs and waits for Angelo to show up. When he arrives, Mikey is sitting in the passenger seat, so Vincent hops in the back.

"How the fuck did you get an appointment to see Jimmy D?" asks Angelo.

"Just drive," Vincent says. "I don't want to be late."

Angelo drops him off in front of the building. Mikey looks out the window, saying nothing the whole time. They drive off.

Vincent looks down LaSalle Street and in a flash of insight he realizes, watching all the lawyers and other businessmen in suits strutting up and down, that he's standing in the hub of Chicago power. *This is where you can get a foothold in the business,* he thinks. Someday *he* will be talking to these lawyers and other suits.

With the excitement roiling inside him, Vincent enters the building and takes the elevator to the fourth floor. The receptionist, an Italian lady he recognizes from the Neighborhood, sees him come in and points some chairs in the waiting room. People come in and out of offices, paying him no heed. Vincent looks at his watch. It's 2:55. He's five minutes early.

Vincent sits still with his mouth shut and waits. He looks at his watch again. It now reads 4:15 p.m. No one says a word to him. At 5 o'clock, as all the employees begin to leave for the day, the receptionist points him to a doorway.

He walks through and sees Jimmy D sitting at his desk with an older, gray-haired, gentleman on his right, both men dressed in expensive suits and ties. Jimmy D, fifty-five years old, a major fatso with a blood-lit nose, lights up a huge cigar and motions Vincent to a chair. Vincent sits. Jimmy D glances over to the man, who radiates power and confidence, then blows a great plume of smoke into the air for effect.

"Okay kid, we got the call. You're on. Explain to us what you want and need."

Vincent looks at the two august gentlemen in front of him. He addresses Jimmy D directly, though from time to time, he glances at the other man.

"To get a private investigator's license in the state of Illinois, you have to put in three years at a detective agency. They have to assist you by giving your work records to the state, and then you have to take a test. If you pass the test and meet all of the other requirements, you pay a $100 fee and you get your license. I'm getting resistance from those in the business. I'm sure they do not want me to have a license. I cannot even get over the first hurdle."

Jimmy D glances over to the older gentlemen and a look passes between them. They nod at each other. The fatso Jimmy D struggles but eventually manages to lift his rotund mass out of his chair. He gestures his cigar toward the doorway.

"Okay kid, someone will get in touch with you and tell you what you need to do. In the meantime, keep your mouth shut. Do not discuss this with anyone or even tell them that you came to us."

The whole meeting lasts about fifteen minutes—*Fast,* Vincent thinks.

As he leaves, he waves goodbye to the receptionist, who smiles sweetly at him. Vincent strolls around LaSalle Street to get a feel for it. Never in his life has he dealt with lawyers. But he's going to be his own man, start a business, and make a name for himself. If he can actually get the license, that is. One step at a time.

Vincent takes a cab back to the Neighborhood. Outside The Patio, his buddies greet him. He tells them absolutely nothing. He walks down the street to the grocery store. Tony's not to be found, so he asks Rina.

"He had a doctor's appointment, honey, but he'll be back in the morning."

"Should I show up at six a.m. tomorrow?" Vincent asks.

"Yes, come in at six. We're expecting two more trucks. Say hi to your mom."

"I will."

Vincent's mind wanders as he walks. This will be a big opportunity if it comes through, and he believes it will, but he cannot stop thinking about what it will cost.

13

SHOES

As Vincent walks past the barber shop, "Shoes" Aiello calls out and waves him in. Shoes directs him into the back room. Vincent has never formally met Shoes. At 68, Shoes is well known in the Neighborhood, because of his large collection of exotic shoes—alligator, crocodile, snake, and other skins and leathers—always shined to brilliance, but never matching the clothing he wears. This is odd, but then again, Shoes is odd himself. In any event, Shoes has been around for as long as Vincent or anyone else can remember and has the blessings of the old man for his sports book.

In the back room, Vincent is amazed to see the flurry of activity. He is led to a corner table. They both sit down.

"I hear you know how to find people," Shoes says.

"Who told you that?"

"Are you being a smartass? Who the fuck you think?"

"You need something?"

"Yeah, there are two stiffs who owe. I will give you all the information I got on them and I want you to find them and tell me where they are."

Vincent wants to say no, but obviously word has spread that he is now in debt himself. Obviously, from time to time, Outfit guys are going to approach him. He makes a mental note to talk to Tony about this, but best just to go along for now until he knows what is what.

"Okay, give me the names and whatever information you got and I'll look into it."

"Yeah, but you do nothing else, you understand me?" Shoes says. "You do nothing but find them and tell me. You got that?"

Vincent nods as Shoes walks over to another guy, who takes out a pencil and paper and writes out the information. Then this guy takes more papers out of his pocket and writes down more information. Shoes hands the papers to Vincent.

"You tell nobody about this. You find these guys and you report back to me, you understand?"

Vincent nods and Shoes points to the doorway.

"Let me know when you got something."

Vincent thinks about this. He's offered no money. It's like an order, like being back in the Army. He could not refuse. *Strange.* He will wait until the morning and talk to Tony about this. Telling "nobody" cannot include Tony, he figures.

Vincent's mother is at home, setting the table for dinner. She looks at him with questioning eyes, but says nothing.

"Go wash up. Dinner is almost ready. By the way, a Valerie called you. This a Neighborhood girl?"

"Nah, she used to work with me and actually trained me. I quit, and she probably wants to know what's what."

"You quit? Why didn't you tell me?"

"Tony told me to quit. He didn't really give me no choice. He said that I have to work for him for a while."

"Go wash up," his mother says, without any further comment.

After dinner, he helps his mother with the dishes, then they sit down and watch Jackie Gleason in *The Honeymooners*. Spending time with his mother seems to please her, but he's bored with what's on TV. He announces he's going to bed because he has to work at six the next morning. She nods and he goes off to his bedroom.

He calls Valerie. She wants to see him. He tells her he'll see her tomorrow night.

The following morning, he dresses in old clothes and heads to the grocery store. When he arrives at six, the doors are locked. Tony is nowhere to be seen.

Vincent sits on the doorjamb. About fifteen minutes later, a car drives up and Tony gets out of the passenger side. Vincent doesn't recognize the driver. Tony does not say a word to Vincent, just unlocks the door and walks in. Vincent follows him, and they go to the back to open the dock doors. There's already a truck waiting. Tony points to the truck. He doesn't need to say anything.

Vincent unloads this truck and the one that comes an hour later. Tony comes out and points to where the boxes should be stored. When he's done, Tony walks out of his office, points to Vincent, and curls a finger toward him. Vincent follows Tony to his office, sits down, and waits for Tony to speak.

"In about a week from now you're going to meet with a lawyer. Don't ask me who, because I don't know, but this lawyer is going to take care of some things."

Vincent waits for Tony to say more and when he does not, Vincent asks if he can talk to him about something else. Tony nods and waits for Vincent to explain.

"Shoes grabbed me yesterday. He told me that he wanted me to find a couple of guys who owe him money. It seems as though he did not give me a choice, but that I would have to do this."

Tony looks at Vincent. A few moments go by. "Do it."

Tony gets up from his desk. At the door to his office, he turns around.

"Do it now. Leave now and get it done. When you find them, you come and see me first, you understand?"

"You first?"

Tony frowns, so that the lines in his face look like canyons.

"Okay, okay," says Vincent. "Do you want to know who these guys are?"

"It's none of my business. Just tell me when you find them." Tony walks off.

Vincent does not have his work tools—books or equipment—that were at the Catalog Company. But he's still got his contacts. He calls his old office and asks for Valerie. Once on the phone, she asks him when she's going to see him. Vincent ignores her question.

"I need you to help me with something and I'm going to give you some information. I'll call you again in an hour, and you can let me know what you found out."

"What's this all about, Vincent?"

"Don't ask, just do this for me. I need to get the cross-reference directory information and a few other things from there. I'm also going to need a car. I'll figure all that stuff out but get this done for me, sweetheart."

He gives her the names and hangs up. Then he calls his other contacts and asks for the favors. He needs to set up shop somehow. But he's got no money. He walks out into the Neighborhood to find Mikey and Angelo.

They have a job to do.

14

THE BENEFITS OF A CHOP SHOP

Angelo Ragatta and Mikey Solanotti are quite a pair. They do almost everything together, but mostly crime. Three years older than Vincent, Angelo is an absolute family man with two kids. He married his high school sweetheart immediately out of high school. Angelo has solid muscles—athletic and dangerous.

Mikey, four years older than Vincent, but in no way as mature or streetwise, fucks anything with a heartbeat. Mikey is thin and wiry, moving only when necessary. The two really have nothing in common, except crime and a loyalty to each other.

Angelo's wife, Jessica, thinks Mikey is a bad influence. She's fine with him at a distance—just not in her house. She hates that he smokes excessively. She knows that her Angelo is a dyed-in-the-wool gangster, but she never asks questions. Never. She's a great wife, loving and caring, so she lets her husband be and is always pleasant to Mikey when she sees him.

Vincent walks up to the pair with a frown on his face.

"What's got you?" Angelo asks.

"I need a car."

"Yeah, so?" says Mikey.

They go off to find Fat Louie Cosenza. Louie is a made man. He's got body shops all over the city, but in reality, it's a huge chop shop operation.

What is a chop shop? Let's say the owner of a white Oldsmobile Cutlass with a beige interior needs to get the bashed-in driver's side door fixed. Once the order—or request—comes in, Louie sends out his crew to look for a different white Oldsmobile Cutlass, one that is clean and undamaged. After such a car has been found and inspected, the team steals the vehicle and delivers it to one of Louie's many garages. There it's stripped and broken down for parts—as in "chopped." The door is delivered to the requesting body shop, and Louie sells the rest of the parts to other body shops around the city. They all place orders from Louie.

It doesn't take too long to find these cars, either. Louie has contacts at all the large parking lots, including the huge lot at the airport. Most times it's as simple as calling those contacts, getting a confirmation, and sending out a theft crew of two or three guys in an untraceable car with phony license plates. The theft crew carries all the tools of the trade and can steal any car, no matter the make or model. It's a wonderful deal for all, except, of course, the poor scrub who loses his car. Louie's body shop doesn't have to spend money getting a replacement door from the manufacturer. Actually, it's better for the customer, too, since the manufacturer charges more and takes a long time to fill orders.

Vincent, Angelo, and Mikey pull up to the shop as Fat Louie is giving an estimate to a customer.

"Hey Louie, what's what?" Angelo says. "Hey, you look like you lost some weight."

"Fuck you, Angelo. You lookin' for a beating?" Louie says, turning back to his customer.

The three laugh and then wait. When Louie's finished, he walks over to the trio.

"What's up?"

"Vincent needs a car," Mikey says, "and he has no money to pay for it yet. You know the score."

The fat man looks right at Vincent. "You're Teri's kid, right?"

"You know my mother?"

"Yeah, my younger sister Connie and she are friends. Come inside."

The deal is simple. Louie will outfit a car for Vincent, and in return, he and the other two will do something for Louie. One, two, three.

"Come by tomorrow at three, and something will be ready for you, Vincent. Say hello to your ma for me."

Vincent now has a car to track down the two compulsive gambler welches for Shoes.

But these favors are adding up.

15

MICROWAVES

The next morning Vincent goes back to work at six and tells Tony that he has to leave early that afternoon. He also tells him that he has a lead on one of Shoe's debtors and needs to take the next couple of days off. Tony grunts. That is the most Vincent gets out of him.

Valerie has come through. She has information on one of the names, a Henry Woljokowski. Vincent's credit card contact, Mary Donovan, has got even more information, including the fact that Henry recently purchased a late model used Cadillac for cash, using a new address for registration. Vincent wonders how Henry got the cash to buy the car but puts it out of his mind. He makes a note of the information about the car and the new address.

Mikey drives him to Fat Louie's where one of the employees takes Vincent in the back and hands him the keys to a shiny black '62 Ford

Thunderbird. Mikey whistles. Vincent takes the keys, gets in, and follows Mikey back to the Neighborhood.

About eight that night, Vincent picks up Mikey in his Thunderbird. No Angelo tonight. He's at home babysitting the kids while his wife attends a baby shower. Vincent and Mikey laugh about that as they drive to Henry Woljokowski's new address. When they arrive, they spot Henry's Cadillac parked in front of his apartment building. Vincent and Mikey look at each other knowingly and drive off.

"That's one," says Vincent.

"Nice ride, and it's clean," says Mikey. "I bet it's a one-owner car, probably some old Jew broad."

Back in the Neighborhood, they stop at Baba's for beef and sausage sandwiches. A bunch of people are milling outside. Mikey asks what's going on.

"Microwave ovens" says one of the guys.

"What the hell is a microwave?" Mikey responds.

"No idea," says the same guy. "But Baba says they're the wave of the future, no pun intended. He says every woman in town is going to want one. He's selling them for $300 each."

Mikey whistles. "Glad I'm not married."

"I'll bet they have serial numbers on them," Vincent says. "I think I'll wait. My mother would never use one anyways."

16

PRIME PICKINGS

The next day around noon, Vincent goes to see Tony. He drives up in his car and sees Tony walking up Taylor Street. He parks in front of the store. Tony looks at the Thunderbird, frowns, but says nothing. Vincent leans forward and tells him what he learned.

"What do you want me to do now, Papa Tony?"

Tony hesitates, looks up to the sky, then gestures down the block. "C'mon with me."

They go next door and see Shoes in the alley berating one of his guys.

"I'm telling you, this fuck is past posting! If I find out Larry is in on this, I'm taking him up to see the pig farmer. Now get out and find out what's what," Shoes says.

Shoes looks back and sees Tony and Vincent waiting for him to end his tirade. He glares at Vincent and smiles warmly at Tony.

"To what do I owe this pleasure, Tony? I paid the rent and got the toilet fixed," Shoes says.

Tony says nothing but gestures for them all to walk farther down the alley, out of ear shot. Once there, he looks around and nods to Vincent.

"Tell him," Tony says calmly.

Vincent looks over to Shoes and tells him most of what he's learned. But he does not tell Shoes that Henry paid cash for the car. Shoes takes the information Vincent has written out for him and looks at the kid with newfound respect.

"Son of a gun. Good job, good job. What about the other thing?"

"I'm working on it," Vincent replies.

Tony, now impatient, growls, "C'mon" to Vincent. He doesn't speak until they're back in his office.

"He didn't say a word about any payment, Papa Tony."

Tony nods and says, "Find the other guy. Where did you get the car?"

"Fat Louie."

Tony frowns and gets up.

"Find the other guy, Vincenzo, and come to me first when you do."

Vincent sits there momentarily, gets up, deep in thought, and walks out the door. He's unnerved, confused, and pissed about Shoes. He meets his friends who are standing outside The Patio talking among a group of guys.

Vincent gestures to Angelo and Mikey. "Whaddya think that Caddy was worth, Mikey?"

"I dunno, Vincent, maybe around three Gs. Why?"

"No, I meant to say how much is it worth chopped. Whaddya think?"

"A lot more than that. It looked clean and I saw no damage. Why?"

Vincent smiles and says, "I'm gonna make a call. Then let's take a ride to see Fat Louie."

It's late by the time they arrive at Louie's. Always to the point, Louie asks, "What's up?"

Vincent hands him a piece of paper with all the information about the Caddy.

"This is prime pickings, Louie. A cherry. Send out a crew and deduct what you can from my debt."

Louie frowns. He looks Vincent over, confused and a little suspicious. But he pockets the information, nonetheless.

"I don't understand, but sure, I'll send someone out right away," Louie says shaking his head.

"What the fuck are you up to, Vincent?" Mikey says as they drive off. Vincent doesn't even hear as he steers the car towards Mikey's house.

His mind is on the other thing he has to do for Shoes.

17

A SCOPE OUT

While Vincent was dealing with the Caddy, Valerie has been busy on his behalf. She's been looking into the other guy Shoes wants found, Manny Valdes, a master welder and safe cracker.

Valerie tracks down Valdes' sister, Gloria, and then gags her by telling her a story about a fake romance she had with Manny. Gloria tells her that Manny moved to East Chicago, Indiana, about twenty-five miles outside of Chicago proper—another world. Manny's sister doesn't know his new address, but she does have Manny's new telephone number, in case his frail mother has to reach him. Gloria gives it to Valerie who swears her to secrecy, saying that she wants to surprise Manny. She and Valerie even giggle about it.

Vincent feels a thrill when Valerie tells him the whole story later. There's something he finds sexy about a woman who uses her brain, but there's also something else about her. In any event, they're a good match. Vincent then calls Todd Billings, his contact at the phone company. He gives the phone number to Todd, who tracks down the address. *It's good to have friends,* thinks Vincent.

Vincent, Mikey, and Angelo drive to East Chicago. On the way, Mikey asks, "What do you hear from Paulie the G, Vincent?"

"They think he's gonna be a superstar and he's going for more training. He may be home for Christmas, him and his new girlfriend, some white bread chick he's got the hearts for. His mother is thrilled, but I get ice cream headaches thinking about it. I love him like a brother, though, so keep your comments to yourself."

"Jeez, don't be so sensitive, Vincent, I was only asking."

Mikey looks over his shoulder to Angelo, who merely shrugs.

Manny's basement apartment is in a bad neighborhood and from the outside looks even worse than they thought.

"What a fucking pigsty, Vincent. I doubt this guy has two pennies to rub together. I cannot imagine how he got into Shoes for two large."

Mikey leans back. "There are no lights that I can see, Vincent. Drop me off at the corner. I want to scope out his place."

"Why? We know where he lives. That's all I need to give Shoes."

"I gotta feeling," Mikey says. "This is a safe guy, right? Didn't he used to work with the North Avenue crew with Larry Rosselli?"

"Yeah, so what?"

Angelo says, "Let him look, Vincent. What harm can it do?"

If Mikey suggests doing anything, it means he actually has to move, the lazy fuck, thinks Vincent, so he drives to the end of the block and drops Mikey off. Angelo climbs up front. They circle the block and park with the basement apartment in view.

A few minutes later, Mikey gets back in the car. His shirt and pants are soiled. He looks at Vincent and says, "I knew it. It's a work pad.

There's only a mattress, some other junk, a shit load of tools, drills, and other shit. There is a telephone in there with an active dial tone."

Vincent shrugs and says, "So?"

Mikey looks at Angelo and says, "Maybe we should trail this fuck and check out his route. If he's lining up a score, maybe we should bump into him, whaddya think?"

Vincent says, "You guys do what you want, but after I give this information to Shoes, I want to be done with him."

They drive back to Chicago. Vincent drops them off in the Neighborhood and drives to Valerie's place. Valerie Franck lives in an apartment in Lincoln Park, the near north side. She has a small, modest, really tidy apartment, which pleases Vincent, a bit of a neat freak himself.

When Vincent arrives, Valerie is downstairs talking to a neighbor. She sees Vincent and walks over to the car.

"Nice wheels," she says. "Am I ever going to meet any of your friends or family, Vincent?"

"No," he replies.

Valerie looks at him agape but says nothing. She knows better. He won't give her any information, anyway.

Their relationship evolved from training at work to friendship. Now it's evolving into something more. Vincent's not ready for this, but Valerie definitely is, which might be a problem. Sometimes he thinks about introducing her to his mother. But he knows Teri would latch onto Valerie and hear wedding bells. Valerie herself has spoken from time to time about her divorced parents. Vincent doesn't pry because he doesn't care. He wants to enjoy this relationship as long as it lasts, but he has no intention of taking it much further. He has too many plans for his own future. No way is he going to introduce Valerie to his mother.

18

THE GIRL WANTS TOO MUCH

The next afternoon Vincent fills in Tony about Manny Valdes. They go next door to find Shoes. He's where they saw him last, in the alley confronting yet another employee.

"Are you fucking kidding me?" Shoes barks at the cowering bookie. "He was out there talking to the police about his car being stolen? What about my fucking money?"

Shoes turns, sees them, and walks over.

"Tell him," Tony says.

Vincent gives all the information he has on Manny, including the possibly bogus address. Shoes looks troubled.

"So, you think this is just a phony address and that he lives somewhere else, or what? You think he's staging a score?"

"Yeah, I do. But now you know where to find him. His sister uses that number to call him. She takes care of their elderly mother, so she needs to reach him from time to time. Maybe he just crashes there for now."

Deep in thought, Shoes says nothing.

"Anyway," Vincent continues. "I did as you asked, so I'm done."

Suddenly Shoes' entire demeanor changes. He's about to explode. But when he looks at Tony, whose face has hardened, he has a change of heart.

"Yeah, well, okay. Maybe I can call you if something else comes up."

Tony grabs Vincent by the arm before he can respond, and they leave Shoes standing there.

Vincent goes home and calls Valerie. It's Friday night and they have plans: dinner and a show.

After he picks up Valerie, they drive off to the restaurant. Vincent is moody and silent. He's like that sometimes, and his mood is contagious. Valerie is stewing. Finally, she comes out with it.

"You always talk about your friend who is away at college or something. Paulie, right? You talk about him like he's your brother, but you never give me any details or anything. And it's not just him. You keep everything inside. What do you want from this relationship, if that's what we're calling it, Vincent? I mean, we go out, we fuck, and that's about it."

Vincent abruptly pulls the car over to the side of the road, wheels screeching to a stop. He shifts the Thunderbird into park.

"Look, Valerie," he says, turning to face her. "I like you a lot. But you don't know anything about me, about my background, the neighborhood I grew up in—*nothing*. I don't think you would like my friends, so I don't introduce you. If you're not satisfied with what we have, then say so, but don't bug me about it. I've got plans that don't include you. No offense, but that's what it is."

Valerie is stunned. She looks over at Vincent and starts to weep.

"Take me home, Vincent."

"C'mon, can't we just be friends with no drama? Can't we just enjoy each other's company and have a good time?"

She looks out the window and says nothing.

"You sure?" he asks.

"Take me home, Vincent. And forget my number. No more favors, either. Just leave me alone."

Vincent frowns. He takes her home. On the way back to the Neighborhood, he wonders why he acted like such a jerk. He's never had a meaningful relationship with any woman. He just likes the company, the sex, and that's about it. Maybe he'll call Valerie later and try to make up with her. Or maybe not.

He wonders about Paulie and his new love and how he makes it work.

19

THE COLLEGE BOY

Since Vincent's return home, he and Paulie banter on the phone like they used to. Though their bond doesn't waver, it is increasingly clear that they're on fundamentally conflicting paths.

At college in North Carolina, Paulie tries desperately to cloak his Italian background, so that he fits in better with the student body. He's one of only three Italian-named students enrolled in the school, and the others are third and fourth generation—Italian in name only. They have nothing in common with Paulie. He's from the Neighborhood, and this is the south. For the most part, the attitudes are grossly different from anything he has ever encountered—or even anticipated, for that matter.

People constantly mispronounce his last name and ask some really stupid questions about "EYEtalians." When word gets out that he is from Chicago, the notorious gangster breeding ground, plenty of people wonder if Paulie is related to mobsters. He's constantly defending himself against the prejudice by reminding his classmates that his goal in life is to become an FBI agent.

On that score, he's the real deal. Paulie majors in criminal justice and often visits courtrooms to listen in on criminal cases. He even takes special courses outside of his core curriculum to further enhance his chances.

On their phone calls, Vincent listens to his friend talk of his intention to become an FBI agent with sincere interest. In his heart, Vincent would like nothing more than for Paulie to never come back to the Neighborhood. He knows that the distance between them, in all matters, will widen. Vincent also knows that after Paulie graduates from college, he'll attend the FBI Academy, and that nothing Vincent says can make him change course.

From time to time, Vincent tries to broach the subject of Paulie with Tony, who only shrugs his shoulders and says nothing. Vincent knows that Tony has paid for Paulie's college and truly cares about his grandson. Tony does not want Paulie to work for the FBI, either. But, because of his intense love for Paulie, he reluctantly encourages him, something that Vincent cannot bring himself to do.

On the phone, Paulie tells Vincent more about his new girlfriend. Everything Paulie says makes her sound like she's pure WASP, especially with a name like Carolyn Arrington. But Vincent also senses that Paulie genuinely cares for Carolyn and he wants Paulie to be happy, so he listens, though he's doubtful it will last.

His perception is reinforced when he hears Paulie talk about her family, and in particular, her father, Winston Arrington III, a deputy U.S. attorney with designs on an even higher office. Connected and with powerful political skills, Winston does not initially accept his daughter's relationship with Paulie.

On his part, Paulie is always polite and courteous to Carolyn's parents and especially respectful to Mr. Arrington. Carolyn's father slowly learns to accept Paulie, seeing how hard he works. Of course, the fact that Paulie's sole ambition is to become an FBI agent helps solidify their relationship, since Winston Arrington is dyed-in-the wool law enforcement, as close to the justice system as Paulie's grandfather Tony is to the Outfit. Frequently, Paulie and Winston have long, involved conversations about the law, about the cases Paulie's seen in court, or precedents he's reviewed during long nights reading in the university stack.

During Paulie's senior year, Winston introduces the young man to a couple of FBI agents that he's worked with. They are surprised and even intrigued that he wants to become an agent, given his Neighborhood background. Impressed by his dedication, they offer him sincere encouragement to move forward. They speak for hours about the obstacles Paulie might face becoming an agent, most importantly his family's association with the Neighborhood. They acknowledge that his Italian heritage, in particular, might make joining the Bureau more difficult. On the other hand, they hint that his Italian background *could* be an asset.

Of course, on their phone calls, Paulie tells none of this to his friend. He doesn't want to give Vincent any more cause to disparage his FBI dreams.

20

WHAT'S IN A NAME?

By 1967, while Vincent is working to start his private detective business, Paulie, after four years of college, has forged friendships throughout his community. For the most part, he's been accepted by the student body. He's done his best to shed the stereotype that's associated with his ethnicity and is happy that he now commands a measure of respect.

Ever since his conversation with the FBI agents, Paulie has toyed with the idea of changing his name. But when he thinks about his grandfather and the others back in the Neighborhood, he hesitates.

One day on the phone, he discusses this with Vincent.

"Have you gone fucking crazy?" his friend explodes. "Have some of your feeble brains seeped out? Why in the world would you even consider that?"

He and Vincent argue, and Vincent finally surrenders.

"Do what the fuck you want, you dummy," Vincent says. "I personally don't care if you change your name to Elliot Ness—it will just give me more to rag on you. You never listen to me anyhow." Then, his voice changes. "But think about who it would hurt. Think about that, Paulie," he says earnestly.

This is the only argument they've ever had, and they quickly change the subject. Their friendship has suffered from years apart. Each think that the other has changed dramatically.

In truth, they both have.

21

A FATEFUL DECISION

Just before graduation, Paulie thinks seriously about proposing to Carolyn. Before he takes that step, though, he considers what that might mean to both of them. He decides the time has come to change his name. He convinces himself that if he does, it will be better for himself and for his future with Carolyn: the FBI will take him more seriously, improving his chances to become an agent for the Bureau.

He asks Carolyn's father what steps are needed to change his name. He wants to do this before applying to the Academy. Winston Arrington, smiling inwardly, asks Paulie if he's ashamed of his ethnicity. Paulie politely, though forcefully, states that no, he is not. But, he explains that he wants more than anything to become an FBI agent.

Carolyn's father likes the idea. He encourages Paulie because of his daughter, whom he knows is in love with the young man. If they ever get married—a thought that Winston dreads and certainly hopes will not come to pass—he'd find consolation in the fact that his daughter and grandchildren would not bear an Italian name.

Arrington promptly takes Paulie to the courthouse and tells him how to proceed with his name change application. Shortly thereafter, Paulie appears before a judge, who grants him leave to legally change his name. That day he becomes Paul A. Andrews.

That night, Paulie calls Carolyn to tell her what he's done.

"Why?" she asks, confused.

"You know that I want a career with the FBI," he responds. "And I don't want my name holding me back."

"Why do you think that would make a difference?"

"Believe me, it will. Your father agrees."

"My *father*?"

"I asked for his advice."

"Why would you ask him and not *me*?" she cries, unable to disguise the hurt in her voice.

"Carolyn, he is law enforcement. And after I graduate, I intend to propose to you. I want your father to know that my intentions are real. I want his respect."

Carolyn says, "Paul, I loved your name and would have been proud to carry it. And I love you no matter what, but I am sorry you made this decision."

She hangs up the phone, disheartened. Why did Paul bend to her father? She actually feels some disgust.

22

TUFF PHONE CALLS

That evening, Paulie cannot sleep. He tosses and turns with guilt and anxiety. He's borne his grandfather's name proudly since birth, but now he is an Andriano no longer. He needs to call his "Nonno" and let him know. He also needs to tell his mother.

At seven the next morning, he groggily gets out of bed and calls the store, knowing that his grandfather will be there. When Papa Tony comes to the phone, he is excited as always to hear from his grandson. Paulie clears his throat, trying not to choke on his words. He tells his grandfather of his name change.

Tony pulls the phone handset from his ear and stares at it in utter disbelief. His hand begins to shake as he slowly places the handset back against his ear and quietly says, "Paulie, why? Why?"

Paulie swallows hard, holding down the bile that begins to erupt from his stomach and says, "Nonno, I want to advance within the

Bureau, and they have always had an attitude against Italians, thinking that we are all part of organized crime. I want to succeed as an FBI agent without having to justify my heritage."

"Paul Andrews." Tony repeats the name with sorrow in his voice. "So, I no longer have a grandson named Andriano—my name, my honor, my family."

"I am so sorry if this hurts you, Nonno. That is not my intention."

"I will miss my grandson and I will grieve," responds Tony before hanging up. He walks out to the alley behind the store to hide his anguish.

Paulie thinks his heart will break, but he's not finished. He calls his mother.

After he stops speaking, she remains silent. She finally says, "You're your own man now, Paulie. The choices you make are yours and yours alone. I will always love you. I don't know what to do about your grandfather's hurt and pain, but I know he loves you. I think that time will tell. In the meantime, just succeed. That success will help heal the wounds, my son. Have you told Vincent?"

"I dread that, but I will, today. I love you, mom. Please try to understand and tell Nonno I love him and will always honor him no matter what my name is."

Paulie hangs up. He has one more call to make. He waits a while, recovering himself, then dials Vincent's number.

"Hey, Paulie the G, did they teach you how to shoot yet?" Vincent jokes before his friend can speak. "Tell them to run for cover when they do because you may shoot them. You're fucking cockeyed, could never hit a fast ball."

There is silence on the line, before Vincent asks, "What's going on?"

Paulie hesitates for another moment, then shares his news with Vincent. Now it is Paulie's turn to hear silence at the other end.

"Paulie, you are so incredibly stupid," Vincent finally erupts. "Why in the world would you do such a stupid thing knowing it would hurt everyone? Papa Tony must be devastated."

"Vincent, please try to understand. I truly believe that if I have to constantly defend my name and ethnicity, it will become even harder to become the best FBI agent I can. Please try to understand and support me."

"Paulie, you are like my brother and I love you, but this was a very serious mistake. You could have kept your name and continued to be proud of being Italian. You could have fought for to keep your good name and birthright, but you bowed to them, Paulie. That I cannot forgive. But I will always be there for you. You are who you are. Go on, be Paulie the G. That is what you always wanted and now you will get your wish."

Vincent hangs up, thinking *If the neighborhood ever hears about this…*

"What a fucking nightmare!" he yells at the ceiling of his mother's kitchen.

Paulie, alone at school, stares at the ceiling, too. Guilt-ridden, he tries not to hate himself.

23

THE SACRIFICE FOR A DREAM

Vincent goes to the grocery store. There he sees Rina, but she cannot look at him. He walks up to her anyway and kisses her cheek, as always. She throws her arms around him. She's never done that before.

"Oh Vincent," she sobs.

"It will be okay." he says, awkwardly holding her. "Hopefully this will work out. He always wanted this."

"But changing his name? Why in the world?" she utters.

"That's Paulie," Vincent says, as if it's some kind of an answer.

"But why?" Rina asks again.

"I will never know," Vincent responds. "This dream of his to be an FBI agent is one thing. But turning his back on his family name? I can't think about it without wanting to throw up."

Rina strokes Vincent's head, then withdraws from their embrace,

"Where's Papa Tony?" he asks.

Rina wipes her eyes and points to the rear of the store. Vincent walks toward the loading dock and sees the old man. When their eyes meet, Tony tears up. Then he stiffens and points to a truck parked at the dock.

"Unload that," he says curtly and walks out the back to the alleyway. Vincent watches him go, the old man wiping his eyes with his handkerchief.

When Vincent later meets up with the Neighborhood guys, he does not say a word. They will find out on their own someday.

24

A CHANGE IN STATION

Still reeling from his conversation with Paulie, Vincent walks over to The Patio later that afternoon and sees Angelo and Mikey. Angelo comes up to him and waves Mikey over.

"We tailed Manny and found out his score. We're going to wait for him to bust open the safe and then rob him."

"What?"

"Yeah, it's a good score. The company gets a delivery from Brinks, then stores the payroll in a safe for Friday. It's pay day and they cash a lot of checks. Can you believe that? They charge them for cashing their own money, the Jew bastards!"

"When is this going to happen? This Thursday?"

"Yeah," says Angelo, in a sort of manic glee. "You want in?"

"No," Vincent replies. "Don't get caught, you two. Try not to do anything stupid. And whatever you do, do not let him know who you are. We do not want the bosses to know. In a week or so, assuming it is what you think, we'll go and pay the tax, but not until then. You two understand?"

"Yeah, yeah."

Tired of The Patio, Vincent makes his way home.

"Ma?" he calls out.

She's in the kitchen. She points to the stove and says, "We'll eat in about an hour. Why the sad face?"

He doesn't want to burden her with Paulie's secret, but this will be just one more for her. Too many. So, he sits her down and tells her everything.

She frowns and says, "So Rina and Papa Tony know also?"

"Yeah, he told them. The old man took it hard."

She shakes her head, gets up, and goes to the stove. Over her shoulder, she says, "Give it time, Vincent, give it time. He's still Paulie, no matter what name he uses. Remember that. You want some Ovaltine?"

They eat and watch *The Honeymooners*. Halfway through the show, Vincent stands up and leaves. He's in no mood. He goes out to his car and drives over to Valerie's apartment building.

Vincent parks outside her building, then walks over to the front stoop, but stops himself from ringing her doorbell. Instead, he sits on the stoop to think. After a while he asks himself, *What am I doing here?* He gets up, goes back to the car, and drives away. From her window, Valerie sees it all, heartbroken.

The next morning, Vincent arrives at the grocery store at about seven o'clock. He's surprised to find that the front door is locked. He walks around to the loading area in the back. He peeks in and sees Tony leaning against the walk-in freezer door. He has a photo in his hand and tears in his eyes.

Vincent feigns tripping over a box to announce his presence. Papa Tony quickly puts the photo back in his pocket. He sits down on a crate and calls Vincent over. He looks into Vincent's eyes but says nothing. It seems like he cannot speak.

Vincent wants to say, *He will be okay, Papa Tony, don't worry. He'll come around.* But he says nothing. Let this go and let's see what happens. He has a lot to work out.

Tony looks at Vincent in a new light. He shakes his head, wipes his eyes, and says, "There's a truck coming in now, and this afternoon you will have to go see someone. I will let you know."

Then Tony walks to the front of the store and lets in some employees. Rina is not among them. He looks out the door, then out on the sidewalk, looking up and down the street for his daughter. She's not in sight. *What's happening to my family?* he wonders.

She's never late.

25

MOVING FORWARD

When Vincent is about to leave the grocery store for the day, Tony calls him into his office.

"Okay, you need to go downtown tomorrow at three o'clock to 11 South LaSalle Street, Suite 901. The lawyer's name is Sidney Ackerman. He will be waiting for you. You just listen to what he has to say and do what he tells you. Do not comment at all and never mention any names, period. You understand? You just listen and follow instructions."

Vincent has a thousand questions, but the look on Papa Tony's face shuts him up.

"Okay," he says.

"He will contact our friends to move this forward. Do not talk about money or anything. We will discuss this later when you come in tomorrow. Don't tell anyone about this."

"Not even my mother?"

"She will know in time. We need to keep this close to the vest for now. We don't know if we can trust this guy or not, but downtown says he's okay, so we wait."

"Papa Tony, thank you."

"Go to work and stop bothering me."

Tony walks away, and a tremendous grin crosses Vincent's face. Papa Tony turns around.

"You say something?"

Vincent's smile quickly vanishes, "Nothing, nothing at all."

26

AN UGLY OFFICE

The next day Vincent gets a ride downtown from Angelo.

"What's this about?" Angelo asks, wondering why Vincent didn't drive himself.

Vincent looks directly at Angelo but says nothing.

At the building, Vincent rides the elevator to the ninth floor, walks into the reception area, and approaches the receptionist, a gray-haired older woman with a sourpuss, hatchet face.

"I'm Vincent Scalise," he says.

"Take a seat."

Vincent does what he's told. As he waits, he eyes the cheap lithographs on the walls. He's not impressed with the office at all. *Low rent,* he thinks.

About fifteen minutes later, a dapper guy, about forty-five years old, with gray, slicked-back hair and tinted glasses, strides into the room and holds out his hand to Vincent.

"Sidney Ackerman. How the hell are you?"

Vincent shakes it, and Sidney walks Vincent back through the doors. Inside the office, they're met by another man. He has black hair and huge, thick glasses that give his eyes a fish-like look. Vincent immediately dubs him, "Bottle Glasses." This second man wears a wrinkled leisure suit that's soiled with what appears to be mustard. He says nothing, and indeed, does not acknowledge Vincent at all. For his part, Vincent also says nothing. Ackerman gestures to a seat and Vincent sits.

"Do you have your driver's license with you?" Ackerman asks, holding out his hand.

Vincent hands it to him.

"This where you live now?"

"Yes, sir."

"Okay. You've had some experience I'm told. Did you graduate high school?"

"No, I went into the Army. I got my GED there."

Bottle Glasses looks at Vincent, then to Ackerman, but still remains silent. Ackerman writes down some information from the license, and then hands it back to Vincent.

"Okay," Ackerman says, "We'll let your people know the next step. You can go now."

"That's it?"

"That's it."

Angelo waits for Vincent downstairs.

"Let's go back to the Neighborhood," Vincent says. "I want to pick up my car and run some errands. Is tonight still on?"

"Yeah, you want in or what?"

"No, but just be fucking careful and do not do anything stupid. I have to stay away for a while until I put together some things— hopefully soon."

27

THE FIRST SCORE

It's 11:00 that same night. Mikey and Angelo are parked outside of Manny's apartment with a view of the alleyway and Manny's car. The lights in the apartment go out, and they watch Manny exit the building, a large, heavy duffel bag in each hand.

"Here we go," Angelo says.

Just then, two guys come out of the alley and grab Manny by the shoulders. One punches him in the head while the other starts yelling at him. Manny manages to reach into his pocket and brandishes a wad of bills. The larger of the two men counts the bills and then slaps Manny across the face with the wad. The first guy knees Manny in the stomach, and they leave him shaken, leaning against the car. A few moments later, he pulls himself together enough to open the car door and drive off.

Angelo looks at Mikey. "Shoes."

"Yeah," says Mikey. "Good timing for us, though. He hasn't done the job yet."

Mikey and Angelo smile as they drive off. They know exactly where Manny is headed.

At the job, they see Manny pick the lock on the warehouse door, grab his two sacks, look around, and then enter the building.

Angelo and Mikey wait. After about an hour, Manny peeks his head out the door to see if anyone's there. Then he disappears back inside. This is their cue. Mikey and Angelo cross over to the doorway, one to the right, the other to the left. Manny comes out, a sack in each of his hands.

Mikey swoops in from behind, striking Manny hard with a leather sap on the back of his head. The safecracker crumples to the ground, unconscious. Angelo rifles through his pockets and finds nothing but his wallet and tosses it into the weeds. Then they open one of the sacks. There it is. Fucking stacks of banded cash. Quickly, they transfer the cash into a bag they brought with them and run to the car. They leave Manny his tools. No one sees a thing.

As they drive away, Mikey turns to Angelo, "Should we call the cops? I hit him pretty hard."

Angelo looks at him as if he is insane.

"No fucking way. Let him wake up and try to figure out what happened. I think he'll leave town and not be seen again for a while. At least that's what I would do. He probably thinks Shoes' guys tailed him."

"Works for me."

Neither of them can suppress a big grin.

The next day, Vincent comes upon Mikey and Angelo chatting with some guys outside of Baba's.

"You guys got a minute?" Vincent says, as he gestures to Angelo and Mikey.

They follow him down the block. Vincent can almost sense the shit-eating grins on their faces.

"You want to tell me what the take was or what?" Vincent says.

"Around $58,000, give or take," Mikey says. "Whydya wanna know?

"Numb nuts. You're gonna have to pay a tax, you know that, right? The sooner the better."

"Is that necessary?" Angelo asks.

"Yeah, it is. I'll go talk to the boss and let you know what he says. But whatever he decides, you guys are going to give it up. You understand me?"

They both nod their heads. They really don't want to comply, but they know better. This is the Neighborhood, after all. And this is Vincent.

28

RESPECT

The next morning Vincent goes to see Papa Tony. He explains what his friends have done and asks permission to talk to the street boss as soon as possible.

"I'll let you know," Tony says.

Vincent nods his head, shrugs his shoulders, and goes back to work.

The next morning Tony walks over to Vincent and tells him that Johnny V, the street boss of the Neighborhood, will see him.

"Go to the club and sit and wait. He will see you when he wants to. Don't say anything to anyone. Just sit and wait. Go now."

Vincent walks down to the St. Anthony's Social Club and passes some of the Neighborhood guys, whose eyebrows raise when he walks inside. None of them has ever been inside. They're curious and even a bit jealous.

All eyes turn to Vincent as he walks in the door. Then they go back to what they were doing—playing cards, talking. Vincent finds a seat close to the doorway and sits down. Nobody says anything to him, and he doesn't say anything to anyone.

About an hour later, Johnny Varenzano walks in the club. He briefly glances at Vincent, but says nothing on his way to his office in the back. A few minutes later, a huge hulking mass, Bruno Spolleto, walks up to Vincent. Bruno tells him to go to the back.

In the office, Johnny V gestures for Vincent to sit. His hair is gray and receding. He is muscular in a chubby sort of way—he has a layer of fat but beneath that is pure muscle.

"Tony says you need to talk to me. What can I do for you, son?" Johnny is almost friendly.

"Two of my Neighborhood friends scored. I'm here to find out what you want them to do and how much tax to pay," Vincent says.

Johnny grimaces at the word "pay" but says nothing. Vincent waits.

"I'm told you're a good kid. You go find your friends and bring them back here with you with their score, and we'll talk. Do that now."

"Yes sir. I'll be back as soon as I can," Vincent replies.

Vincent goes to Angelo's house and spells out the deal. He tells him to pick up Mikey and to bring the money in a large, brown paper bag to the club. Vincent will meet them there.

When they gather in front of St. Anthony's, Vincent tells them to wait outside and he walks in. He sees Bruno who nods to him and gestures to the office.

"They're outside. Do you want me to bring them in?" says Vincent.

Johnny nods. Vincent walks outside and then leads his two friends back to Johnny V's office. All three of them stand, waiting. Bruno walks in behind them and closes the door. His hulking mass and demeanor are scary. Mikey is extremely nervous, while Angelo has a stone face. Vincent says nothing.

Johnny V sits at his desk and places his hands behind his thick neck.

"Tell me," he says finally. He rubs his cold black eyes and waits for a response.

Vincent gestures to Angelo, the calmer of the two, to speak. Angelo describes everything except for identifying Manny as the welcher that Vincent was asked to find for Shoes. He purposely leaves that detail out. He then holds out the paper bag and places it on the desk in front of Johnny.

"It's all there, sir. Vincent told us that we must report this to you," says Angelo.

Johnny looks directly at Vincent.

"So, you knew this was going to happen and didn't tell anybody?"

"Yes sir," Vincent says looking directly at Johnny. "We weren't sure that we would score, but we did."

"So, there's fifty-eight grand in the bag?"

"Yes. That's the whole score," Vincent replies.

"You were in on this, then? You were there?" questions Johnny.

"No sir. I was not there."

"But you told your friends that they must report this to me?" Johnny asks, calmly.

"That's right."

They wait for the explosion. Instead, Johnny V calmy announces, "You two rob again without getting permission, and I'm not gonna be happy."

All three of them nod.

"Bruno, take these two outside and have them wait. Vincent, you stay here. I want to talk to you," says Johnny.

Bruno walks Angelo and Mikey out the front door and tells them to wait on the sidewalk. He walks back to the office. He looks over at Johnny, and Johnny gestures to the bag. Bruno takes the bag and counts out the money.

"Fifty-eight Gs," he confirms.

"You did good, son, by coming to me and showing respect. I will remember that. Take fifty to your boys and tell them if they don't ask for permission in the future, no matter what the fuck they do, they're in trouble."

Vincent nods.

"Now, what's your cut?"

"Nothing sir. It's all theirs," says Vincent.

"Bruno, give him two of the eight," Johnny V says.

Vincent shakes his head. "No, sir. I understand respect and mean to show you that I do."

Johnny V's cold black eyes narrow. Then he smiles warmly.

"I'll remember you and your demonstration of respect," says Johnny. "You're a good friend to these guys, but if you vouch for them and they screw up again, it is on you."

Again, Vincent nods.

"You're a good kid, Vincent. Give my regards to Tony," Johnny says, ending the meeting.

Vincent picks up the bag and walks outside to his friends. Angelo makes a grab for the bag.

"Not here. Let's head to Baba's," Vincent advises. Once there, he hands them the bag. Mikey frowns when he learns how much tax was taken, but Vincent reassures them.

"Guys, this was a good thing, what you did, and now you have a measure of respect, which is a good thing in itself."

"You should take an end, Vincent," Angelo says, with Mikey nodding.

Vincent shakes his head and walks off. The two thank him and head to Angelo's house to split the money.

Vincent walks to the grocery store. He finds Tony and tells him exactly what happened.

Tony acknowledges with a simple nod.

29

MISPLACED AFFECTIONS

Despite everything that's going on in his life, Vincent cannot shake his feelings for Valerie. The girl has gotten under his skin, and a few days after the meeting with Johnny V, Vincent decides to do something about it. After helping Tony at the store, he drives to Valerie's house. It is almost six-thirty, and she must be home from work.

After he's parked the car, he gazes up at her brick apartment building and picks out her window. He sighs and almost turns around to leave. He stops himself, screws up his courage, and rings the doorbell. A few moments pass, his heart pounds in his chest, and then, blessedly, the buzzer chimes. He pushes the door open and walks up to her apartment.

She is waiting in her doorway, hand on her thrust-out hip, glaring daggers at him. He cannot help but think of how unbelievably sexy she looks. He loves a spirited woman.

"What do you want, Vincent?"

He starts to smile, and her glare intensifies. The smile vanishes.

"Look, I know I was a jerk, but I care about you."

Valerie sends Vincent a look that stuns him. A blind man could see that her eyes say, *Drop dead.*

She slams the door in his face.

As he turns back to the stairs, he says to himself, *Well, you deserved that.*

He'll send her flowers in a few days. He hopes that she will at least talk to him again. He does owe her for all the training and help she gave him. Once he establishes himself, he will find something for her at his firm—that is, if she doesn't shoot him first.

30

CICERO

Two weeks pass without incident. Vincent is becoming increasingly anxious about the status of his private investigator's license. He hasn't heard a thing since his meeting with Sidney Ackerman.

All the while, his own resources are dwindling. He works for Papa Tony every day, without pay—and without complaint. But something needs to change. Eventually, he gets the nerve to ask Papa Tony for an update about the license.

Tony looks at him sternly. "When I hear something, you'll know about it. This takes time, and there are a lot of people involved. You may not realize that, but that's what's what. Just be patient, Vincent, and quit bothering me about it. Now get back to work."

Around five o'clock, Vincent, tired and sore, leaves the grocery store and goes straight home.

"Ma!" he yells as he walks in the door. "I'm taking a shower."

"Whatever," she replies from the kitchen.

He gets out of the shower, towel wrapped around his waist, surprised to find Papa Tony sitting at the kitchen table.

"Hey, Papa Tony."

"Get dressed Vincent and shut up. We're going to take a drive. We'll take your car."

In the car, Vincent looks over to Tony. "Where to, Papa?"

"Cicero. Get off the expressway at the Austin exit and head south to Roosevelt Road. I'll tell you where from there."

"My grandmother and grandfather live there."

"Don't you think I know that?" Tony whacks Vincent on the arm. "Sometimes I wonder about you and whether or not you have a brain at all."

A half hour later, Papa Tony breaks the silence. "Park over there, about a block away from that restaurant on the corner."

Vincent glides up to the curb. He and Tony walk into the restaurant. As they pass the restaurant's large street-facing window, Vincent notices two men sitting at the corner table facing the doorway. Vincent immediately recognizes one of the men. He looks at Papa Tony, who merely looks back and nods.

Inside the restaurant, they wait by the door. After a few moments, one of the men signals them to come forward. They sit down at the table across from the two men, Marco Angelini—the street boss of Cicero, a very powerful Outfit member—and his top lieutenant, Lonnie DeMeo. Neither looks at Vincent. They speak directly to Tony.

"This him?" asks Marco.

"Yes," replies Tony, without further comment. Now they both eye Vincent up and down.

"You wanna be a fucking private eye?" Angelini asks. "What the fuck?"

"Yes, sir, I do," Vincent replies.

The two men look at each other for a long moment. Then suddenly they both start to laugh. Vincent does nothing, neither does Tony. Just as abruptly as they started, Angelini and DeMeo become very serious.

DeMeo gestures to Tony. The two of them get up and leave the table. Vincent hears the front door close behind him.

"Why should we help you? What good is it going to do us?" Marco inquires.

Vincent looks this powerful boss in the eye.

"You never know. One day I may be of help to you," he says in a steady voice. "But in the meantime, I need the license to work. It's as simple as that."

"Simple, eh?" Marco responds.

"This is what I want to do," says Vincent, "instead of running around committing crimes just to earn."

Marco glares at him for a few moments with a cold, calculating stare. Vincent does not flinch, showing no fear.

"We'll see," Marco says. "Go find Tony and go home."

Outside the restaurant, Vincent stands to the side as Tony shakes hands with DeMeo. Without another word, they drive back to the Neighborhood. When they arrive at the grocery store, Vincent asks Tony, "Now what?"

Tony shrugs his shoulders and gets out of the car. More confused than before, Vincent asks nothing else.

I'm learning, he thinks, *but what a pain in the ass*. He just has to keep his mouth shut and wait. But that's the hardest part.

31

THE POLYGRAPH

The FBI agents Paulie had met through Carolyn's father come through for him. They help him prequalify for the FBI Academy, then assist him in filling out the necessary applications for enrollment. Carolyn's father even writes Paulie a letter of recommendation.

Paulie tries not to think about the impact of forging a new identity, about how changing his name is seen as a betrayal by those closest to him, about the hurt he's inflicted on his grandfather in particular. Despite his misgivings, Paul Andrews enters the FBI Academy at Quantico filled with enthusiasm.

Throughout his first weeks of intensive training, Paulie does not come down off of his cloud. He loves every minute of it. The intellectual rigor, the heightened sense of moral purpose, the expectation and drive for physical excellence—everything is just as he had imagined it would be in his dreams. In fact, there is nothing about the Bureau that he doesn't like.

But he cannot shake the feeling that there's a problem. There are awkward moments in class or at the mess hall when someone calls out "Andrews!" and he doesn't reply. Shame fills him in those moments, and his conscience will not let him rest.

Am I lying to myself? he wonders during sleepless nights. *Will Papa ever forgive me?*

But he remembers the words his mother told him, that success will heal the wounds. And that fills him with ambition. And so, one night early on, he makes a solemn vow to be the best he can be. Then, maybe his grandfather will look at things differently, will see Paulie differently. Maybe.

After six weeks, a senior agent approaches Paulie in the cavernous entrance hall of the FBI Academy.

"Andrews? They're ready for you now."

Paulie steps into a windowless and colorless meeting room. The polygraph operator sits waiting.

"Agent Andrews, take off your jacket and tie, and let's get started. My name is Agent Elias Jones, and I will be conducting this polygraph test and interview. Please sit down."

Paulie sits in the chair provided. The agent straps him into the apparatus and resumes his own seat.

"This procedure is relatively simple. I am going to ask you a series of questions in a particular format, then change to another format and move on. You look nervous. Are you nervous, Agent Andrews?"

"No, sir, I am not."

Agent Jones looks over at the polygraph, as if to confirm. "Good. Let's get started. Is your name Paul Anthony Andrews?"

"Yes," Paulie slowly responds.

The polygraph operator lets out a quiet cough and then looks up at Paulie.

"You reacted negatively to that response, Andrews. It was a matter-of-fact question. People don't usually get those wrong."

Paulie pauses. He didn't expect that his guilt would seep through so easily, so obviously. All of a sudden, he's extremely nervous, but he doesn't let it show. He takes a deep breath.

"I recently changed my name, sir, legally, from Andriano to Andrews," Paulie says. "I thought that the Bureau would have noted that in my file."

"I'm sure they have. But that still does not explain why your response registers as negative. Is there something about your name change that stresses you?"

"Yes, sir."

Agent Jones glances over at the machine. His face is impassive.

"Go on."

"It displeased my grandfather, who raised me. It is his name I changed, and he is upset with my decision."

Agent Jones rubs his chin.

"I see. Before I continue, are there any other questions that would cause a similar response?"

"No, sir. I told you the truth and will continue to tell you the truth. That was a stumbling block, as I love my grandfather dearly. But I have made my choice."

As he speaks, his mind instantly races with all of the things he wishes he could say but knows he shouldn't. *To be frank with you, I changed it from an Italian name to further my chances within the Bureau and for no other reason. I am proud of my heritage, but I thought it best to have a less ethnic name.* Then he thinks, *Am I really proud? Would a proud man have changed his name? Fuck this system for making me compromise my heritage for my dreams.*

Through sheer power of will, Paulie forces these negative thoughts to recede just as fast as they flood in. He imagines himself back home in the Neighborhood, sitting at his mother's kitchen table, waiting for dinner to be served. He remembers his resolve, his childhood dreams, and his vow to be great. In a matter of seconds, he's calm again and ready to continue.

"Okay, let's move on," Agent Jones says.

The rest of the interview proceeds without event. When Agent Jones dismisses Paulie, he shakes his hand and tells him that he's done well.

32

THE MIND AND THE GUT

After his reckoning with the polygraph test, Paulie exudes a new strength. He excels and even distinguishes himself throughout the remaining training. He's singled out for praise by many of his instructors. His fellow trainees look to him for advice and leadership.

However, all is not entirely well. His worries over his identity are eclipsed by a new fear—that he'll be sent to Chicago for his duty assignment. He wonders why he feels so apprehensive about working in his hometown. He believes fervently in the mission of the FBI, in the righteousness of the law, that the might of the Outfit does not equal right, and that wrongdoers should be punished for their transgressions.

But, he wonders, *if that is so, then why does the idea of going up against the guys back in the Neighborhood fill me with such dread?*

Intellectually, he finds no answers. In his gut, he doesn't know that he'll be able to oppose his family and friends. He looks forward to his graduation day with a potent mix of apprehension, confusion, and excitement. On that day, he'll receive his orders.

Paulie graduates top of his class. After the ceremony, he and the rest of the new agents in his class flock to the bulletin board to see their new assignments. As he scans the list of names, though, Paulie doesn't see his own.

"Agent Andrews." A firm voice comes from behind him. Paulie swivels around. He's met by a tall, impeccably dressed agent, whom he has seen many times but has never met personally.

"Yes, sir."

"My name is Randolph Peters, and I am the Supervising Agent here at the Academy. Come with me."

"Yes, sir."

"I've looked through your file. Your testing and training are exemplary," Agent Peters says, as he leads Paulie to a quiet part of the building, the sounds of their leather shoes echoing off the walls of the empty halls. "I want to compliment you, Agent Andrews. A few of your instructors reached out to me singing your praises. They believe you have what it takes to become one of the Bureau's top assets."

"Thank you, sir."

"We're placing you in the Los Angeles, California office. The unit's Supervising Agent, Agent Orosco, is a personal friend of mine. You'll learn a lot from her."

Without thinking, Paulie grins from ear to ear.

"Does that please you, Agent Andrews?"

Paulie holds out his hand. Agent Peters takes it.

"More than you know, sir. I will make you proud," Paulie says, his smile intensifying. *I guess that settles it*, he thinks, *I don't want to go up against the Neighborhood.* But then his smile fades.

"One other thing, Agent Andrews," Peters continues. "I noticed that none of your relatives were present today."

"My girlfriend was in attendance, as well as her mother and her father, Deputy U.S. Attorney Winston Arrington."

"Yes, I saw them. But no one from Chicago?"

"I asked them not to attend sir. I have my reasons."

Supervising Agent Peters frowns but doesn't push. "They would have been proud."

Paulie stifles a frown at this deception, "They are, sir. I know it."

"Good. And good luck, Andrews," Peters says, before leaving to speak with other graduates.

"Thank you."

Outside, Paulie spots the Arringtons and makes a beeline to them. He hugs Carolyn.

"I'm so proud of you!" she says, kissing him on the cheek. Then she looks over to her father.

"Congratulations, Paul. You've really done well," he says, shaking Paulie's hand.

"Thank you, Mr. Arrington. That means a lot coming from you."

"We have two things to be proud of today, Paul," continues Winston, while beaming at his daughter. "Carolyn was accepted to Georgetown."

Paulie feels his heart drop. But he tries not to let his disappointment show. Arrington senses his distress. He then rests his hand on his daughter's shoulder, as if to encourage her. Carolyn looks at her father and then to Paul.

"Paul, I know we made some plans," she says, "but I want to get my law degree. I hope you will understand."

"I do, and you should," Paulie replies, the pain steadily rising within him. "We each have our dreams, and you deserve to pursue yours, Carolyn. I suppose we both need to be patient and wait. It will be hard for me, but if this is what you want, I'll support you."

Arrington looks at Paulie, as if trying to gauge how badly he has been hurt by this sudden news. He fully expects that the physical distance between his daughter and Paulie will make them reconsider their plans together, and indeed, move on. Although he likes Paul, he doesn't want his daughter to marry him. So what if the Guinea changed his name? He could dye his hair blonde and join the country club for all he cares. A Wop is a Wop is a Wop, and that cannot change any more than a leopard can shed its spots.

33

WAY OUT WEST

Four days later, a Tuesday, Paulie boards a United flight to a new city. As he checks for the umpteenth time that his orders are safe in his briefcase, he cannot help but think that he is traveling to a new life. He knows nothing about Los Angeles. He doesn't have any friends there—no grandfather, no mother, no Carolyn. It makes him feel sad and very uneasy. But he's resolved to succeed.

He spends his first night on the West Coast in a cheap motel near his new office. He speaks to no one. The following morning, he reports to the office and is told that he's a day early, so he takes a cab to Venice Beach where he gets a sunburn. That night he calls the Arringtons back east. Mrs. Arrington tells him that Carolyn is out with friends. He leaves the number of his hotel. Then he calls Vincent.

They haven't spoken since his graduation. They talk for over an hour. Vincent says he's proud of Paulie and doesn't hesitate to express how overjoyed he is that Paulie has been assigned to the Los Angeles office.

"You're just happy I'm anywhere but Chicago, you idiot."

"Hey, it's not that I don't miss you," Vincent replies. "You meet any movie stars yet? Who am I kidding? They wouldn't give you a second look, G-Man. They like he-men like me. Leave the pretty girls to me and go out and fight crime. Do they even have crime in Los Angeles? I mean you'll probably get really good at tracking down jay-walkers."

They both laugh.

Paulie tells Vincent about Carolyn's choice to go to law school. Vincent is silent for a moment then says, "You're better off being on your own—for now, anyway," Vincent assures him. "Get settled into that fucked-up job. You've been training so intensely, give yourself a break." Paulie says he agrees, but he's not so sure.

"Let me know when you get settled, and I will come visit. Then you can introduce me to all the stars you've made friends with. And I don't mean Mr. Ed, the horse, you fuck."

They laugh some more before hanging up. For the first time since he arrived in California, Paulie feels good.

The next day he reports to the office where he meets his new Supervising Agent, Natalie Orosco. Paulie can tell from her tailored, form-fitting, business suit, stern face, and black hair tied up in a tight bun that she's all business. He guesses she's in her mid-forties. She informs him that he will be training with the white-collar crime unit. He'll meet his training partner the following week. In the meantime, she says, find an apartment and settle in.

He thanks her. Then he's cut loose again. *Great*, he thinks, *just what I need, more time to kill.* He buys a newspaper and flicks through the classifieds. Taxis take him to look at a couple of apartments. He settles on a small studio in Santa Monica. Moving takes about twenty minutes, since everything he owns fits in one duffel bag. And besides, he doesn't plan on spending much time there anyway.

34

PAPERS

The day after Vincent's conversation with Paulie in California, he goes to see Papa Tony. They sit down at a table outside the grocery store and sip lemonade that Paulie's mother brings them. Tony looks at Vincent with envy. He has not spoken to his grandson since Paulie told him about his name change.

Vincent senses that Tony wants to talk. Otherwise, he'd be barking at him to get to work. So, Vincent shares everything that's going on with Paulie. Rina comes in and sits next to Vincent as he speaks. She has spoken to Paulie a couple of times since he moved out to L.A. and knows most of what's going on. But she still misses him and wants to talk.

"I will wait until he gets settled out there and then go pay him a visit," Vincent says. "I'll make sure that he's okay."

Papa Tony looks away as the tears well in his eyes. He gets up and goes back inside to his office.

"I will make this better, Rina," Vincent assures her. "First, I need to go out there and look him in the eye. He needs to mend this rift with Papa Tony. I will make sure that happens, Rina, I promise."

Rina bows her head, then says, "Vincent, that would mean the world to me." She tousles his hair and lets him kiss her cheek.

Just then they hear Papa Tony's voice boom from inside. "Vincent! Get over here."

Vincent gets up and goes.

"Go see that lawyer at three o'clock this afternoon," Tony says. "Take your birth certificate, discharge papers, your GED, and anything else official. Do you have your social security card?"

"Yes. Can you tell me what's happening?"

Tony shrugs his shoulders and walks back into his office.

Vincent goes home to shave and take a shower. When he gets out of the shower his mother is not home, and he wonders where she is. He looks out at the street and sees that his car is gone, too.

He gets dressed and goes into the kitchen where he notices an old manila folder sitting on the table. He opens it up and finds copies of his birth certificate, his Army discharge papers, his GED scores, and other documents. In fact, it's everything that he needs. He hears the front door shut, and his mother approach from the hall. He kisses her.

"Did Papa Tony ask you to do this, Ma?" He nods toward the folder.

"Yes, this morning."

"Really? Because he went all through this with me a little while ago."

His mother shrugs and says, "Me too. So, I went to my friend Joyce's office, and she let me photocopy everything. I put the originals back in your dresser drawer, along with two other sets of copies in case you need them."

"Papa Tony told me I had to go see that lawyer this afternoon."

"So, what are you talking to me for? Go see him. Now you have everything you need, I think."

Something doesn't seem right. Vincent takes his car keys, kisses her goodbye, and sets off to see the attorney.

35

HATCHET FACE AND BOTTLE GLASSES

Vincent Scalise to see Mr. Ackerman, ma'am."

If Vincent isn't seeing her with his own eyes, he would not have thought it possible for a person's face to crinkle and harden in place to such an unnerving extent. *She would do well in a horror movie*, he thinks, *and probably scares the shit out of kids every Halloween*. This hatchet face tells him to have a seat. He looks at his watch—it's 3:01 p.m.

About ten minutes later, the outer door of the office opens, and the man from the previous meeting strolls in. This time, instead of velour, he's wearing a suit. But he still has food stains on his tie—*good old Bottle Glasses*. He looks at Vincent, but does not utter a word, nor otherwise acknowledge Vincent's presence. He disappears into one of the back offices.

"Excuse me, Ma'am? Who is that person?" Vincent asks.

She looks at him, her eyes tighten, and then goes back to her work.

Fuck this, Vincent thinks. He's about to get up and leave, but thinks better of it. He's the one who asked for the favor, after all.

By 4:30 there's still no sign of Ackerman. Vincent busies himself by memorizing the captions of the lithographs on the wall. There's one of Abraham Lincoln and another of the Great Chicago Fire of 1871. *Would it have killed them to spring for some magazines for the waiting room?*

Then Ackerman comes in. He looks at Vincent, as though trying to place him.

"Sorry! Got held up in court. I'll be with you in a moment."

Vincent has no time to say anything as Ackerman streams directly back to his office. A few moments later, he hears a buzz. Hatchet Face picks up the phone.

"You can go in now."

Bottle Glasses is perched on the arm of a chair next to Ackerman's desk. He points to the chair opposite the desk. Vincent sits down. The lawyer holds out his hand to Vincent, but not to shake. Vincent gets the message, and hands him the manila folder.

"These are not the originals," Ackerman says, flipping through the documents, more to himself than to Vincent.

"No."

"Okay, they will have to do," Ackerman says. "Listen, kid. You will get a notice in the mail that will tell you where to take the test. This should occur in about two weeks. Don't call me in two weeks complaining that it hasn't come. Sometimes it's a little early, sometimes a little late. Then you will need to bring a $100 money order for the test fee. Now go see Mr. D'Amico. I just got off the phone with him. He's waiting for you in his office."

Vincent hesitates, not sure if Ackerman has more to say.

"What are you waiting for?"

On his way out of the office Vincent grins to himself and thinks, *One day I'm going to throw those three out of a window and watch them bounce.* He shakes his head. *Fucking lawyers.*

At Fat Jimmy D'Amico's First Ward office, the friendly receptionist shows Vincent in almost immediately. The fat man sits behind his desk.

"Take a seat," Jimmy D says. "Okay, it's gonna cost you $6,000—five grand to Ackerman and another grand to some Jewish organization, so that they can plant trees in Israel in Ackerman's mother's name. I have no idea what the fuck that's about, but that's it."

Jimmy puffs on his cigar but gets nothing. He holds it away from his face and realizes he hasn't lit it. He looks over to Vincent for a response.

"I don't have six grand," Vincent says.

"I know. It's taken care of, but you owe. You will take a test and then you will get your license."

Once again, he waits for Vincent's response, but there's none.

Then his voice changes register, and he leans forward.

"You tell no one how this happened, understand?" The fat man says sternly, looking Vincent directly in the eye.

Vincent nods.

"I don't even *know* what the fuck happened, so there is nothing to tell, sir."

Fat Jimmy frowns.

"Ackerman will get the cash, his mother will get the trees, and you will get your license. Everything will be legal, and the world will still keep turning. You should be grateful and happy, but you do not look happy."

"I am. I just have to raise the six grand. When I have it, do I bring it to you?"

Jimmy D looks like he's going to explode.

"No, you dumb fuck. They told me you were up on things. I told you it's taken care of. You need to go back and talk to your people in the Neighborhood—they will tell you what to do. There is no rush."

Jimmy's voice changes again. "Now all you gotta do is do good. Earn and help out when you can and even when you cannot, understand? Above all, stay loyal."

"Thank you. Yes, I will," Vincent stands to shake Jimmy D's hand. "I can't tell you how grateful I am."

"Don't mention it."

"Hey, just before I go. What kind of cigars you like?"

"Ha. You know, if in your travels you come across some real Cuban cigars, perhaps you might think of me."

The fat man rocks himself back and forth to get up from his seat. He puts his arm around Vincent's shoulders and walks him out of his office, where he shakes Vincent's hand once again. Vincent walks out to the lobby and gets a smile from the receptionist. She looks really familiar.

Six fucking grand, when the license fee is only a C note. I've been fucking robbed, but it feels so good.

Vincent walks to his car, unable to suppress the grin across his face. He needs to know who fronted the money for him, but that can wait.

He drives back to the Neighborhood and finds Angelo and Mikey outside The Patio— where else? He motions for them to come to his car.

"I need to score large," he says.

The two look at each other, shrug, and nod. Enough said. Vincent goes home and is met at the door by his mother.

"Well?" She says, her eyes bright and sincere.
"I guess it's done, Ma. But I owe six grand."
She nods.
"I made dinner, so eat. Oh, and that girl called again."

36

AN EMPTY BOTTLE OF WINE

After he eats and helps his mom with the dishes, Vincent calls Valerie. She's not home, so he leaves a message that he'll come by around nine that evening. Then he goes back to the table.

"Ma, who fronted the six grand for me?"

"Papa Tony."

"Why didn't you tell me? I don't want to take money from him. I don't know how soon I can pay him back. I wish you had told me beforehand."

"He did not want you to owe money to the boys," Teri replies calmly. "We talked about it, and I agreed. He knows that you will pay him back when you can. Don't be unappreciative."

"I don't like this, but I'm going do my best to pay him back as soon as possible. Can I at least thank him?"

"Of course, you can, but don't make a big deal out of it. You should not feel guilty about this, because he cares about you, even if he doesn't show it. Just be nice and thank him."

"You're right. Thank you, Ma."

Vincent kisses his mother goodbye and walks to his car. Twenty minutes later he's outside Valerie's place. He looks up to her window and sees that the lights are on, so he figures she's home. He walks up to the building and rings the doorbell. No response. He starts to walk away, but turns, and rings the bell again. This time, the buzzer comes through.

Her apartment door is slightly ajar. For a moment, he wishes he was strapped. He knocks and calls out, "Valerie?"

There's no answer. He pushes the door open a little wider. "Valerie? You in there?"

Still nothing.

"Fuck it, I'm coming in!" He springs into the room to see her sitting on her couch, her arms folded across her chest, glaring at him hatefully. A nearly empty bottle of red wine sits on her brown wood coffee table.

"Jesus fuck, Valerie! I thought you were getting robbed or something."

"What are you doing here, Vincent?"

"My mom said you called."

"I called you twice and you never called me back!" Valerie cries, her eyes welling with tears.

"Well, I'm here now. Last time you gave me the impression that you never wanted to see me again. You looked at me as if you wanted me to drop dead. Well, I didn't, so I'm here."

"Why do you have to be such a jerk, Vincent. Why?"

"You know, I'm sorry." He cannot help himself. "But I meant what I said. I've got lots going on and I can't really commit to anything serious right now. It would not be fair to you. I like you a lot and want to be with you, but I don't want the pressure of a relationship. You did a lot for me, Valerie, and I will never forget that, and I will always be there for you. You are a friend, so can't we just continue our friendship and enjoy each other's company?"

"Yeah, sure. Whatever you want, Vincent," Valerie sighs, her voice weak. She starts to cry again.

Vincent sits down next to her and puts his arms around her shoulders. She leans her head onto his shoulder, and he gently strokes her hair. She stops crying.

"I guess you're the boss."

And then, looking up with her wide eyes, she grabs his hand and walks him into the bedroom.

A couple of hours later, Vincent quietly slips out of Valerie's apartment while she sleeps. He's happy that they are still close, but he warns himself to be careful and not give her hope.

37

SOFT LOVE

The next morning, Vincent's mom fixes him breakfast, along with a glass of milk with Ovaltine.

"I want to go see Papa Tony this morning, Ma. I'll do exactly what you said—thank him just like you told me."

"Good."

"But I am going to insist on paying him back on a regular basis until we're square. I'm not gonna work there anymore, Ma. I gotta get my business started. I'm going to start making inquiries and see if I can generate some business right away."

"Okay, honey."

He finishes his breakfast, drinks his Ovaltine, and washes the dishes. Then he sits down with a pad of paper and pencil and starts outlining what he needs to get started.

At around nine o'clock, he walks down to the grocery store, kisses Rina, and asks where the old man is. She points to the back office.

"Morning, Papa Tony."

Papa Tony looks up at him standing in the doorway.

"I want to thank you for fronting that money for me. That's a lot of dough, but I will pay you back as soon as I can. I really appreciate you doing that. My ma told me why."

Before Tony can respond, Vincent blurts out. "I can't work here any longer. You've been kind to my mother and me for the longest time, and there is nothing that you could ask me to do that I won't do. But what I really need to do now is to get my business started.

Papa Tony looks at Vincent and nods his head slowly. Then, very deliberately, he walks over to Vincent, puts his arms around him and hugs him tight. Then he looks directly in Vincent's eyes before gently pushing him away. He does not say a word. He goes back to his desk.

Vincent walks quickly out to the loading dock, his eyes filling with tears. The old man does love him, he does.

38

MASSIVE DETAIL

Vincent wipes his eyes and collects himself in the alleyway, then leaves to find Angelo and Mikey. They're at their office—the bench on the sidewalk outside The Patio.

"So, what's what?" Vincent asks as he approaches them. Angelo looks at Mikey, then speaks. "Do we have to tell Johnny V what we are up to?"

"First, tell me what it is," answers Vincent.

Mikey and Angelo shrug at each other, then Angelo motions Vincent to come closer. In a huddle, Angelo and Mikey sketch a rough idea for a robbery that they've been planning. After they finish, they look at Vincent for a response.

"So, way up in Skokie?" asks Vincent, after consideration.

"Yeah, we know this guy has got a whole shitload of gold coins—and supposedly a major league stamp collection worth a ton. I don't know what we could do with that, but the gold coins alone are worth the price of admission. I'm sure that this guy is not connected—he's a Polish Jew—but if he *does* know someone, we will find out really quick, won't we?" says Mikey with a wry laugh.

"Okay," Vincent replies. "I gotta see what's what. If this guy's not protected and no one knows him, maybe. Then maybe I'll just talk to Johnny about it and see what he says. But if he says we must kick up, we have to kick up. He's the boss in this neighborhood, and we have to give him the respect."

Angelo frowns. "I loved it when we just robbed, and nobody knew nothing,"

"Yeah, but if we give the respect we're supposed to, we are protected and can earn without any problems," says Vincent. "Everybody kicks up and you know that. Without a blessing, we may face problems that we don't even fucking know exist. So, let's do it my way and see what happens. Now lay this all out for me in massive detail."

For another forty-five minutes, they outline their plans to Vincent. The job will take place that Friday night. Angelo and Mikey will go see Fat Louie first and get an untraceable "work" car for the job. Once the job is done, the car will be chopped and cease to exist. Vincent will get the equipment and other necessities.

When they're through talking, Vincent heads home. He feels uneasy about this score, knowing what he has to do, but quickly puts the thought out of his mind. Soon, he won't have to take part in these scores again. Or at least not as often.

39

BURIED TREASURE

Without traffic, it takes about a half hour or so to get to Skokie from the Neighborhood. On Friday night, around midnight, the three of them park four doors down from the target's home in a residential area of fully detached houses. They sit for ten minutes and listen to the Skokie Police Department's "air"—slang for the police radio channels. They carefully scope out the block. Most of the lights in the windows are out, but not all. It appears that their intended target, Charles Jakowski—a seventy-six-year-old retired iron worker and union leader—is burning the midnight oil. In the car, they go over their plan one more time.

"What I'm told," Mikey says, "is that since his wife died, Jakowski spends most of his time in his finished basement. So, it's simple. We pick the lock of the back door, slip in quietly, listen, then race down into the basement and go in strong."

"Angelo, you grab him, duct tape his mouth closed, and secure him to something right away," Vincent says.

"Got it."

"Good. Let's go."

Wearing dark clothes, Vincent, Mikey, and Angelo make their way around the house through the darkness to the covered back doorway. They look around the area and listen carefully. It's all quiet. Nothing to worry about. Mikey has earphones on and listens intently to his portable police band scanner. After about five minutes, they look to each other, nod, then put on black ski masks.

They each carry a canvas bag. Vincent opens his, takes out some tools, and picks the deadbolt lock. It takes him longer than he expected, but he gets it. Mikey and Angelo enter the house. Vincent looks out from the backyard one last time, and seeing nothing of concern, closes the door behind him.

Inside, they all hear the TV blaring from the basement, which is a very good sign. The old guy must have hearing problems. Taking no chances, Vincent quietly steps through the kitchen to the living room. There's no one there. Without speaking, he points out the stairs to Angelo, who passes him and goes up. About a minute later he returns and gestures: There's no one up there, either.

The three of them stand at the door to the basement. Angelo goes down first, slowly. As soon as he sees the back of the old man's head, he explodes in a burst of speed to the easy chair. Angelo surprises him and socks Jakowski hard on the side of his head to stun him, then grabs him from behind just as Mikey falls in and helps Angelo secure the old man's mouth with duct tape. The John Wayne movie keeps playing on the TV.

Jakowski is bigger and stronger than they thought, and he fights like crazy, twisting and turning every which way. Vincent grabs his kicking legs and tightly secures them with duct tape.

"Calm the fuck down!" Vincent snaps. He then whispers in the old man's ear, "We're just gonna rob you. We're not gonna hurt you."

They lay him down on the floor as he continues to thrash around. Then they take a step back to wait him out. Vincent grabs a pillow from a couch and gingerly places it under Jakowski's head. They do not want him injuring himself. That would just cause more problems. Soon, the old man stops thrashing. Angelo walks over to a desk and pulls out the high-backed desk chair on casters.

But Jakowski is hardly worn out. He glares at the three with a rage they did not expect—palpable hatred in his eyes. They thought he would just acquiesce. No chance.

Vincent leans over him and says, in a slightly disguised voice, "Calm the fuck down. Accept that this is happening, and we won't hurt you. But if you keep trashing around, you're going to hurt yourself. If you do, then we will walk away with what we take, and leave you bleeding and hurt. Calm down and let us get busy. We'll leave you with a knife to cut yourself free after we're gone. Do you understand, Mr. Jakowski?"

Jakowski nods, but his eyes show utter defiance. Mikey and Angelo prop him up onto the desk chair and secure him to it with more duct tape. Once finished, the trio stand over him in a semicircle.

Vincent continues, still with a disguised voice, "Now just tell us where the gold coins are. With or without your help, we will find them, but the easier you make it for us, the easier it will be for you, got it?"

Jakowski neither nods his head yes nor shakes it no, so Vincent continues.

"I'm going to remove the tape from your mouth. If you start to scream, I'll just put it back and wait you out. We have all night, so just cooperate, and let's get this done."

At a signal from Vincent, Angelo carefully removes the duct tape from Jakowski's mouth.

"Okay, so, where are they?" says Vincent.

Jakowski smiles. "Fuck you," he says, beginning almost in a sing-song voice. "Fuck your mother and your entire fucking family. I won't tell you shit! Do the fuck you want, you will not find them, and you can just go fuck yourself!"

The three look at each other and shake their heads. Vincent re-tapes Jakowski's mouth and glares down at him. Meanwhile, Angelo and Mikey head upstairs to tear the house apart for the coins.

Jakowski sits still, his eyes never ceasing to glare at Vincent with absolute malice and defiance. Vincent, remaining calm, says nothing. Soon enough, Mikey and Angelo come downstairs and shake their heads at Vincent. Mikey holds up some old jewelry, including a diamond wedding setting, and shows it to Vincent. This is all they found.

At the sight of the jewelry, Jakowski starts ranting under the tape, and Vincent removes it once again.

"Those are my dead wife's, you fucks!"

"Put them back where you found them," Vincent says, gesturing to Mikey. Then he says to Jakowski, "We will not dishonor your wife. But we want the coins, so stop stalling."

"Fuck you!" Jakowski spits.

Rolling his eyes, Vincent wraps the old man's mouth again. This time he doubles the tape. By the time he's through, Mikey has returned. He and Angelo look to Vincent as if to say, *"Now what?"*

"Search the basement."

They do so, taking the furniture apart, the drop ceiling tiles, everything. They search the laundry room and storage areas. They even take the TV apart and still they find nothing. Vincent then examines the elaborate wood-paneled walls.

"You did a wonderful job paneling this basement. It would be a shame to tear down all of this," Vincent says, rapping on the panels with his knuckles.

Jakowski, unable to speak, looks at him with even more defiance.

With Jakowski watching his every move, Vincent sweeps the basement again with more intensity. He walks up the stairs and sits down at the highest step, so that he can look over everything below him. With his hands cupping his chin, he concentrates, his eyes continuously flitting back to Jakowski's as they scan the room. That's when he pays particular attention to the flooring.

The basement floor is covered in black and white tiles. On the right side of the basement, the side farthest from him, the tiles are placed true, in line with the wall. But the tiles in front of him, on the left side, seem to slant inward, toward the back of the long basement. Vincent stands up to study this further. As he steps to the back wall, he's sure that the end tiles are about a half a foot narrower at the very end of the basement.

Jakowski starts going crazy. He twists and turns so much that he topples off the chair and onto the floor.

"So, I'm getting warmer, huh, Mr. Jakowski?" says Vincent. The old man pathetically tries to propel himself toward Vincent, who simply looks on. Angelo and Mikey try to right the chair but are rebuffed by an angry Jakowski who jerks his head from side to side.

"Calm him down," Vincent orders. "He's going to hurt himself. Hold him down on the couch."

They do so as Jakowski tries to scream through the duct tape. Vincent then walks to the end of the basement. Jakowski goes quiet, his eyes never leaving Vincent. As Vincent feels his way along, he keeps pressing his hands against the wood panels. Suddenly there's a sound of a latch clicking. The wall opens outward.

Jakowski moans loudly through the duct tape and begins to cry. Angelo and Mikey look on with amusement and walk over to see what Vincent has discovered.

There in the wall, on custom made shelves, are about twenty or thirty long plastic tubes, each filled with gold coins. Vincent calculates at least 300, maybe much more.

"Holy fucking mother of God," Angelo says, "will you look at that!"

"Jesus!" says Mikey.

Jakowski is now sobbing uncontrollably.

Vincent also sees two leather-bound portfolios on the bottom shelf. Inside are page after page of stamps—old stamps with elephants, iconic structures, and long forgotten and famous faces. Some are in languages he doesn't recognize. He draws a long, slow whistle.

"This may be worth a fortune," says Angelo.

"Let's take it, too," joins Mikey.

"Load up the coins," Vincent orders. "We're getting out of here."

As the two gleefully gather the coins, tubes and all, in their large canvas bags, Vincent picks up the two portfolios and walks over to Jakowski.

Vincent calls over to Angelo, and together, they set Jakowski upright on the tiles in his chair. Vincent tenderly removes the tear-soaked duct tape from Jakowski's mouth and pulls up his T-shirt to wipe the old man's face.

"My whole life, you fuck, my whole life I've had that collection. It was passed down to me by my father. And now they're lost to you pieces of shit," he says, spitting at Vincent through broken tears.

"You two go upstairs and load up the car," Vincent says. "I'll be out in about ten minutes. Give me that box cutter in the bag."

"What are you going to do, Vincent?" asks Mikey.

"You two just go. I'll be out soon."

They leave. Vincent kneels in front of Jakowski.

"We're not taking the stamps, old man. They're yours. If you are smart, you will treat this as a gift and keep your mouth shut. I don't know about the coins, but my guess is they were pay-offs while you were with the union. So, I doubt you ever declared them on your tax returns or insured them. That's a tough break. But I'm also guessing the stamps have been insured and if they were to go missing, well… you can decide if you want to declare them stolen or not. In any event, they'll remain with you."

Vincent places the portfolios on the desk.

"You're one tough old man. Now I'm going to punch you in the nose, so it bleeds. Then, I'm gonna leave this box cutter, too. "

Vincent holds the tool a few feet from the old man's face.

"It'll take you a while to completely cut through the duct tape and free yourself. Once you do, call the cops immediately. Remember this gift I'm giving you when you talk to them."

Vincent cuts an eighth of an inch of tape and then wipes the box cutter, so that no prints remain. He stands and smacks the old man in the nose and just as Vincent promised, his nose begins to bleed. Vincent smacks him again and says, "That's for spitting at me."

Jakowski looks up at Vincent.

"So long tough guy," says Vincent.

Jakowski looks down at his beloved stamp collection, then up at Vincent, and quietly says, "Fuck you."

Angelo drives away nice and slow. But Mikey is hot.

"Are you fucking crazy, you left the stamps?"

"No, I did the smart thing, Mikey. If we took those stamps, they may have led the police directly to us. Who were we going to fence them through, anyway—Ali Baba? Yeah, right. We couldn't trust anyone, and I mean anyone, with them, and they would just bring all kinds of heat on us if we kept them. It was the smart thing to do."

Angelo taps the steering wheel with his knuckles. Mikey stews for a few moments.

"When you're right, you're right," Mikey says.

He reaches from the back seat and tousles Vincent's hair. Vincent bats his hand away.

"Let's just get back to the Neighborhood."

40

MEETING AGENT CALDWELL

"You're late, Agent Andrews," Supervising Agent Natalie Orosco barks at Paulie from behind her cluttered desk. "Take a seat."

"Sorry, ma'am," Paulie says, sitting in the open armchair. "I thought this meeting was at nine o'clock."

He checks his watch. It's nine o'clock to the minute.

"In this unit, five minutes early means you're on time."

"Sorry, it won't happen again."

"See that it doesn't."

Next to him sits an attractive black woman, about five feet five, with her hair tied in a bun. Like Agent Orosco, she also wears a form-fitting suit favored by the women in the office.

"Meet Agent Caldwell, your new partner."

Paulie nods to Caldwell. She remains rigid, not returning the greeting, her eyes fixed on Orosco.

"You two are to report directly to Agent Thomas Baranson, your direct supervisor. You'll be briefed by him at 15:00 hours. You both have been assigned desks in sub-office number twelve. That's all, you are dismissed."

"Pleasant lady," says Paulie to Caldwell in the hallway outside the commander's office.

"She is a decorated agent worthy of respect," Agent Caldwell responds. "She is no nonsense, and neither am I."

"Got you," says Paul. *Wonderful, two alpha females.*

Their office space is a plain cubicle of gray fabric walls with two old, gray metal desks facing each other. Agent Caldwell chooses the far desk, leaving Paulie with the desk that faces Caldwell and the gray cubicle wall—his back exposed to the cubicle entrance.

Agent Caldwell starts arranging her desk, pulling out a framed photo from a large handbag, pointedly placing it so that Paulie cannot see the image. She then gets to work reading and sorting the files that are on her desk. The entire morning passes without a word between them, not even a *Where are you from?* It's frosty.

At noon, Caldwell breaks the ice first. "It's time for lunch, and I have some errands to run. See you at Agent Baranson's office at 15:00," she says and then immediately leaves.

As he watches her leave, he sincerely wonders if he's said something to offend her. He tries to let it go. In any event, *A man's gotta eat.*

He exits the building and walks toward the Westwood shopping area. Entering the manicured area of shops, restaurants, and theaters cheers him up. Aside from the iciness of his new partner, he loves it here. He loves the sunshine, the absence of bugs and lack of humidity—even the wannabe actors don't bother him.

He spots a pizza place and goes in out of a sense of nostalgia. As he sits, he makes a note to call his mother and Vincent after work.

He then remembers that they're two hours ahead. They'll be eating dinner. He wonders who he will have dinner with. He thinks about Carolyn. He hasn't heard from her since the move. *How are we going to manage this long distance?* But then he snaps out of it. He needs to get his career going, get to know the lay of the land, and actually start working. *Enough with the dilly-dallying.*

A dark-haired waitress comes to the table.

"Hey," he says. "I'm new in town, and let me tell you, it's great to see a fellow *paisan.*"

"I'm German and from Connecticut," she replies flatly.

"Oh."

After a couple of slices of cheese pizza and an orange soda, he returns to headquarters. He arrives at his new supervisor's office fifteen minutes early. Agent Caldwell is already there. He nods and they both wait.

"Do I keep calling you Agent Caldwell?" asks Paulie. "Or am I permitted to call you by your first name?"

"You can call me Tania. That's pronounced Ta-nee-ah, not Tan-ee-ah, okay?"

"Sure, pleasure to make your acquaintance. I'm Paul."

They hear him before they see him. A loud, coarse voice booms and fills the halls. Paulie turns and sees a huge man, almost six foot five, with his hair cropped high and tight, and a mustache too small for his face. He strides toward them, talking to another agent. At the doorway to his office, he shakes hands with his colleague, sees the two waiting for him, and gestures for them to come in.

"Take a seat."

Baranson parks his huge body behind his desk and gets right to the point.

"Okay, I'm assigning you five cases: two bank fraud matters, one money laundering case, and two wire fraud matters. You are now responsible for these cases. They are yours alone. I'm sure you've already had time to read the files on your desks. Remember, though, the files are for reference only. They're only the beginning of a learning experience. Sure, they will help guide you, but you need to actively pursue these cases."

"Got it, boss," replies Paulie.

Caldwell sits ramrod and says nothing.

"Agent Andrews, I know you're new in town. I assume you have not secured a vehicle yet, am I correct?"

"Yes, sir. I plan to get one this weekend."

"And you, Agent Caldwell, I understand that you're a native of the area. Am I correct in assuming you pretty much know your way around?"

"Yes, sir, I am familiar with all of the L.A. area. I was born and raised in Compton. I put myself through college at UCLA and graduated with a degree in Criminal Justice before attending the Academy."

"I don't need to know your life story, Caldwell," Baranson replies, cutting her off, though with good humor.

"Wait, did you just graduate from the Academy?" Paulie interjects.

"I did."

"I don't think I saw you there."

"I knew who you were."

"That's enough fraternizing," says Baranson. "In any event, good. Then you are well-suited to help Agent Andrews get acquainted with the city."

"Yes, sir," Caldwell replies, with a palpable lack of enthusiasm.

I'd better get a map, Paulie thinks.

"You're both green, so I have assigned Agent Anton Boswhite to show you the ropes. He's a twelve-year veteran of white-collar crime and knows the law and the lawless as well as anyone in this office. He will be your guide, your guru, your counselor—everything. Are there any questions?"

"Yes sir," Paulie says. "Is it common for two rookie agents to be assigned together?"

"Do you not like your assignment, Andrews?"

"No, no. That's not it at all, sir."

"Well, then, good. Anything else? No? Fine. Get to know those files, and you'll review them with Boswhite at 08:00 hours tomorrow. Good luck to you both and make us proud."

Caldwell gets up without a word and walks out. Paulie shakes Baranson's catcher's mitt of a hand and follows behind her.

They both return to their cubicle.

"Do you have time for a cup of coffee? I'm buying. Maybe we can get more acquainted."

"Look, we're going to work together, fine. But I don't need to be your friend. And you don't need to be mine."

"Tania," he says, conscious to pronounce her name accurately, "I just want us to be a team. So why don't we go somewhere and get a bite to eat? I will tell you what's wrong with me, although there is very little, and you can tell me all about yourself. What do you say, partner?"

A glimmer of a smile.

"I'll see you tomorrow, white bread. By the way, I suspect there is lots wrong with you. Nice question to Baranson, by the way."

As she walks away, Paulie feels, for the first time, that maybe, just maybe, this will work out.

41

MORE RESPECT

After the Jakowski grab, Angelo and Mikey fence the gold coins out of state. They slowly and deliberately sell them off piece-meal to avoid attention. It's a hell of a score, and they split the money up three ways, but Vincent is adamant that they don't spend all of it until he's spoken to Johnny V. The two obviously resent this, but they do as Vincent says.

When the final pieces have been sold, Vincent's first stop is the grocery store. He finds Papa Tony on the loading dock, yelling at some driver. Vincent waits out the tirade.

"What'd he do, Papa Tony?"

"None of your business. What are you doing here and why aren't you out doing that private eye shit?"

"Haven't got the license yet but working on a bunch of things," Vincent says, while withdrawing an envelope from his pocket. He hands it to Tony.

"What's this?

"It's what you fronted for me, Papa. Thank you." Papa Tony looks at the envelope in Vincent's outstretched hand and frowns deeply.

"Where did this come from?" he asks, frowning even deeper as he looks inside.

"I earned it, Papa, that is all you need to know. Now I need to see Johnny V."

"So, go see him," Papa Tony says and walks away, ignoring the envelope. *No use in arguing,* Vincent thinks, *I'll give this to Ma and let her handle it.*

Vincent walks to St. Anthony's Social Club but is told that Johnny V is at The Patio, so he goes there. He sees Bruno inside, who acknowledges him but doesn't say much. After about fifteen minutes, Bruno waves him into the back office.

"I have something to tell you," Vincent says, looking directly at Johnny V. "My buddies and I scored up in Skokie the other night."

Johnny slowly looks over at Bruno, says nothing, and just looks back at Vincent.

"So," Vincent continues, "I'm here to show respect."

"No one called from up there as of yet," Johnny V shrugs his shoulders. "So, go home. Tell the others to bring Bruno five percent of their end, yours too, and that's that. I don't want any details whatsoever. You understand?"

Vincent indicates yes.

"From this day forward," Johnny V says with emphasis, "you see Bruno—you don't need to see me unless it is important—and I mean fucking important. You did good, now get out."

Vincent nods, gets up, and walks out.

That was strange, he thinks. But great news for all. He'll tell Mikey and Angelo to deliver the money to Bruno directly, so they all get in better with the boss.

He finds his mother at home.

He sits her down on the couch and hands her the envelope meant for Papa Tony. She doesn't ask where the money came from. She would never. She takes the envelope and places it under a seat cushion, out of sight.

"You are a good son, and you did the right thing. Don't say another word to Tony about it. By the way, that girl Valerie called again. Why don't you bring her here for dinner? I'd like to meet her."

"Ma, it's not like that."

"Fine," she says, standing up and retreating to her kitchen.

42

THE MENDOZA CASE

After three meetings in three days with Agent Boswhite, both Caldwell and Paulie feel very fortunate to have him as their guide. He's undoubtably a straight arrow—forthright and generous with his knowledge.

For their first case, Boswhite recommends that they tackle a money laundering scheme for the Sinaloa Cartel. Boswhite advises them to tread carefully since the target is a civic leader, a young and philanthropic owner of a rapidly expanding chain of Mexican supermarkets. Boswhite reminds them to come to him if they have any questions. In any event, he's available to help guide them through the investigation.

The new partners dig into the files of José Medina Mendoza, the 30-year-old superstar businessman. They're told that much of the information comes from an informant, a former employee who swore that he overheard Mendoza laying out his scheme. But the information is vague at best—just enough to pique the interest of the FBI, but nowhere near sufficient for an arrest, let alone a grand jury investigation.

On paper, Mendoza is exemplary. Born in Sinaloa, Mexico, the boy was smuggled into the United States at the age of six by his mother Sylvia, then just 22 years old. Mendoza excelled in school but dropped out of college in his second year to join the Marines, serving in Vietnam. He was decorated, gained his citizenship, and came home a hero to his family and his country.

Everything changed for Mendoza when, according to the informant, his uncle Eduardo, his mother's brother, brought him down to Mexico. There Eduardo introduced the 22-year-old José to his friends in the Cartel, who quickly recognized his intelligence. They lent him money to start his grocery store business, which flourished.

Today, José, now known simply as Joe, is the owner and operator of twenty-two stores throughout Mexican communities in the Los Angeles area. No one knows exactly how he's doing it, but it's clear that the businesses continue to flourish, as more and more stores open each year.

What's more, the papers and the Hispanic media love him. He contributes to political campaigns and charities and aligns himself with respectable businesspeople and law enforcement leaders. In other words, if there is some wrongdoing, he'll be a tough nut to crack.

There seems to be no way in. Paulie, with his extensive experience in the grocery business on account of his grandfather's store, is especially frustrated. Weeks go by, but still no results.

Then, one Sunday afternoon, while walking along the beach in Santa Monica, Paulie recalls the countless cases of canned Italian plum tomatoes that were constantly being delivered to his grandfather's store. When he was younger, it seemed like he and Vincent were always unloading dozens and dozens of cases of tomatoes. He gets that the Neighborhood loves their gravy, but there's no way they went through that much.

Paulie considers this on his way home and calls Vincent.

"Hey, you remember all those cases of tomatoes we used to unload at Papa Tony's?" he asks.

"Yeah, so what?"

"Remember how they just seemed to disappear so fast, and we wondered how it was possible for the Neighborhood to go through so many so quickly? Papa Tony must have sold them to other Italian grocery stores, right?"

"Again, so what?"

"Well, I'm working on this big operation and trying to figure out how they are laundering so much money."

"Have you lost your mind? Are you really trying to get me involved in a Federal investigation? There's no fucking way."

"Take it easy. I was just interested in your thoughts. You always were good at figuring out things. But, you know, fuhgedddaboudit. I'll just talk to you later."

"Don't be so fucking sensitive, G-Man. Let me think about it for a fucking minute, okay? First off, how do you know if they are actually laundering money? Do you have any fucking facts or are you just harassing people the way you guys do here in Chicago?"

"My gut tells me that they are. I'm trying to figure out how—which is my job, by the way."

"Let me roll this around in my mind for a minute. Tell me all you know and don't spare the details."

When Paulie finishes laying it out, Vincent says he'll give it some thought and get back to him.

"But, don't tell anyone, boy scout," Vinnie warns his friend. "That's all I need is for word to get out that I am helping you."

He hangs up. Paulie looks out the window, frustrated. Vincent, on the other hand, has an idea.

43

THE MARK'S NEPHEW

The next day, as Vincent walks to the grocery store, he's stopped by Mikey and Angelo, who have been waiting for him.

"I got good news and bad news, Vincent," says Mikey, unusually nervous. Angelo just looks pissed.

"What's up?"

"The good news is that we gave the cash to Bruno, who treated us with actual gratitude. He smiled at us and said to bring more when we got it," Angelo says.

"Yeah, but the guy who gave us the tip is pissed and wants more money," Mikey jumps in. "He told us we were crazy not to get the stamp collection, because it's worth hundreds of thousands of dollars, if not a million. He wants us to go back and get it."

"Who is this fuck, and why are we having this conversation?" Vincent says with anger.

"He's the nephew of the mark. He thought he would get the collection as his end so he could sell it, but we never had that conversation. We never gave him the impression that we would give him the collection, only that he would get his end of the score when we fenced it out. I guess he learned that his uncle was filing a claim with the insurance company as part of his loss. The nephew thought we had taken the stamps until I convinced him otherwise. But now he's threatening to find someone else to grab the collection from his uncle."

"I told him not to even try," says Angelo, "not to even think about it again, that fuck."

Vincent looks at the two.

"Mikey, call him up and tell him nicely we want to talk this over, that we will get this straightened out. Angelo, do not threaten him. Get him to meet us in Melrose Park at Cassini's restaurant. I will call there and set things up. I don't want him seen in the Neighborhood. We will straighten this out then. Now I need you to tell me all about this guy and how you got the lead."

They talk for over a half hour. When they finish, Vincent says to Mikey, "Call me at home when you get through to him. Let's get this done tonight."

At 8:45 p.m., the three walk into Cassini's in Melrose Park. Sitting at the front by the cash register is 82-year-old Mama Cassini. Her grandfather, an Italian immigrant, opened the restaurant back in the 1800s. They greet and endear themselves to Mama Cassini, who is loved by all. Her husband, Giovanni, was a bookmaker all his life. These days, he enjoys his retirement years at the restaurant acting as the head waiter, ordering his staff around. He leads the three to the table farthest from the front door.

"No funny business here. Understand?" he says.

The three nod and wait for the tipster. At nine sharp, Stanley Jakowski walks in and looks around. He's ushered to their table by Giovanni, who gives them another stern look, before walking off.

"Sit down, Stanley. You hungry?" Mikey asks.

Stanley sits down, taking in Angelo and Vincent, whom he had not met or seen before. They keep their lips sealed.

"Nah, I ate a burger earlier. Is it safe to talk here? That waiter keeps looking over," he says.

"Okay, we're going to order a couple of pizzas and then we can go talk."

"My uncle is making an ass of himself, Mikey. I hope he doesn't fuck things up. He's a screwball Polack," Stanley says, looking around, unable to keep still.

"Save it for later, Stanley. We can't just walk in here, order nothing, and leave," Mikey says.

While they wait for their pizzas, Vincent asks Stanley, "You work up in Skokie?"

"No, I work in Evanston," replies Stanley, lightening up a bit. "My friend owns a body shop and I work there, but my mother owns a dry cleaner place, so I go back and forth between the two."

They talk about sports and other mundane things until they finish the pizzas. They pay Mama Cassini, say goodbye, and leave. On their way out, Giovanni nods ever so slightly at Vincent to show that he appreciates their restraint.

"Take the front seat," Mikey says to Stanley, pointing to a Volkswagen van stolen for the purpose of this conversation.

"Where are we going?" Stanley replies.

"Just for a drive," says Vincent, so we can talk this out in private.

"Yeah, okay, sounds good."

With Angelo and Vincent in the back seat of the van, Mikey drives for about fifteen minutes. He turns into a wooded area and shuts off the engine. Then he turns to Stanley.

"So, you gonna threaten us again?"

"I, I didn't threaten you guys," says Stanley, suddenly nervous. "I just thought that it was really stupid not to take the stamp collection, that's all. I would have taken that as my end, like I told you."

"We never, ever had that conversation, Stan," Mikey says. "We didn't even know if the collection was at the house. We were there for the gold."

"Yeah, but once you knew, you should have taken it. Now you guys have to go back and get it," Stanley replies, filled with bravado, trying to act tough.

Vincent slaps him hard on the back of his head.

"Listen, you fuck, you don't order anyone around. We are not going to go back, and you're gonna keep your mouth shut. You open your mouth about any of this and you're going to need a lot of body work yourself. You told Mikey that you might get the collection after your uncle dies, so wait. Either that, or we use the collection to mail your body parts to other states. You understand me?"

Angelo pulls out a revolver.

"Let's just end this now because this fuck is going to cause us problems."

"NO! NO!" cries Stanley. "I won't cause any problems, I promise! Don't hurt me!"

"Fuck this!" Angelo says as he cocks the hammer.

"Please, I didn't say anything," Stanley begs, "and I won't. I'll wait, I'll wait, I promise!"

"I don't fucking believe you," Mikey cuts in, yelling now. "You threatened us and now you want us to let you live?"

Tears stream down Stanley's face. Vincent reaches over and places a hand on his shoulder.

"Okay, Stanley, calm down. We'll let this go but you better realize who you're dealing with and what we can do to you. It will not take but a fucking moment to decide. You set this up, and you got your end, so be satisfied, be smart. Deal?"

Vincent suddenly grabs Stanley's shoulder roughly.

"Look at me, you stupid fuck! Do you fucking understand?"

Stanley nervously nods his head up and down. Angelo uncocks the revolver and puts it away.

"Be smart, Stanley," sighs Mikey.

They drive him a block away from the restaurant and set him free. He walks away, his shoulders sagging, relieved beyond measure.

Back in the car, the guys are laughing.

"Use the stamp collection to mail his body parts?"

"Where did that line come from, Vincent?"

"I've been known to come up with a phrase or two."

They park the stolen van, wipe it down for prints, and leave. One of Fat Louie's guys will pick it up tomorrow, and it will never be seen again.

When they get back to the Neighborhood, Vincent steps out and turns to Mikey.

"Keep an eye on this guy for a while, will ya? I don't think he will be a problem. But you know where he lives. Maybe run into him in about a week just to say 'Hello.'"

"Sure thing," says Mikey.

Vincent gets in his car and drives off. Angelo and Mikey look at each other. They have newfound respect for their pal.

44

THE TEST

On the morning of the private investigator's test, Vincent is awakened by the familiar smell of his mother's breakfast. He eats with relish, brimming with confidence. He says goodbye to his mother, who kisses his cheek and pinches it. She looks deep into his eyes. The message is clear.

Angelo drives him downtown.

"You know that Alphonse is getting out next week, right?" asks Angelo.

Next to his mother and Paulie, there is no one in the world that Vincent trusts more than Alphonse Guidini. A few years older than Vincent, Alphonse looked after him when he was younger.

"Yeah, I know. I've missed him. I wrote him dozens of times and never got an answer, but that's Alphonse for you. I told his mother and Ralphie that I would drive out to Statesville to pick him up. Ralphie understood."

A prolific and highly regarded jewel thief, Alphonse was fucked over by one of the guys he did a robbery with. Alphonse was not actually caught in the act. Mario Collino, who had gotten picked up on another job, gave up the entire crew—Alphonse, as well as Jake Battaglia and Mark Gregorio—for a reduction in his sentence. Before that, the cops had no suspects.

In any event, Alphonse stood tall. He never cooperated with law enforcement, never gave up a single bit of information on Jake or Mark. When Jake heard that Alphonse got pinched, he skipped town, taking all the jewels with him. No one has heard from him since. The third guy, Mark Gregorio, never served time for the job either. He died in a freak car accident just a month before the trial started.

None of that mattered to Alphonse. To the cops, he didn't even acknowledge that the others existed. He was tried, convicted, and sentenced to five years. Alphonse did a little over two-and-a-half years of his sentence before he was paroled. He had never been convicted before, so it was an easy decision for the parole board.

But that left Mario Collino, the fucking sniveling rat, still in the wind. No one from the Neighborhood had heard from or about him in years. However, that changed just a few months ago. Vincent reached out to Mario's friends and got the name of his girlfriend, and from there he found the rat living in Wisconsin under another name. The dumb shit was still using his own date of birth. Vincent keeps this information to himself but plans to give it to Alphonse at the appropriate time. For the rest of the drive downtown, Vincent thinks about Alphonse in silence.

Angelo drops Vincent off at the state office building, wishing him luck. At the doorway to the room where he's about to take the test, Vincent is approached by one of his future competitors. Edward Braylord, owner of the largest investigative firm in Chicago, derisively looks at Vincent.

"I don't know how you pulled this off, Scalise, but we will put you out of business before you even get a foot hold," says Braylord, another ex-FBI agent with lots of corporate clients. "We're looking into how you pulled this off and we will find out, I assure you."

"And I assure you that you can go fuck yourself. We'll see who ends up on top. Now get out of my fucking way." Braylord can only glare at Vincent's back as he enters the room. Vincent never glances back.

The test is scheduled to last an hour, but Vincent is finished in forty minutes, lingering longer to double check his answers. He walks out, pretty much happy with himself. He takes a bus back to the Neighborhood just for the hell of it. It will give him time to think as he watches the city go by.

Later that evening he calls Paulie, who is not home. Vincent leaves an insulting message on Paulie's answering machine, then heads out to meet with the fellows at Ali Baba's.

45

A DEAD END

Paulie comes home from work and presses play on his answering machine. He smiles at the message from Vincent. He looks up at the clock, but knows that it's too late to call back. He and Tania were on a stakeout of José Medina Mendoza. It had turned up absolutely nothing—and not for the first time.

Mendoza conducted his business as he did every day, making the rounds of his supermarkets, before returning to his flagship store on Sunset Boulevard in the mid-afternoon. At six p.m., he left in his Ford Mustang and went home. They watched him walk up his driveway and get greeted by his wife, Maria, and their two children, Matthew and Dorita. Three times, Paulie and Tania stayed in the car all night to see if Mendoza left for some midnight rendezvous. But he never did.

Paulie calls Vincent back the next day.

"We did another surveillance on this guy," Paulie says. "It turned up nothing. We don't have a goddamn clue, Vincent. Anyway, how did the test go?"

"Piece of cake."

Paulie believes him, the asshole.

"Hey," Vincent continues. "I'm planning to come out there within the next couple of weeks."

"That sounds great, but I don't know if I should expose you to my partner—or to anyone else I know for that matter."

"Yeah, yeah G-Man. No problem. I have absolutely no interest in meeting your boy scout troop, anyway."

They laugh and hang up.

Teri calls her son into the kitchen and they eat breakfast.

"Are you really going to go out to California to see Paulie?"

"Yeah, Ma. I want to see him in person. We have to get the situation with Papa Tony resolved."

Teri smooths back her son's hair in a loving fashion and smiles.

46

ALPHONSE

The night before Alphonse is released, Angelo and Mikey go to Vincent's house. They each hand him two hundred and fifty dollars to give to Alphonse. Vincent looks at the two, hugs them, and shakes their hands.

"You didn't need to do this," Vincent says, "but I certainly appreciate the gesture—and I'm sure Alphonse will, too. We need to keep him out of trouble for as long as we can."

They volunteer to go with Vincent, but he wants time alone with his friend. Vincent promises they will all get together soon.

Vincent packs a bag with clothes, shoes, and other necessities for Alphonse. He stuffs an envelope with the five hundred dollars from Angelo and Mikey, along with another thousand dollars of his own. Then he kisses his mother goodnight, sets his alarm clock, and goes to sleep.

He arrives at the prison at 5:30 a.m. He's told to wait in the parking lot. They'll notify him when and where to pick up Alphonse. At 6:30, he's called over and led to a gate. Soon he sees Alphonse approaching with a frown on his face. But upon seeing Vincent, he breaks into a wide, crooked smile. His curly hair is cut shorter, and maybe he has added another ten pounds of muscle to his five-foot-seven frame, but he looks basically the same since the last time Vincent saw him. Even his green eyes have the same intense shine. They bear no sign of sorrow or fatigue.

"You look great, you piece of shit. What did they feed you in there?"

"Shit, but that's that."

They embrace. Alphonse looks over Vincent's shoulder to see if anyone else is with him.

"You must have convinced my mother and Ralphie to stay home."

"When you see your mom, you should look human—I mean, at least as close to looking human as that freakshow mug of yours can get. I got some clothes and stuff for you in the car."

They drive to a restaurant, and Alphonse changes in the bathroom before breakfast. When he gets back to the table, Vincent hands him the envelope.

"What's this?"

"Something from me, Angelo, and Mikey to help you out. Don't say anything. Just take it and shut the fuck up."

A pearl of a tear shines in Alphonse's eyes. He nods his head. "Thank you, pal. I really appreciate this."

While they eat, Alphonse tells Vincent some jailhouse stories. "I only got one shot while I was in."

"Wait, you got shot?"

"No, no. A shot is like a disciplinary action or some shit. I don't fucking know. Anyway, I got a shot for *reckless eyeballing*," he says, trying hard to stifle a laugh.

"What the fuck is reckless eyeballing?"

"The bosses, that's what you call the guards, do not like it when inmates stare or give them looks, which they call eyeballing. You can also get a shot for silent insolence."

They both laugh again.

"But anyway, I became a barber and cut hair. Everyone must get at least one shave and haircut every week, so there was always lots to do. Other than that, I worked out in the yard, read, and pretty much kept to myself, which is the smart thing to do. You don't want to get into jailhouse politics, so I stayed out of all that."

"That's good, Alphonse. Hey, listen, there was another reason why I wanted some time alone with you. I found your rat partner. Mario."

Alphonse does not say a word. He slowly nods his head in acknowledgment. There is nothing more to be said. When Alphonse wants the information, Vincent will give it to him. They talk about other things and finish eating.

The drive home is mostly in silence. Alphonse is eager to see his mother and brother. When they reach his street, Ralphie and his mother are waiting on the stoop. His mother cries out when she sees him get out of Vincent's Thunderbird. She covers him with kisses. His brother hugs him. The neighbors and some of his old buddies congratulate him for graduating "college"—the Neighborhood term for doing time.

Vincent gives him his telephone number and tells him they will see each other later. Before he goes, Alphonse's mother tells Vincent to thank his mother for her. Teri sent over a couple of lemon meringue pies—she remembered that Alphonse loved them.

47

COMING UP SHORT

Slowly, Tania Caldwell begins to warm up to Paulie. His drive for excellence reminds her of herself. One day, she relents and takes him up on his offer to get lunch. Soon, it becomes almost a daily occurrence. He learns that she has good reasons to be private. The photo that stands on her desk is of her 11-year-old son, Tyler. The boy's father, Edgar, had been a gang member, but he disappeared a few months after getting shot. Afraid for his life, he left 17-year-old Tania to fend for herself and their toddler son. Tania's mother watched little Tyler while her daughter went to school and worked. She still does. Tania is someone to be admired, which Paulie frequently tells her.

Meanwhile, the two agents develop a solid rhythm to their working relationship. Six weeks into the job, they are called to Baranson's office for a status report. In preparation for the meeting, they send their recommendations in advance: two of the bank cases are ready for grand juries, and two others are ready to be presented to the U.S. Attorney. They're confident as they make their way to his office.

"Good morning," Agent Baranson says, after they sit down. "I have your reports here. You've made remarkable progress on these four cases."

Paulie and Tania share a look. Here comes the praise. "But," Baranson continues, picking up another report on his desk, "you seem unable to land a foothold in the Mendoza money-laundering case. How do you explain yourselves?"

Apparently, Baranson doesn't subscribe to the coddling technique of management.

"We have ceased active visual surveillance on him," Paulie says. "From the outside, he's as innocent as a baby. His routine is rigidly disciplined, like an unending loop. Essentially, we're stuck, unless we can set up audio surveillance and wiretaps. But we need your go ahead for that."

"We'll also need access to the informant," Tania adds. "If you'll note in our reports, we've requested access for both the audio surveillance and the informant multiple times."

"As to both of those issues," Baranson frowns, "confer with Boswhite. And show more initiative in the future. I want an update later this week. That'll be all."

Back in their cubicle, they discuss the meeting.

"Did Baranson seem," Tania pauses, "not upset exactly, but sort of short with us? It's weird he had no interest in discussing the other cases, only Mendoza."

"Maybe this is a test to see if we can solve this without wiretaps. But that seems strange, too. We should call Anton and ask him what's what. And it's definitely odd that we have no access to the informant."

Caldwell's phone rings.

"Yes, this is Tania Caldwell. What? Yes, of course, I'll be right there."

"Everything okay?"

"Yeah. I don't know. That was the principal of Tyler's school. I've got to go over there now," she says, packing up her things.

"Is there anything I can do?"

"I don't even know what's wrong."

"Okay, let me know."

After she leaves, Paulie glances at his calendar. Knowing Vincent will be in town the next week brings Paulie a feeling of calm. Vincent always has an unorthodox view of things, but his intuitions are very often right. In any event, it'll be good to see his "brother."

48

CANNED TOMATOES

Hey, Ma… Ma!"

Vincent bumps into her as he turns through the kitchen door. "Whaddya yelling for?"

"Nothing, I just was looking for you."

"Don't yell in my house."

"Alright, jeez. Hey, listen, have you talked to Rina lately? I went by the store to say hello to her and Papa Tony. She looks really depressed, Ma, and so does Papa Tony. Do you know what's going on?"

She does, but Teri cannot discuss it with her son, at least not yet.

"They both just miss Paulie," she says truthfully. "Sometimes it hurts them more than other times."

"Alright, Ma," Vincent says, not entirely convinced.

"And maybe they don't understand why he was so obsessed with becoming an FBI agent in the first place," she offers. "To be honest, I don't either. Did you boys ever discuss it?"

Her arms across her chest—a signal to Vincent that she means business—Teri waits for his reply.

"Not much. He constantly got ragged about it by the guys in the Neighborhood, so I didn't press him. It was like he had this dream and wanted it to become reality. As close as we are, I have no clue. Anyway, when I see him next Tuesday, I'll get everything resolved, believe me."

His mother stares him down.

"Are you going to tell Rina and Papa Tony that you're going out there?"

"Yes, I'm going to see them now. But I won't tell them the reason why. In any event, I'm not coming home until he finds a way to settle things with Papa Tony. This has gone on too long."

"They're both stubborn."

Vincent begins to pace.

"I think he will listen to me and reach out for his Nonno. Believe me, I will make his life miserable if he does not."

"Good luck with that," his mother says.

Vincent heads out. He leaves the car and walks to the grocery store. He needs time to think about how he'll approach the old man. On his walk, Vincent hears his name called. He turns and sees Shoes outside the barber shop waving him over.

"Hey kid, I'm glad I saw ya. I was actually thinking about you."

"What's up?" asks Vincent.

"Did you get your license yet?"

"No, but I should in a couple of days."

"Come and see me the moment you get it. I want you to meet a couple of people, okay?"

"You bet. I will let you know."

Rina is at the counter when he gets to the grocery store. "Hi, honey," she says, as he gives her a kiss.

"Hey, you know I'm going to see Paulie next Tuesday."

"You're what?" Rina looks overjoyed at first, but then she frowns. "Are you going to tell my father?"

"Yes, I'm going to see him right now. Is he in the back?"

Rina bites her lip.

"He's got a lot on his mind right now, Vinny. Just tell him you're going out there but try not to get into any discussion about it. He's in a nasty mood."

So, what else is new? Vincent thinks as he walks to the loading area.

Vincent sees Papa Tony talking to a truck driver, waving his hands around. *Rina was right about his mood.* He sees Vincent and abruptly waves off the driver. Then he brushes past Vincent without a word and goes inside.

The new guy, Peter Dante, is unloading boxes of canned tomatoes from the truck and setting them against the wall. Vincent looks at him with sympathy. Then he thinks about the question Paulie asked him, about what happens to the thousands of cans of tomatoes they used to stack up right there.

"You ever think about why we never bring those cans inside?" Vincent asks Dante. "Someone might take them out here."

Not that they ever would, considering the respect Tuff Tony commands in the Neighborhood. But then again, why is it only the canned tomatoes that are stored out on the loading dock and nothing else? The new guy looks at Vincent, surprised to be spoken to.

"I dunno. Someone will come with another truck and pick them up later."

"Oh yeah, obviously."

Vincent turns and goes back inside. Papa Tony in his office, looking intently at a photo of a young Paulie sitting on his lap. Vincent has seen it a hundred times—little chunky Paulie, with a big grin on his face.

"Papa, what if someone in the grocery business wanted to hide or launder money without risking the withdrawal of cash? In other words, how could a grocery owner secretly hide his profits—or lack thereof—from his store?"

Papa Tony scowls at Vincent before answering.

"Why you asking?"

"Just curious," says Vincent.

"You can leave out the produce, bread, meat, and all the other things, but the only way to get cash in and out is to rotate the canned goods stock."

Of course.

Then Tony looks over, placing the photo face down on his desk.

"Why do you ask?"

"Like I said, just curious."

"This is what you think about? Get out of here, I'm busy."

"Wait, I gotta tell you something. There's a reason I came over here. I want to let you know that I am going out to see Paulie next Tuesday."

Tony looks Vincent in the eye but says nothing. He stands up and pushes Vincent out of the office and closes the door. Vincent walks back over to Rina.

"What's wrong with him?"

Rina wrings her hands together and tears up.

"He's got a lot on his mind, honey. You go and give my son a big kiss from me. And get him to call me more often."

Vincent heads home even more confused than before. He needs to talk to his mother about this. But, on the bright side, he might have just solved Paulie's money laundering problem.

At the end of the day, Rina locks the door to the store and walks back to her father's office. She knocks lightly on the door.

"Papa, it's Rina. Can I come in?"

A moment later, the door slowly opens. Tony takes her arm gently and sits her down. They look at each other for a moment. Then Tony breaks the silence.

"I just heard for sure. He's getting released in two weeks."

Tony watches her reaction. She doesn't reveal much.

"Papa, he kept his word and did not interfere in any way. But he's going to want to see Paulie, I have no doubt. And he should."

"No," Tony says, anger in his voice. "He should not, and I will not allow it. Paulie is an FBI agent now, for God's sake, not an accountant or a banker. An FBI agent. I will meet with Carmine and explain all of this to him. I will make him understand!"

Rina shakes her head and begins to cry. Her father's anger frightens her. But enough is enough. He cannot control her life forever.

"I should have never agreed to this, Papa. He is Paulie's father."

"Rina, he is a made man and may become even more powerful after he gets released."

"I understand why you made me do what you did. But I felt it was wrong then, and I still do."

"Paulie cannot ever know that his father is an Organized Crime boss. He'd lose his job. He'll be ruined."

"I cannot believe that I kept his son from him. I feel horrible. I've felt horrible every day for twenty-five years."

"Let this be for now. I will talk to Carmine."

He embraces her. They both weep. In his arms, Rina feels like she's suffocating. But what can she do?

49

AGENT BOSWHITE

The morning after their report to Baranson, Paulie and Tania meet with Agent Boswhite. He offers them both coffee, which they decline. He pours himself a cup from a French press he keeps in his office.

"Are you sure I can't tempt you? These beans are imported from Guatemala. You cannot even get them in the city. I get them delivered special."

"No, thanks," says Paulie, for the second time.

"Your loss."

Boswhite walks around his desk and sits.

"How can I—"

"Why won't you let us interview the informant for the Mendoza case?" interrupts Caldwell.

Boswhite is taken aback. He frowns.

"Obviously, that was not my decision. That came from down the hall."

He jerks his head toward Baranson's office.

"I don't know who the informant is. I also don't know whether he's been designated as a confidential informant, a paid informant, or what. I can certainly try to find out. Was there anything else?"

"Yes," Paulie replies. "We'd like to begin some audio surveillance on Mendoza. But neither of us is an expert and we don't know how to proceed. When I was in the Academy, I met the head tech, David Logan.

"Yes, I know David."

"I was thinking about reaching out to him. But I wanted to check with you first."

"Audio surveillance is a complicated issue," Boswhite says. "I'll have to get back to you on that. Anything else?"

Paulie and Caldwell look at each other.

"I don't think so," says Paulie.

"Great. Keep up the good work. You both have done a stellar job so far."

Boswhite smiles at them.

"I think that just about wraps things up, no?"

"Yes, sir, of course."

Agent Caldwell stops Paulie in the hall.

"That was fucking weird, right? It's not just me?"

Paulie begins to pace.

"No, you're right. Something feels off. I've got an idea, though."

"I'm all ears."

"I'm just gonna bounce this whole situation off someone I trust. He might have some good thoughts."

"Someone in the Bureau?" Tania asks, raising her eyebrows.

"No."

"You're making me nervous."

"Trust me on this."

Tania frowns and looks at her watch.

"Oh shit. I have to go back to my son's school again. I have a meeting with the principal. I'll be back in about an hour. We'll discuss this then."

"Want me to tag along?"

"You want to come to a meeting with my son's principal? That's ridiculous."

"What? I'm interested."

Caldwell considers "You know what, why not? It might be interesting to hear your thoughts on the whole thing. But you won't, uh, say anything, right?"

"Scout's honor."

"You're a weird guy, Paul. Anybody ever tell you that?"

"You should hear what they say about me back home."

50

EDGAR

Mrs. Caldwell, nice to see you again," says Perry Hamlin, the school principal.

"It's actually *Agent* Caldwell."

"Oh yes, of course, my apologies." Hamlin looks over at Paulie. "And you are?"

"My colleague, Agent Andrews," says Tania.

"Okay. So good to have close friends at work. Please take a seat."

"Thanks."

Hamlin looks at Paulie, then back to Caldwell.

"May I speak freely?"

"Please do. So, what is this regarding? No one explained it to me when I picked Tyler up yesterday."

"For the most part Mrs.—I mean, Agent Caldwell—your son Tyler is a great kid. Very upbeat and well adjusted—in short, he's a pleasure to teach. But recently he's become increasingly sullen and antisocial. And yesterday, of course, the nurse wanted to send him home. He said he was sick. She spoke with me afterwards, and she believes Tyler may be depressed. Has something changed at home? Anything that we should know about?"

Agent Caldwell takes a moment.

"Actually, yes. Tyler's father came by the house recently—after walking out on the two of us several years ago. I let him see Tyler, because he's the boy's father, but Edgar is bad news. There was a physical confrontation between the two of us, and Tyler saw it all go down."

"I see. Did you call the police?"

"I'm an agent in the Federal Bureau of Investigation, Principal Hamlin. I'm perfectly capable of handling myself. Of course, I feel awful that Tyler had to witness any of it. But at least he saw his father's true colors. In any event, Edgar won't be a problem anymore, I can assure you of that."

"Yes, of course. But as regards Tyler, I think he should speak with someone. I have the names of a couple of very highly respected therapists he could speak to."

Caldwell sighs.

"I will have a talk with Tyler this evening. And yes, I'll take those names, thank you."

"Please let me know if I can be of any assistance."

"Yes, thank you, Principal Hamlin."

Paulie and Tania walk out to the car.

"You never told me any of this," Paulie says.

"It's not your business, Andrews. I must have been crazy to bring you along."

"Stop. Stop!" He reaches out for her arm, which she pulls away fiercely.

"What do you want from me?"

He looks her dead in the eye.

"I'll kill that guy if he puts another hand on you."

"You're not allowed to say things like that, Andrews. This is my problem to handle, not yours. Get in the car."

They drive back to the office in silence. Paulie thinks about how they would solve this situation back in the Neighborhood. For the first time in his life, Paulie thinks that there might be something to the Outfit's particular brand of justice.

51

MOTHERLY ADVICE

As Vincent prepares for his trip, he finds that he's actually looking forward to it. He's never traveled as a civilian. In between scouting hotels, comparing air fares, and shopping for swim trunks, he checks the mail five times a day to see if his private detective's license has shown up. It cannot come quick enough.

He is, indeed, checking the mail when his mother returns home. She says nothing about where she's been, as usual.

"Hey, Ma. Just so you know, I talked to Rina and Papa Tony about the trip, so they know."

She nods her head and goes to the kitchen. He follows. "Ma, I sense something is going on. Can you tell me what's what?"

She looks at her son and hesitates. "No."

Since she won't tell him, and he can see that she's upset, he lets it go. He wonders why, but there's no sense in pursuing this. He changes the subject to engage her in conversation.

"I'm all set to leave on Tuesday, and I'm really looking forward to it. Do you want me to bring you back a souvenir?" She shakes her head no, so he pursues another topic. "Jeez, I hope my test results and license are waiting for me when I return."

But it's no use. She fusses around in the kitchen for a few more minutes. Then she looks at him with blank eyes.

"That girl called when you were out this morning."

Then she walks into her bedroom and closes the door.

"Ma," Vincent calls, loud enough so she can hear it through the door. "I'm going out to see the guys."

No response. *What's going on with her?*

As Vincent walks through the Neighborhood, he spots Mikey pacing around, looking nervous.

"Hey Mikey, what's going on?"

Mikey jolts, startled. He looks over to his friend.

"What? Oh, hey, Vin."

"You look scared!"

"I gotta tell you something. Stanley just disappeared, and no one knows where the fuck he is."

"Yeah, so?"

"I've been checking. It's just strange that he never went to work or to his mother's cleaners. He's just disappeared. What the fuck!"

"Calm down, Mikey! Don't worry about this. Wait till I come back from California, and we'll look into it together."

"Yeah, okay. I'll tell Angelo."

"What's with the crowd at Baba's?"

"More microwaves. He cannot get enough of them."

Vincent looks over to the beef stand, frowns, and shakes his head. *Fucking progress.*

The next morning, Vincent lies in bed.

"Ma?"

"In here, Vincent."

He gets up. She's in the kitchen making meatballs.

"You want breakfast, sleepy head?" she asks without turning from the stove.

"Maybe some toast and Ovaltine. I'm not really hungry. Listen, Ma, I have to talk to you about Papa Tony and Rina. I know you know something about what's troubling them. I think I need to know what before I go see Paulie."

She washes her hands, turns around, and then slowly sits down across the table from him. He looks directly into his mother's eyes.

"They asked me not to tell you, my son. I cannot break my word to them. It is not something you can involve yourself with anyway. Just trust that it is something the two of them need to work out. Maybe soon, they will let you know."

"But Ma—"

"I repeat: It's important that you understand that this is something that only the two of them can work out. Please do not press them or even hint that you suspect something. Let them think that your only concern is Paulie. If you want to help, go out there and convince him to reconcile with his Nonno. That would be a big help, believe me."

She looks at him with love and care. He knows she's sincere. So, he resolves himself to do just as she asks. But his curiosity is killing him.

"Okay, Ma."

Teri gets up and continues making meatballs. Vincent makes himself some Italian bread toast, eats it, drinks his Ovaltine, and leaves to take a shower. After he gets dressed, he checks the mail. Nothing.

52

OUTSIDE ASSISTANCE

Although he really should not have paid for first class, Vincent enjoys the attention and service. He vows that he'll make enough money to do this often. He feels spoiled and loves it.

At the hotel, he leaves a message on Paulie's machine.

"Paulie, I'm here. It's about 4:30 p.m., I guess. I'm in room 620 at Shutters right on the beach. Fucking beautiful. You have gotta love it out here."

Paulie picks him up at seven to take him to a good Italian restaurant that he knows. They have not seen each other since Vincent left for the Army all those years ago. As good friends do, they fall into easy conversation immediately.

"The food is pretty good here. There are all kinds of Italian restaurants in L.A., and I intend on going to all of them."

"We'll see," says Vincent, inspecting the menu, a task made more difficult by an endless number of gorgeous women in the restaurant. Vincent has never seen so many platinum blondes in one place.

"Vincent, keep your eyes on the menu. Those women would not give you a second glance, anyway."

They talk for more than two hours, mostly about the Neighborhood and what everyone is doing. Paulie tells Vincent that he has not heard from Carolyn, except for a few letters and a rare phone call now and then. These days, he doesn't know where they stand. Vincent doesn't tell Paulie about Valerie. It's just not worth it. All the while, Vincent picks up on the fact that Paulie seems to gloss over his family.

"Why don't you take me back to the hotel," Vincent suggests, after coffee. "We can walk along the beach and talk about your problem. Okay?"

"Yeah, sure."

The moon shines bright, and it's warm on the beach as they stroll and talk. Paulie lays out what he knows, and Vincent listens intently, as he always does. He wants all the details.

"What time does Mendoza leave the main store in the morning?"

"It varies. Why?"

"I want to get a look at him—his operation and everything. Let's go out there together, first thing tomorrow morning."

"I'll have to tell my partner what I'm up to."

"And why is that, G-Man? Can't you do things on your own? I think you still need a wet nurse."

"Vincent, this is not a caper. This is an FBI investigation, and she is my partner. I have to tell her."

"Suit yourself but leave me out of it. Does tomorrow morning work or what?"

"Yeah, okay. I'll handle her."

They walk in silence for a few steps, then Vincent asks him to sit down. Paulie senses there's going to be more to this walk.

"Okay, what?"

"You have to make up with Papa Tony. He is suffering, as is your mother. You messed up big time when you changed your name, fuck-head. Papa Tony is embarrassed and saddened by your choice—and by the way, I agree with him. What's wrong with the name Agent Andriano anyhow? What, the FBI only hires white bread?"

Paulie thinks of Agent Orosco, and indeed, of his partner, Agent Caldwell. He feels even more shame. But Vincent is not done.

"It's *his* name you changed, Paulie, and *his* honor. It was a big mistake and an insult, and you need to make it up to him. You have to at least talk to him. You should be fucking ashamed of yourself. You are my brother, but you piss me off with this FBI shit. Be an agent but give the old man the respect he deserves."

Paulie hangs his head lower and lower, and a tear forms in his eye.

"Okay, Vincent, enough. I get it. I will call him, I promise, but not just yet. I'm under a lot of pressure with this case now. I want to see Papa Tony in person, anyway. Once this case is finalized, I will go back home."

"Good. And just so you know: Nobody in the neighborhood or anyone else knows what you've done. I have not told a soul."

Vincent looks up at the full moon. He puts his head in his hands and sighs.

"You are one stubborn fuck and always have been, G-Man. Okay, let's solve this case. The sooner we do, the sooner I can get the fuck back to Chicago and get some decent food."

Vincent gets up, brushes the sand off his pants, and heads back to the hotel.

"The earlier you pick me up, the better. Deliveries to grocery stores usually occur first thing. Take me to the busiest and largest store—other than the main one."

"Alright, I'll pick you up at six, okay?"

Vincent nods. "One more thing? Don't dress like a Fed. You'll stick out like a sore thumb."

53

ITALIAN Ts

At six the next morning, Vincent waits outside his hotel wearing large sunglasses, blue jeans, boots, and a sleeveless white undershirt—aka an Italian T, aka a wifebeater.

Paulie pulls up. Through the car window, Vincent sees his friend wearing a pressed white short-sleeve dress shirt. He couldn't look more dorkish or like a Fed if he tried. Without a word, Vincent turns around and goes back to his room. When he returns, he throws a Chicago emblemed T-shirt at Paulie's face.

"Take off that fucking shirt and put this on, dummy. I said not to look like a Fed, but I don't want you to look like a vacuum cleaner salesman, either."

"This shirt screams Chicago. I'll look like a tourist."

"Shut up and just put it on. Do you want my help or what?"

Paulie changes then and there. It's a little tight. Vincent laughs when he sees Paulie's new look.

"Now there's my buddy from the Neighborhood. Where you been all these years?"

"Shut up."

"Alright, fuck you, too. Let's go."

They drive out to Mendoza's second largest store and pull up to the loading area in the back. Several trucks parked in the slots are being unloaded.

"Don't pay attention to the name brand trucks, anything with a logo, or other advertisements. We're looking only for plain trucks. There won't be any advertising or artwork on the vehicle, period."

It takes about an hour, but sure enough, a 26-foot truck pulls up to the back of the store with no markings or advertising on the body whatsoever.

Paulie pulls out a camera and is about to start taking pictures when Vincent slaps his camera hand down.

"Think like a thief, not a fucking G-Man, will you? You do not want anyone seeing you taking photos. Take down the license number instead."

A Mexican guy wearing a multicolored, sleeved T-shirt and a large straw hat comes off the truck and waves a store worker over. They talk for fifteen minutes before the driver returns to his truck and waits for all the other trucks to unload.

About twenty minutes later, after the last truck leaves, the Mexican backs his truck into the vacant slot. He leaves the vehicle and goes into the store. Fifteen minutes later, he and three workers return. He opens the back doors of the truck and they begin loading pallets with boxes into the cargo of the truck.

"Wait here and don't get out for any reason," says Vincent.

Paulie watches as Vincent strides up the stairs to the loading dock and approaches the crew. The workers don't seem to pay much attention to him.

"Hey fellows, can I get an application for work?" Vincent asks them.

One of the workers tells him to come back during the week—the foreman has left for the day. The Mexican with the straw hat glances at Vincent but otherwise ignores him. Vincent looks at the pallets being loaded and notes the brand name stenciled on the boxes. It's a Spanish brand— probably from Mexico—that Vincent doesn't recognize. Some boxes are open, and inside them are cans, just as he suspected.

"Alright, see ya."

Vincent takes a roundabout way back to the car.

"Hey Paulie, you ever tail anyone before? I mean, without getting spotted?"

Paulie gives him a nasty look. "So, we're going to tail this guy?"

"Duh? You think?"

"Fuck you, Vincent."

They wait for the truck to leave. It's an easy tail: the guy keeps under the speed limit, driving like he's worried the cops might stop him at any moment. He gets on the highway. They follow.

When he exits at Riverside, Paulie checks his notes. "I bet he's going to one of the other stores."

Sure enough, the Mexican leads them to another branch of the supermarket chain. Instead of driving to the loading dock, though, he pulls the truck into the parking lot. Then he walks to the front entrance and returns twenty minutes later. He then drives around to the back of the store and pulls into an open slot.

"He's going to unload what he just loaded up at the last store. Give him time to start unloading, then drive by—slowly, but do not stop. I want to see if I'm right. I'm going to slump down in the back seat. Keep your eyes forward and do not look at them."

Paulie follows Vincent's instructions.

"Okay let's go back to the hotel," Vincent says. On the drive, Vincent lays out his theory.

"They're taking canned goods from one store and delivering them to another. They are rotating their stock. They probably claim to have sold all those canned goods. The store they deliver them to claims to get new deliveries. I would bet that the vendor is the one actually laundering the money."

Paulie looks at Vincent with awe. He figured this out in one day, but Paulie isn't quite sure he understands.

"Jeez, Vincent. Can it be that fucking simple?"

"Yeah, it's a classic scheme."

"Classic? I'm not sure I even *follow* it."

"You don't need to. Just get one of your pencil pushers on it—you know, those guys who sort through receipts, invoices, and shit."

"You mean forensic accountants?" Paulie asks.

"Yep, that's them. Those geniuses should be able to figure out the rest. It can't be hard to do, especially for boy scouts with pocket protectors. But I'll give you a clue. I bet the vendor is down in Mexico. Then once you boy scouts find out who the fucking seller of those goods is, you can put out the campfire. Or you can just keep selling cookies or whatever it is you actually do."

They get breakfast near Venice Beach, gawking at the girls and the street shows. Paulie and Vincent love being together again, and, afterwards, stroll shoulder to shoulder, constantly bantering and laughing.

After about an hour, Paulie must leave. He has to meet up with Agent Caldwell and share with her the details of what he and Vincent have uncovered. Vincent rolls his eyes. But they make plans to get dinner that night.

Before he goes, Vincent takes Paulie's chin in his hand.

"Remember to take some time today to think about what you're going to say to Papa Tony," he says firmly.

54

THE CRIMINAL MIND

After he leaves Vincent, Paulie finds a pay phone and calls Agent Caldwell at home. Tania answers and is taken aback by the call.

"Why are you calling me at home, Andrews?"

"Do you have a minute to talk shop?"

"Sure, what is it?"

"My friend is here from Chicago. Long story short: We think we know how Mendoza is laundering the money."

"You brought an outsider into a Bureau investigation? Are you crazy? We have to report this."

"No, I'm not crazy. And it's just a theory for now. I suggest that me and you follow the same steps my friend and I did today. Okay?"

"I need to meet this person first."

"Sure. It will be memorable, believe me," Paulie says, stifling a laugh.

At seven the following morning, Monday, they meet at a coffee shop in Westwood. Agent Caldwell is already at a table nursing a coffee when Paulie and Vincent walk in. When Paulie points in Caldwell's direction, Vincent is dumbfounded.

"This is my best friend, Vincent. He's like my brother," Paulie says to Caldwell. They take their seats at the table.

"Paulie said you were pretty," Vincent jumps in. "But that's an understatement, sweetheart. You're beautiful."

Tania looks at Vincent, then at Paulie.

"Is this a fucking joke?"

Vincent holds up his hands, as if to ward off the shrew. Then he looks at Paulie, gesturing that he should explain.

"Vincent is a private investigator from Chicago," Paulie almost chokes on his words. "And he has a lot of experience with the grocery business. He's out here on an assignment, and I asked his opinion."

Vincent folds his hands in front of him and looks Tania in the eyes.

"Look, I am not going to cause any problems. Paulie and I are as close as two buddies can get. We trust each other, and I truly want to help. As soon as you guys are up to speed, I will step aside. In reality, all the hard work is ahead of you two."

"Andrews," says Caldwell, turning away from Vincent, "Are you serious?"

"Tania, if not for Vincent we'd still be in the dark and floundering," Paulie reasons. "Give him a break."

Caldwell takes a long sip of her coffee as she considers Paul's plea. "If I hadn't seen for myself how well you handled our first few cases, I would shut this down in an instant." She emphasizes this with a snap of her fingers. Then she holds the same two fingers in front of Vincent's face, not quite squeezing them together.

"As for you, Vincent, or whatever your name really is, I'm this close to charging you with unlawful interference of an ongoing investigation," she says. "But, for Andrews' sake, I'll let you go on."

Paulie is red in the face. At first Vincent winces slightly at the sound of Paulie's new name, but then he smiles warmly at Caldwell and begins to lay out the scenario.

They talk for over an hour. Vincent articulates what he suspects, as well as suggests the next steps the three of them should take. Tania listens with increasing interest. She slowly gains a measure of respect for Vincent and his rough street sense. *He must be some sort of criminal,* she thinks. *If not, he certainly has a criminal mind.* In the end, she agrees to try his proposal. The plan is to tail Mendoza as before.

"Why don't we take two cars?" Vincent suggests. "Paulie and I in one and you in the other. I suspect that you have a means to communicate with each other—you know G-men walkie talkies or whatever—so we can further plot," Vincent says.

"Plot?" asks Caldwell.

He and Paulie ignore her comment. Vincent continues outlining his plan. When they get to the first stop, he and Paulie will look for a truck similar to the one they saw the day before. If one appears, Paulie will drop Vincent off to scout the area. Then he and Paulie will follow the truck after it has been loaded with goods. Meanwhile, Tania will stay on Mendoza. She'll wait to hear from Paulie to determine if the truck is headed toward her location. If so, they'll regroup there.

They pick up Mendoza as he leaves the main office on Sunset Boulevard, as he does every morning. They follow him, careful not to get made. When he arrives at his Bakersfield location, he enters the store. Tania finds a suitable lookout space, and Paulie lets Vincent out.

Vincent walks around the store to the loading area. He's about to approach the workers when he spots the Mexican man in the straw hat.

He hides himself from view, while the guy chats with the workers. Then Mendoza appears. This is enough for Vincent. He runs back to the car.

"That Mexican guy, the same guy from yesterday, is here. I just saw him talk to Mendoza. We need to identify this guy. Let's tail him to the next stop."

Paulie radios Tania, and she acknowledges the plan. About fifteen minutes later, Mendoza leaves with Tania in pursuit. About an hour later, she calls and gives Mendoza's new location to Paulie.

Meanwhile, the Mexican in the straw hat hangs around for over two hours. When he finally leaves, Paulie and Vincent are on him.

"That's the same truck, Paulie. Same license plate and all. He must have made another pickup after he left the store yesterday."

Paulie thinks for a moment then radios Tania, who tells him that Mendoza has gone to a third store but left after twenty minutes. Maybe he was just making an appearance for his employees, she suggests. Paulie asks her to go to the Bureau office and run the Mexican's plate.

Vincent leans over into the mike and says, "I'm going back home tomorrow morning. Take good care of my brother. Hope to see you again someday, pretty girl."

"Jesus. Alright, Vincent. Safe flight," she replies.

Vincent and Paulie drive south for hours toward the border. They watch the truck approach the border guards who let it through.

Paulie pulls the car over at the station. He gets out, flashes his badge, and speaks with the Border Patrol agents.

"I gave them the license number of the truck, and they told me that they'd watch out for it," he reports to Vincent. "They asked me if this was drug related. I told them no, but didn't give them any more information than they needed."

On their way back from the border, they stop at a seafood restaurant in San Diego and then drive to Vincent's hotel. At the curb, Paulie gets out of the car and the two warmly embrace. They promise to call each other often, before Vincent sternly reminds Paulie to contact his Nonno.

"No fucking excuses, Paulie. You understand?"

"I heard you, I got it!"

55

HEALTH

Rina returns from her doctor's appointment. She walks to the back of the store to her father's office. He looks up at her, sits her down, and closes the office door.

"He wants me to see a specialist, Papa. He looked worried but smiled and told me not to get excited."

"This is Doctor Alito, right?"

"Yes. He said to say 'hello.' He scheduled an appointment with a specialist for me next Friday. We just have to wait, Papa," Rina says.

Her father stares at the ceiling, his face radiating worry and apprehension.

"Go home, sweetheart. I'm going to speak with Dr. Alito."

She nods and leaves the store.

Rina doesn't go home. Instead, she goes to see Teri, who invites her in for tea. They sit at her kitchen table drinking Chamomile. Rina begins to cry. Teri leads her into her living room and sits her down on the couch. She holds Rina in her arms as Rina continues to weep.

Tony drives to Dr. Alito's house in Oak Park. When he sees him pull into his driveway, Tony gets out. As the doctor unloads files from the back seat of his car, Tony calmly taps him on the shoulder.

Alito turns and flinches when he sees that it's Tony.

"Tony, what are you doing here?"

"You know, Salvatore, you know. Why don't you invite me in for a cup of coffee, let me say 'Hi' to Lena, and we can talk?"

Dr. Alito frowns heavily, but he cannot refuse. It would be a huge mistake. He gestures Tony toward the house. Once inside, his wife Lena greets them, and they engage in small talk. Then Dr. Alito leads Tony to his home office.

"Okay, tell me," Tony says.

Dr. Alito leans forward in his office chair, folds his hands on the desk, and sighs.

"I don't know for sure, but I think it's cancer," he says. Tony starts to pace, making Dr. Alito apprehensive.

"So, you don't know for sure and that's why you're sending her to a specialist?"

"Of course. He's an oncologist. I did not tell her any of this, but I think she has an idea. I wish she had come to me sooner."

Tony leaves the doctor sitting in his office chair. Alito rubs his wrinkled forehead and breathes a sigh of relief.

When Tony returns home, he hopes to find Rina, but she's not there. He picks up the phone and calls Teri, who answers on the third ring.

"My daughter there, Teri?"

"Yes, Papa, she's here with me. Do you want to talk to her?"

"No. I'll wait until she gets home. Is she okay?"

"I think so, yes. We're just talking and I fixed her something to eat. I'll call you when she leaves."

Tony hangs up and sits at the kitchen table. Then he leans over and puts his face in his hands. So much is happening and all of it too fast. *I wish Paulie was here.* Then he thinks about it and shakes his head. *No.* He reaches under the table for the jug of Italian wine, pours a glass, and drinks it.

"You know I'm here for you Rina," Teri says, opening the front door to let her friend out.

They hug each other tightly at the threshold. Rina dreads going home to her father, knowing he'll have all kinds of questions for her. Sometimes she wishes that she'd made a life for herself and not obsessed on her one true love. She hopes everything will work out.

56

SUSPICIONS

The morning after Vincent returned to Chicago, Paulie and Caldwell sit in their cubicle and discuss the weekend's events.

"I ran the plate," says Caldwell. "The car belongs to some corporation in L.A. We're running that information as we speak, though I'm not too hopeful. Also, I didn't get the information on the driver yet, but have some of the LAPD checking to see if the truck has any traffic violations. Maybe that will give us some more leads."

"Andrews! Caldwell!"

Baranson's unmistakable booming voice cascades over the office. Over the tops of the cubicles, they see him, followed by two other agents, making a beeline toward them. A few seconds later, he's at the entrance to their cubicle.

"I spoke with Anton. Just to be very clear, you *do not* have authority to speak to the informant. I don't want to hear anymore crap about this from either of you. If I want you to gain access, I'll let you know." He turns to the agents who are with him, "Now, where were we?"

The trio walk away while Paulie and Tania absorb Baranson's words.

"What do you think that's about?" Paulie asks.

"I really don't know. Maybe there's a leak? Maybe he's protecting the informant?"

Paulie looks over to her, leans back, rubs his eyes.

"Anyway, I'll write up a progress report for Baranson about what we found this weekend." Then she leans in, and in a quieter voice, says, "How are we going to explain Vincent, Paul?"

"Hold on, let's go for a walk."

Once outside on Wilshire, Paulie continues.

"We're not saying a word about Vincent. There is no reason to, and it will only muddy the waters. We will simply state that we got a lead and followed through on it."

"Excuse me? Who put you in charge?"

Paulie lets out an exasperated sigh.

"Look, right now we need to tread cautiously," Paulie says. "I know we spoke about it before, but I can't shake the question: Why would Baranson put two green agents, two rookies, on this case in the first place? I mean, Baranson himself basically admitted that we were not experienced enough when he gave us this assignment. And why have Agent Boswhite mentor us? Anton isn't even in our section."

"Well, we did solve those other cases pretty quick," replies Caldwell.

"Yes, but those were pretty much routine, and we were permitted to go to the SEC, remember? Why aren't we authorized to involve other agencies in this case? Or get audio surveillance set up, for that matter? There's another thing: When we gave our status report, he seemed to disapprove of our lack of progress—but I can't shake the thought that he wasn't really bothered, maybe even pleased."

"Paul, there's no way of verifying that."

"I don't know what to say. My gut instinct is telling me I'm right about Baranson. And that means we don't say anything about Vincent's participation."

"You're starting to concern me. This goes completely against protocol."

"I know. So, here is what I suggest: We put this all together in a fashion to present to the U.S. Attorney, which means we'll still need more information. At that stage, we bring in Boswhite. Agreed?"

"Okay, go on."

"Only after we speak to Boswhite, do we go to Baranson."

"I can live with that," Caldwell says. "We'll need Boswhite's say so, but also his experience to make sure we put together an air-tight case. He'll know what to do, and I feel like we can rely on him."

"I agree," says Paulie. "Okay, let's go through our checklist once more. We have the Mexican driver, we have the owner of the truck, and we have the Mexican vendor. We need to subpoena records to trace the cash flow. If Vincent's theory is correct, Mendoza is simply rotating the stock and paying the vendor for stock that he has transferred to another store as if he sold all of it. And the receiving store is stocking the goods as if they got it from the vendor. Then the cycle continues."

Caldwell nods in agreement to all of this. "I wonder if we should go to Mexico," she offers.

"Let's ask Boswhite when we meet with him. First, let's get everything we can in L.A."

They continue their tails of targets. About a week later, the man in the straw hat lets his guard down, and they track him to an apartment in East L.A. where he's living with a girlfriend, Carla Guzman, who works at one of the Mendoza-owned stores. They tentatively identify him as Juan Lopez-Martinez and that he works for a canning company that operates out of Sinaloa. It's not such a stretch to imagine that he's involved with the Cartel.

"We need to tie this all down before we approach him," Caldwell suggests. "That is, if we ever do."

"We need the paper trail," Paulie agrees. "Specifically, the invoices and receipts between the canning company and Mendoza's supermarkets."

"Yes," says Caldwell. "But also consider how many stores Mendoza operates. This operation might run into hundreds of thousands of dollars a day. Someone inside the stores must oversee the accounts. Do you think it's Mendoza himself?"

"Whoever it is, it's someone smart and someone we want to identify."

"Yes," Tania says, "but to do that, we'll need more manpower. We're fooling ourselves if we think we can tie this up on our own. I think now is the time to tell the bosses what we've uncovered."

Paulie stares up at the ceiling tiles and starts to count them. "You're right. I think it's time we go to Boswhite."

57

THE NEXT STEP

Vincent does not get home from Los Angeles until after midnight. He quietly walks into the house, noticing that the light in his mother's room is still on. He doesn't want to bother her at this late hour, so he goes straight to his room and drops his baggage against the wall. He'll unpack tomorrow. As he undresses, he sees the manila envelope laying across his pillow.

It's from the State. He sits down on the bed and opens it.

"Well?"

Vincent is startled by his mother standing over him with her arms crossed. Then he goes back to the task at hand. He places the contents on his bed carefully, one document at a time, and reads each one.

"They did not give me my score. Maybe they don't do that, maybe they just give you the results." He keeps reading.

"These documents detail what I must do to get the actual license, instructions on getting insurance and all. But the bottom line, Ma," the significance of what's happening suddenly falls upon him, "is that I'm in fucking business!"

He jumps off the bed, grabs his mother, and swings her around the room. They both laugh.

"What a relief!"

She kisses her son and goes off to bed with a huge smile on her face.

Vincent is too excited to sleep, even though he's exhausted. He goes into the living room and picks up the phone to call Paulie—but reconsiders, remembering a promise he made to himself. Instead, he watches some television. After an hour or so, he turns off the TV, takes, a shower, and goes to bed. He can barely sleep, though, his mind still racing.

The next morning, he looks at the documents again with pride, and rereads the instructions. He's full of joy and anticipation. He meets his mom in the kitchen.

"What do you want for breakfast, Sherlock?" she asks.

"Everything, Ma!"

She smiles and starts cooking. "Did you call Paulie and tell him?"

"No, I'm gonna tell Papa Tony first. If not for him, this would not have been possible, and I owe him that respect. I want him to be the second person to know—after *you*, Ma."

She smiles, feeling her day brightening. "He will be thrilled, Vincent."

Then she thinks about it some more.

"Do not misinterpret it if he does not seem overjoyed as you are. He has some problems he's working through. You know Tuff Tony—he'll acknowledge this in his own way."

Vincent nods, understanding, and begins eating the gigantic breakfast his mother made him. After he eats, showers, and puts on some nice clothes, he walks over to the store.

Rina is not at the register. He doesn't recognize the woman in her place. She tells him that Rina took the day off. Then he asks about Papa Tony, and she points to his office.

He knocks.

"Come in."

Vincent enters the office. The old man sits at his desk reading some documents. He looks up and frowns.

"Hey Papa, I just got back from Los Angeles. Paulie sends his love."

Tony leans back in his chair. He looks at Vincent but says nothing.

"He looks great and really seems to love what he is doing. I thought you would like to know."

Again, nothing.

"Anyway, I'm also here to thank you once again for helping me get my license. I got a letter from the State today. I have to jump through a few more hoops, nothing unexpected, and then I will be issued my license. I am so grateful to you, you cannot imagine. I will never forget this."

Tony looks at Vincent and the edge of his mouth begins to form a smile.

"Okay, private eye. Go to work, make some money, and make your mother proud. I did this for her as much as for you."

"I will, and I will make *you* proud, too! By the way, is Rina home? I promised Paulie I'd give her a big hug from him."

"She's at a doctor's appointment, but she'll be home this afternoon. Try not to upset her."

With that, Tony gets up and walks out of his office to the loading dock. *Something is wrong*, Vincent feels, hoping that it's not serious. "*Doctor's appointment?*"

58

FUCKHEAD RETURNS

The next morning, Vincent gets up early. His mother is awake, as usual. But Vincent passes on breakfast.

"I'm going downtown, Ma," he says, "to set up things in my office. I have to order telephone lines, get a typewriter, etcetera, etcetera—lots of things to do."

He's rented a space in the same building as Sidney Ackerman, a real LaSalle Street office.

"Have you got money for all of that, honey?"

"We'll see, but I gotta get going."

As he walks out the door, Angelo and Mikey are approaching his house. They look pissed.

"What's up?"

"Fuckhead is up in Wisconsin," Mikey sighs. "He said that he was going to take care of things."

"You mean braindead Stanley?"

"Who else? He hadn't checked in lately, so I gave him a call."

"What is he taking care of?"

"He learned that his uncle is meeting with some people in Wisconsin to sell his stamp collection. Once his uncle sells it and gets the money, Stanley will never see a dime. So, he plans to grab the collection before his uncle can seal the deal."

Vincent looks at Angelo, who is really pissed. Not a good thing. "When is all this supposed to happen?"

"His uncle has a condo on Lake Geneva and is up there now. He's supposed to meet with a buyer over the weekend. Stanley learned all of this from his mother, so now he's up there watching and waiting to make his move."

Vincent looks at the two of them. "And we are worried about this why exactly?"

"You kidding me? If he gets caught, he may tell his uncle everything and put the finger on us," says Angelo.

"Okay, okay," Vincent says, knowing Angelo is probably right. "Call him right away and tell him that he can't pull it off alone and that we will help him. And tell him not do *any*thing until we get up there. Do that now and make sure he believes you. I'm going downtown and will be back in about two hours."

After Angelo and Mikey walk away, Vincent mumbles "Fuck!"

On the way downtown, he considers the situation. Something in Vincent's streetwise mind is telling him there is something very wrong here. The collection, and maybe even the gold, was insured and maybe Jakowski got paid already. That's not what bothers Vincent. But what if the so-called buyers are not legit? What if they are actually insurance investigators looking to see the collection and then hammer the uncle?

Vincent makes a sudden turn, tires screeching, and drives back to the Neighborhood. His first stop is St. Anthony's Social Club, where he gets some information from Bruno. Then he sees Mikey and Angelo by the beef stand and waves them over.

"Get in," he barks. "We are not waiting. We're going up there now."

"Stop by my place first, so I can tell my wife and pick something up," Angelo says.

Vincent looks at Angelo and a message is passed between them. He nods and drives Angelo home.

On the drive to Wisconsin, Vincent gets more details from Mikey.

"When I spoke to fuckhead, he sounded kind of excited," Mikey says. "I told him he was probably right about his uncle stiffing him. I told him he had a good idea. And after a little persuasion, he believes we want to help. He realizes he's over his head with this, anyhow."

Not much else is said. Mikey and Angelo exchange looks and watch Vincent who is deep in thought, planning as always.

Outside Waukegan, Vincent stops for gas and to make a phone call. He dials the number Bruno gave him. For about ten minutes he chats with an Outfit associate in Milwaukee. Vincent smiles grimly and goes back to the car.

Vincent drives for about five minutes but doesn't get back on the highway. Instead, he stops at a public park. He sits back, leans against the driver's door, and looks at Angelo in the front seat, then Mikey in the back.

"You guys are going to think that I have lost it but listen: I don't think those guys who are meeting Stanley's uncle are legit. I'm guessing they're insurance investigators who are setting up the old guy."

Angelo and Mikey glance at each other, then back at Vincent.

"What the fuck?" says Mikey.

"Yeah, I could be wrong but that is what I believe. I called a couple of guys up here to babysit Stanley while we do our thing."

"And what's our thing, Vincent?" asks Mikey.

"I don't know," replies Vincent. "I'm still working it out."

59

LAKE GENEVA

Vincent and his crew meet Stanley in a cheap motel near Lake Geneva. After Stanley lets them into his room, Mikey and Angelo stand with their backs against the door, arms folded. Vincent directs Stanley to sit on the bed while he pulls up the lone chair in the room and sits across from him.

"Stanley," Vincent says, "Tell me what you know, and I mean *everything*."

Stanley's forehead is laced with sweat. He smells awful, like he hasn't showered in days.

"Okay, okay,' Stanley begins. "My uncle told my mother that he was meeting with some people that an old union guy put him onto. I don't know the guy's name, but I got the impression from my mother that he was connected somehow, that he and my uncle did lots of union business before my uncle retired—under the table stuff." Stanley pauses. "My mother has… well, she's not always with it, so half the time I don't know what she remembers or when this all happened. Anyway, my uncle has a condo near the lake, where he also has a boat slip, so I drove up here to see for myself."

"Do you think he has the stamps with him?"

"I don't know, maybe. When I saw him, he was talking to the boat owner in the next slip, and he was all smiles. He looked really happy, so that makes me think something is going down this weekend. Believe me, he don't smile often, so something must be up."

Vincent sits back and thinks for a few minutes.

"Okay," he says, breaking the silence. "I have something to do, but I'll be back in a while. Mikey and Angelo will wait here with you. Don't call anyone while I'm gone. In the meantime, relax. We're here now, so we have it covered."

Vincent gets up from the chair and walks over to the door. Angelo and Mikey make room for him to pass.

"And, Stanley," Vincent adds before leaving, "take a fucking shower!"

Vincent leaves the motel, gets in his car, and drives to a nearby gas station, parking next to a pay phone. He calls the two guys in Milwaukee—Gino and Gus—and gives them the address of Stanley's motel. Vincent tells them they should get a room at a motel nearby and he'll meet them there that night.

Before hanging up, Vincent says, "I know this is a big favor, Gino, but there may be some money involved. If not, I'll find another way to repay you."

Vincent arrives back at the motel. Stanley's showered, but he's wearing the same smelly clothes from earlier.

"What, you don't have any other clothes?"

"This is all I got."

"Jeez. Sit down, Stanley," Vincent directs. He then hands Stanley the phone. "Call your mother but be casual. Don't tell her where you are. Just tell her you're checking in on her or whatever it is that you say when you talk to her. Ask her about your uncle, but play it cool. Do not make it obvious that you are seeking information. Do you think you can do that?"

"Yeah, sure. My mother loves me. Me and my uncle are the only family she's got left. I sometimes wonder why my uncle tells her shit, but he does."

"Good."

After the phone call, Stanley relates to Vincent everything he's learned from his mother. Vincent seems pleased.

"Okay, now give me all the details about your uncle's condo, including the slip number for his boat."

Stanley shares the information, then they leave to get something to eat—but not before Vincent opens the windows to air out the room from Stanley's stink. After they eat, they go to a department store and buy clothes for the next few days. Vincent pays for Stanley, who's broke, as usual. Back at the motel, Vincent makes Stanley throw his old clothes into the dumpster out back.

"I'll be back in an hour," he tells Mikey and Angelo. Vincent goes to another motel and finds Gino and Gus in the coffee shop.

"You only need to babysit this guy for maybe four hours. Did you clear this with the boss?"

"Yeah," Gus says. "He wanted to know what's going on. He's not pleased this is on his turf, let me tell you."

"I promise that I will have Johnny V call him when we get back. Like I said, I owe."

After they talk, Vincent books another room. Then he tells Gino and Gus he'll bring the chump over around midnight. Vincent drives back to Stanley's motel.

"Mikey, you and I are going to take a run. We'll be back in about two hours. Angelo, babysit Stanley. And try not to kill him."

Stanley sits up, startled. Vincent smiles at him and winks. That seems to satisfy Stanley, but he still looks over at Angelo in abject fear.

Mikey and Vincent scout out Jakowski's boat slip. The grouchy old man isn't there. Then they scout out his condo and the surrounding area. Carefully peeking in the ground-level window, they see Jakowski leaning back on his couch with the TV on, looking like he's sound asleep. On their way back to the motel, they pick up pizzas, meatball sandwiches, and sodas.

Vincent knocks five times, then enters the room. They find Stanley sprawled on the floor and Angelo laying on the bed, both watching the TV.

"We're all set, Ange," Mikey says.

Angelo just nods and looks down at Stanley in disgust. Vincent is half surprised to see Stanley in one piece.

60

JAKOWSKI REPRISE

At 11:30 that evening, all four men pile into Vincent's Thunderbird and drive over to the other motel. They push Stanley into the room that Vincent has rented. Angelo unplugs the phone cord, wraps it around the phone, and then sits Stanley down on the bed. Vincent leaves to get Gus and Gino. When they enter the room, Stanley's ashen face grows even paler, and he loses it.

"Calm down, Stanley," Vincent says. "My friends here are just going to babysit you until this is all over. Behave yourself and they won't have to snip off your toes, okay?"

Vincent's demeanor causes Stanley to relax a bit.

Gino hands Vincent the keys to the work car they've brought with them, a large, four-door Ford Galaxie. On the way out, Vincent winks at Stanley and tells Gino to start with Stanley's pinkie toe if he gives them any trouble. Angelo frowns at him.

Vincent opens the trunk of his car, and Angelo removes two duffle bags. They drive off in the Galaxie to the lake area. At the far end of the condo parking lot, Vincent walks them through his plan one more time. There are no questions.

Vincent and Mikey walk to the condo with Angelo twenty feet behind looking around the area for any signs of problems. They see no one else. Angelo sets the bags down among the trees behind the condo units, extracts some items out of the bags, and joins Vincent and Mikey. The trio hunch down and listen outside Jakowski's condo.

Once they feel secure, they walk around the condo, peering discreetly into each window. The TV is on in the living room, and Jakowski is sitting up now, beer in hand, watching an old black and white movie, with the volume very loud. *Familiar scene.* Mikey checks the windows to the bedroom. One is unlocked and slightly ajar. He puts on a ski mask and climbs in the window, silently and stealthily. Vincent and Angelo wait for the front door to open.

Mikey gets in and steps cautiously to the living room. Just then, Jakowski rises to get another beer, so Mikey whacks him on the back of his head with a heavy leather sap. Disorientated but still standing, Jakowski stares at Mikey who delivers a second blow. The old man falls unconscious across the glass-topped coffee table, shattering it into a thousand pieces. Mikey then opens the door and lets the other two in. Vincent and Angelo put on ski masks, then quickly duct tape Jakowski's mouth and secure his hands and legs. They are ready for the irascible old man this time.

"He's out cold, Mikey. How hard did you hit him?" Angelo asks, with a look of concern at Jakowski's prone body.

"He was getting up and saw me," replies Mikey, clearly agitated.

"Okay," says Vincent. "Lift him onto the couch. Angelo, clean this up some. I'm going to search the place. I doubt he'd have the stamps here, but we need to check."

Vincent closes the blinds and then sets off to search both floors of the condo.

"Hey, Ange," Mikey says, "see if there is any ice in the fridge. I hope I didn't give this guy a fucking concussion. The back of his head has a huge bump and it's swelling."

Angelo finds the ice and wraps the cubes in a dish towel. He kneels down next to Jakowski and applies the ice-towel to the back of his head.

"Jesus, Mikey. Why'd you have to hit him so fucking hard?" Angelo says angrily.

"If he'd screamed, we might have gotten pinched, but yeah, I may have hit him harder than I should have."

"I don't fucking believe it," Vincent says, returning with the two portfolios in his arms, along with a felt Crown Royal bag, heavy with something inside. "He hid them under the mattress for Christ's sake. What the fuck was he thinking?"

Vincent goes into the kitchen, sits down at the table, and marvels once more at the stamps. Mikey follows suit.

"Hey guys," Angelo calls from the other room.

Jakowski is stirring. As his eyes open, the first thing he sees is the three of them looking down on him.

Jakowski then sees the Crown Royal bag and his stamp collection in Vincent's hands. He struggles furiously, whipping himself into a frenzy. As before, the three regard him calmly, waiting for him to wear himself out. They secured him extra tight this time. Exhausted, he finally lays his head down and becomes still, his eyes watering. He's not a problem.

In the kitchen they open the Crown Royal bag. Inside are at least three dozen gold coins. They must have missed them on the first go-round. Mikey and Angelo smile.

Vincent takes a chair and sits down next to the couch and looks at Jakowski, whose face radiates hate, his eyes aflame.

"How fucking stupid are you, Mr. Jakowski?" Vincent says, shaking his head.

Through the hateful stare, there appears a puzzled look on Jakowski's face.

"I'm going to peel back the tape from your mouth. If you scream or yell out, my friend here is going to knock out your front teeth one by one." Vincent points to Angelo, hulking on the side of the couch.

"You understand, Mr. Jakowski?"

Jakowski nods ever so slightly. Vincent takes his chin, pinches it, and looks straight into Jakowski's eyes. The message is received, and Jakowski nods again, this time more pronounced. Vincent rips the tape off. Jakowski grunts in pain. Vincent waits for him to speak.

"I… are you the same fucking guys?"

None of the three answer. They just stare back at him.

"Can I get some water? I don't feel so good," says Jakowski.

Vincent gestures to Mikey, who brings a glass of tap water. Vincent props Jakowski's head up and lets him drink, the water spilling down his face onto his neck.

"I gave you a gift, and what do you do? Invite someone else to rip you off—how fucked up is that?"

"Whaddya mean? I have buyers for the stamps. A friend set it up for me."

"Are you that stupid? Do you really believe the insurance company is just going to pay you without a thorough investigation? Did you even stop to think this out?" Vincent says, gesticulating wildly.

"Why do you give a shit, you fucking thief?"

Vincent shakes his head.

"Prick to the end, huh? Okay, we were just going to take the stamps but leave you the coins. Now you get fucked twice. So long, you stubborn prick," Vincent says, holding up the stamps and the Crown Royal bag.

"Yeah, and you're still a fucking thief."

"Make sure everything is wiped down," Vincent says to the others. "Take the dish towel and stick it in this prick's mouth as a memento."

He turns to Jakowski. "You know you make me do this."

Angelo grabs Jakowski by his hair, pulls his head back, and stuffs in the ice rag. Then they clean up. As they're about to leave, Jakowski shakes his head, trying to get Vincent's attention.

"Take the rag out and let's hear what the prick wants."

Angelo roughly pulls out the dish towel.

"Please don't take the stamps, they're all I got," Jakowski cries. "Please, I'm sorry I said what I said. Please don't take them."

"No, we're taking them, but for safekeeping, you prick. You behave yourself and you will get them back. I give you my word. Shut the fuck up and quit trying to sell them. If the insurance company finds out, you are fucked and could go to jail."

"What about those Cleveland guys coming up here? They're gonna be pissed."

"If you're smart, you won't be here when they arrive. Tell your friend—if he is your friend—some story that will fly with him. Make something up, treat him to dinner—whatever it takes."

Jakowski seems to consider this.

"In any case, we're out of here and we're definitely keeping the coins. I'm going to cut one of your wrists loose. If you yell out or call the police or even God, for that matter, you will never see these little tiny pieces of paper ever again. Do you understand?"

"Fuck you," Jakowski smiles. Angelo stuffs the rag back in.

Back in the car, Mikey asks, "You really gonna give him back the stamps, Vincent?" Angelo shakes his head, knowing the answer already.

"I gave my word. But not right away. I want to see how this works out with the insurance company. If the old prick keeps his mouth shut, they should pay him. I also want to find out what they are insured for."

"What about Stanley?" Angelo asks.

"Well, that's a problem I need to work on. Let's get back to the motel and spring my friends. I have some coins for them."

61

STAYING QUIET

Gino and Gus say goodbye when they trade places with Mikey and Angelo. Vincent walks them back to their car and hands them five gold coins each. They stare at him, then thank him.

"You still owe," Gino says, putting the coins in his pocket, "but this is a nice gesture, Vincent."

"I know and I still acknowledge that. I got my private investigator's license, so pass that around up here. And if you need anything, give me a ring, Gino. Take care."

Gino nods. They give each other a quick embrace. They will take the work car back to Milwaukee.

Vincent goes to gather up Angelo, Mikey, and Stanley.

"So, what happened?" asks Stanley who is sitting on the edge of the bed. "Did you get the stamps?"

Vincent slaps him on the back of his head.

"You are an absolute fuck up, and I do not know what to do with you. Your uncle has seen the light. Now it's *your* turn to let this go. If you don't, we will be feeding little pieces of you to the fish. Do you understand?"

"Yeah, but what about the stamp collection?"

Vincent looks at Angelo who immediately gets the message. He punches Stanley so hard his skull bounces off the headboard.

The three, plus a duct-taped, unconscious Stanley in the trunk of the car, drive back to Chicago. Stanley is quiet and will remain so.

They pull up to Fat Louie's scrap yard. They get out and are greeted by Cosimo Lido, Fat Louie's yard boss. Mikey has called from a gas station. Everything is arranged.

They pull the limp Stanley out of the trunk of Vincent's Thunderbird.

"Vincent, take off," Angelo says.

Vincent is not happy with this outcome, but Stanley is a serious threat to them. They really have no choice. Angelo and Mikey do not want Vincent involved.

Vincent leaves, dreading that he has to bring this incident to Johnny V's attention. He's conflicted whether he should. Things could go badly, but he has no choice. He will try to see Johnny V tomorrow.

62

ICE CREAM

That same night across the country, Agent Caldwell gets home from work to find her son at the kitchen table solving math problems, a concentrated frown on his face. She kisses him. Her mother has been sitting with Tyler. She's laid out a snack of raisins and carrot sticks.

"How's he been?" Caldwell asks her mother.

"He's good," her mother says, and then, under her breath, "a little quiet. I'll be in my room if you need me."

Soon, there's a knock on the door. Through the peephole, Caldwell sees Edgar standing outside the door. She thinks about ignoring his knock, but she knows her ex won't give up. She opens the door. He looks like a stranger as he stands there. She can barely recognize him with all the weight he's put on. He smells like sweat and motor oil, an unpleasant combination that makes him even less attractive.

"What do you want?"

"Tania, hey. I'm so sorry about what happened. I don't know what came over me." His voice is quiet and soft, as it used to be in the best of times between them. He has a beseeching look in his eyes that's possibly genuine. "I was hoping to be able to see my son."

He looks so pathetic she almost feels sorry for him. Just then, Tyler comes up behind her.

"Hi Dad."

"Well, hey there! How's my little man? Want to go for a ride with your pops?"

"Oh yeah!"

"Now hold on—"

"I got a job at Mancuso's Scrap Yard," Edgar interrupts before she can finish her objection. "That's why I look so grubby."

"*Sure,* you did."

"I can show you the pay stub!"

"Alright, let me see it."

"I'm not with the boys anymore," Edgar says, pulling out the stub from his wallet and handing it to her. "See?"

"Well, that's a start, I guess."

"C'mon, Tania, I gotta see my son."

"Yeah, come on, Mom!"

"Alright, come in," Caldwell relents. "You can spend time here with Tyler, help him with his homework."

"Great!" Tyler smiles, opens the screen door, and reaches for his father's hand.

Tania stands aside and lets the hulk enter the living room of her apartment. *Why do I do this?* she thinks, as he stands by the spot where he threw her against the wall. *I don't know. But I know I'm gonna let him.*

"I don't want to sit on your clean sofa," Edgar says. "Maybe Tyler and I can just go for a walk. Do you want ice cream, son?"

"Ice cream!"

"Is that okay?" Edgar asks, his voice all sweetness.

He's such a snake, Tania thinks as she looks at her son and his eager face. *But I suppose a boy should have a relationship with his father. It's more than I ever had.*

"Sure, but be back in an hour," she says, sternly.

"Just an hour?" Edgar asks, but then, reading Tania's expression, adds, "Okay, let's go, Tyler."

He takes his son's hand, and they walk out the front door. Tyler turns and waves at his mother. She smiles and waves back but feels an overwhelming dread.

63

SPEAKING FRANKLY

The following morning, Paulie and Caldwell go to Agent Boswhite's office. This time, they accept his offer for coffee.

They lay out the facts of the Mendoza case. And then they discuss their conclusions. He listens calmly and attentively, but when they're almost finished, he holds up his hand to stop them.

"Okay, it's obvious that the two of you have done an outstanding job. But you know as well as I do that you should report to Agent Baranson with this information."

Paulie looks around the office, as if to see if there is anyone else there, though of course he knows that they're alone.

"As we mentioned," Caldwell says. "The case has evolved to the point that we now need additional manpower to bring it home. We'd like your help recruiting a team."

"Apologies if I'm being dense here, but I don't see why you don't go to Agent Baranson for this requisition."

"Can I speak frankly, sir?" Paulie asks.

Agent Boswhite nods.

"I don't trust him. I can't provide you physical proof why, but I have my suspicions. I believe that Baranson assigned us—*two rookies*—to this case with the expectation that we wouldn't be able to solve it. I believe that if we discuss the details of this case with Baranson, there is a strong possibility that the information might be leaked to the wrong people—namely Mendoza and the Cartel—and the results of this investigation will be swept under the rug."

Boswhite stares intensely at Paulie for a long time, processing this accusation. Paulie can hear the second hand click on the wall clock.

"Do you realize what you're saying, Agent Andrews?"

He lets his question hang in the air.

"How about you, Agent Caldwell? What do you think about all this?"

Tania leans forward in her chair and looks Boswhite in the eye. "I stand with my partner, sir," she says calmly.

"Is that so?" Boswhite replies. "Well, I have your report here."

"Yes, sir, everything is in there," Paulie jumps in, "except for our thoughts on Baranson."

"Good. I'll set up a meeting with the U.S. Attorney as soon as possible to get a sign off on your surveillance. For now, let's keep your suspicions about Baranson to ourselves." Boswhite rises from his chair. He shakes both of their hands and gestures to the door. They are dismissed.

They walk back to their cubicle in silence. Once there, they look at each other, slap their palms in a high five, and then embrace, giddy at what they've just done. But then they stop short, reminded of the gravity of the situation.

The next day, Paulie and Caldwell take turns presenting their case to the deputy U.S. Attorney, Adam Carlson, who keeps repeating, "Great work!" Boswhite sits and smiles.

"This will do," Carlson says, at the end of the presentation. "I can start drawing up search warrants and court orders now."

"Excellent," Boswhite adds, then picks up his telephone and dials. "Boswhite here... we're ready for you." He places the phone back in the receiver. "I took the liberty of assembling a team. I had a feeling that this would go smoothly. They're on their way now."

A few moments later, six FBI agents enter the room, and Boswhite makes the introductions. Led by Boswhite, they plan their next moves, based on Paulie and Caldwell's recommendations. They finish in about two hours.

"Okay, now we take a walk," says Agent Boswhite to Andrews and Caldwell.

Paulie looks at Tania with an expression that says, *Where are we going?* But soon the question is answered when they hear the booming voice in the halls. They stop and look at Boswhite.

"Trust me," he says, before walking through the open door to Baranson's office, without announcing himself.

Baranson is on speaker phone. He looks up and sees the three enter his office.

"I'll call you back," Baranson announces to the other end. "Anton, what's this?"

"I just wanted to bring these two spectacular agents to your attention. They've essentially solved the Mendoza case. You should be proud of these two—not to mention your wisdom in choosing them. They, and by extension, *you*, have done an outstanding job."

The look on Baranson's face betrays both puzzlement and incredulity. Boswhite takes advantage of the silence to continue.

"We just spoke with the assigned deputy U.S. Attorney who found probable cause. And then we briefed the rest of the team I have assembled," Boswhite says, flatly. Then he waits for Baranson's response.

Baranson's face turns a deep red and his eyes bulge out, as he grabs at the knot of his tie to loosen it from his neck. In short, his large head looks as if it will explode.

"Why am I just hearing about this now, Anton?" he says, looking up at Paulie and Caldwell with malice.

"I didn't want to bother you with the little stuff, boss, until we were ready to present our case. I put this all together with these great people."

Baranson manages to recover his composure.

"Well, as long as you were in charge, Anton," he says, trying hard not to show his anger. The blood that just filled his head seems to drain from it, and he turns pale.

"Just wanted to keep you apprised, sir. Back to work, you two," Boswhite says, ushering Paulie and Tania to the door. He pauses as if he suddenly remembered something, then turns to Baranson. "By the way, please see that the Mendoza informant is ready for a formal interview. Andrews and Caldwell will need to speak to him as soon as possible."

Boswhite turns smartly, and walks out the door, with Paulie and Tania close on his heels. Paulie smiles to himself. *Anton is smooth as silk.*

64

THE PRINCE IS FREE

The day Carmine Commaretta is released from prison, he's greeted by his longtime friend, Mario Mancini. A high school teacher, Mancini has absolutely no connection to Organized Crime. He's simply a very dear friend of Carmine's. Mario's family is from the same village in Sicily as Carmine's. And indeed, this is the same village from which the Andrianos hail.

"Carmanuch, you look good," Mario says, as he embraces his friend.

"Thanks for picking me up, Mario."

They drive off. Carmine is quiet as they drive to the YMCA halfway house where he will need to reside temporarily.

Soon after Carmine embraces Mario, Tony sits in the office of his store, awaiting a phone call. He picks it up on the first ring.

"So, did he get out?"

"Yes, he did, and Mario picked him up," the voice on the other end says. "He has to check in at the halfway house—you know, the one close to Taylor Street, on Ashland and Adams."

What is not said, but known to Tony, is that the YMCA handball courts were just remodeled and paid for by the Outfit. So, many of the Outfit members congregate there, along with politicians, judges, and the like. It's perfect for Carmine. Tony is sure that Carmine is looking forward to seeing everyone.

"Okay, thanks," Tony says, as he hangs up the phone. He looks out his office door and sees Rina at the cash register. She's speaking with a customer, but her anxious eyes are focused on Tony. He nods his head. He'll have to arrange to meet with Carmine soon.

65

THE FIRST SECRET

A couple of days after the excursion to Wisconsin, Vincent walks out his front door, intending to take care of some things at his new office. He sees Mikey approaching. Mikey greets his pal and nods his head slowly up and down. The message is delivered: It's done. A certain *someone* won't be heard from anymore. Mikey continues down the street.

With the new information, Vincent decides this is a good time to go see Johnny V. The office errands will have to wait. So, he walks to The Patio, where he encounters Bruno Spolleto. Bruno tells Vincent that Johnny won't arrive until later in the day.

"Something I can help with?" asks Bruno.

"Nah, I have to talk to the boss myself, but thanks."

Vincent turns and walks the three blocks to the grocery store. He kisses Rina.

"I'm glad you stopped by," she says. "I spoke with Paulie last night, and he asked if you can call him soon. He sounded good and upbeat. He's hoping to come home for the holidays, and we can all be together again!"

"I'll call him tonight. I'm sure he just wants to brag about all the shoplifters he arrested," Vincent jokes. Rina clicks her tongue in amusement. Before he can finish asking if Tony is in, she points toward the loading dock.

Tony sees Vincent approach and he frowns. He wants to tell Vincent about Carmine but he's not yet ready to do so.

"Hey, Papa. You got a minute?"

"What about?"

"Shoes told me that when I got my license, I should tell him. He said that he wants me to meet some people. What should I do?"

Tony looks out over the store and thinks about this. "C'mon," he says, pointing down the alley.

Shoes isn't at the barber shop. They turn around and walk back to the store.

"Okay, go look for him later," Tony says. "Find out what he wants but come to me before you do anything. I want to talk to him first."

Tony turns and walks back to the loading area and talks to a driver. Apparently, Vincent is dismissed. He sighs and walks back home.

His mother is waiting for him on her couch.

"Hey, Ma. I'm heading to the office. I'm just picking up some paperwork I forgot I need."

"Sit down for a minute, honey. I want to talk to you about something," she says, with a worried look on her face.

"What's wrong, Ma?

Teri rubs her eyes, then leans forward and takes Vincent's hands in hers.

"Rina is sick. Neither she nor her father will tell you this, but I think you should know."

"How bad is it, Ma?"

"We don't know for sure. She will not tell Paulie nor will her father. You must keep this between you and me for now. Promise me you will not tell Paulie until I tell you it's okay to. Promise me!"

"Yeah, sure. Okay, Ma, but... never mind. I promise."

"Good, now go get things done. Everyone is counting on you, so make me proud."

They embrace. Vincent walks out to his car. Time to deal with the telephone lines.

After spending a few hours in his office, Vincent drives back to the Neighborhood. Johnny V is not at The Patio, so Vincent walks to the social club. Inside, Bruno immediately gestures for him to go to the office.

Johnny looks upset. He gestures for Vincent to sit down, then he leans forward on his desk, waiting for Vincent to speak.

"The guy who gave up the coin score became a big problem."

Bruno sits down in the chair next to Vincent. His hulking presence is enough to make anyone nervous.

"So, we took care of it," Vincent continues. "Out of respect, I am telling you this, so that there is no misunderstanding. I got some names from Bruno and I asked them for a favor, one that I knew I would have to pay back. Our friends up in Milwaukee agreed to babysit this guy, while I took care of some business. I did not know what would happen up there or I would have told you in advance."

Johnny V takes this in information, sensing Vincent has more to say. "And?" he asks.

"And..." Vincent continues, "soon after I concluded my business, it became clear that one last loose end needed to be tied up—so to speak."

Johnny glances at Bruno who nods. He sits back in his chair and stares at Vincent.

"That's it."

"Do the Wisconsin guys know about your decision regarding the loose end?" asks Johnny.

"No."

A knowing smile appears on Johnny's face and he looks up at the ceiling, as if to speak to an unknown listener.

"Well, I have a philosophy: A rat is a rat. Now get out of here and go earn, private dick. And go see Shoes. He has something for you."

Vincent walks out with the weight of the world off his shoulders. He doesn't feel any sympathy for Stanley. In fact, his only concern was this meeting, and now it's behind him. He walks over to the beef stand, sees Mikey, and waves him over.

"Okay, it's done. I saw the boss. Tell Angelo." Mikey nods and walks off.

At Ali Baba's, Vincent orders a beef and sausage combo and sits down to eat. Angelo and Mikey did not tell him what action they took, and they never will. Not a chance. His mind wanders to the stamp collection stored in his bedroom closet. In the next day or two, he'll open a safety deposit box at the bank. But he has to think first. He finishes his meal and buys a second beef and sausage for his mother before walking home to call Paulie.

He drops off the sandwich at the beauty salon, but his mother is busy dyeing the hair of a middle-aged client. Teri nods to him, *thank you*, and he waves back.

"Oh, so *handsome*, Teri," says the lady, a little too hungrily. Vincent blushes as he walks out.

Back at home, he calls Paulie as he pages through the stamp collection in his lap.

"Hey, G-Man. What's what?"

"Hey, Vincent. You seen my mother and Papa Tony? Are they okay? I talked to Ma, and she said she's fine. But I got a feeling all is not well."

"Yeah, she's good, and so is the old grouch." *My first lie to my brother—fuck!* Vincent thinks. "As it happens, your mother asked me today to call you. What's up? Did you get another boy scout badge, or are you going to a jamboree?"

"I need to get your take on something," Paulie says, dead serious.

Vincent listens as Paulie tells him everything about the case and Baranson.

"So, you think this guy is dirty?"

"I don't know, but he looked very nervous when Anton told him to get the informant ready."

"Maybe he's just incompetent or whatever. But your theory makes more sense."

"What do you mean?"

"Well, if I had that large of an operation, I would always wonder if the 'G' had any knowledge of my doings. What could be better than an inside source?"

This is what Paulie has been thinking as well. But what Vincent says next catches Paulie by surprise.

"Based on what you told me, though, there is no fucking informant. Everything Baranson says the informant told him—that's what Mendoza told *Baranson*."

Not for the first time, Paulie marvels at Vincent's unique perception of things, his logical way of working things out.

"Thanks, 'Cenzo'"

"Does this mean I get a merit badge?"

"Fuck you very much," says Paul, as he hangs up.

66

TRUST

After an exhausting, but also particularly satisfying day of work, Agent Tania Caldwell returns home, anxious to spend some time with her son.

"Hello! I got dinner," she calls out, expecting Tyler to come rushing to the door—as much to embrace her as to see what she brought home.

Her mother is on the living room couch, wringing her hands, with tears in her eyes.

"Mom, what's wrong?" she says, immediately casting around for Tyler.

"Edgar came around a couple of hours ago," her mother says. "He asked to take Tyler for some ice cream."

"What did you do?"

"I let him."

"Jesus Christ, mom!"

"You told me that he was acting better!" Her mother says, defensively. "That he had a job and even gave you some money for Tyler."

"Mom! I don't need his money. I make five times what he does! What did I tell you?"

"I thought it was okay. It was just ice cream."

"He's not here, though, *is* he?"

"No, and I'm so scared."

"Why didn't you call me?" her daughter pleads.

"I kept hoping they would return before you got home," her mother answers. "So you wouldn't worry," she adds feebly.

"You can't trust that man, and you know it! I'm gonna deal with you later." But even as Tania chastises her mother, she thinks, *This is my own damn fault. What was I thinking?*

Tania grabs her keys and flies out the door. She gets in her car and is about to race off when she spots Edgar and her son walking toward her. He's holding her little one's hand. They're licking ice cream cones. *Tyler's fine.* Caldwell gets out of the car and races over to them. Edgar sees her approaching.

"Tania!" he calls out, joyfully.

"Are you okay baby?" she says to her son, crouching down, checking his body to see that he hasn't been hurt. Then she stands and addresses Edgar. "Where have you been? My mother is beside herself," she says, as calmly as possible, despite her racing heart.

"Yeah, we stopped by the arcade, and then got ice cream on the way home," Edgar replies. "Tyler wanted to see who was the boss at *Space Invaders*. Let me tell you, he was great."

He sees that she's agitated. "Hey, sorry Tan, we lost track of time. Is this a problem?"

"No, no. It's…fine. I'm glad you had a good time," she replies. *Here I go again. What's wrong with me?* "Say goodbye to your dad, Tyler."

"Bye, Daddy."

"Bye, my little killer," Edgar says, holding his hand low for a high five. Then, seeing the look on Tania's face, adds, "of *aliens.*"

"Alright, baby, let's go," Tania says to Tyler.

"What, no hug for Daddy?" Edgar says to Tania. She glares at him, shakes her head, and walks off with her boy.

67

SEÑOR LOPEZ-MARTINEZ

The next day, Agent Boswhite calls Caldwell and Paulie into his office.

"Baranson wants to have a meeting in a few minutes," he says. "Please keep your composure. In fact, it's better if you don't speak at all. Are we clear?"

Paulie shifts in his seat. Caldwell nods.

At Agent Baranson's office, the large man is cordial. He even has an unnerving smile on his face as he greets them. They sit down. Baranson clasps his hands together and begins.

"The informant's identity must remain confidential," he says, with finality. "You will not be able to interview him, I'm afraid. My source, who brought this to my attention, fears for the informant's life, so I am going to oblige him."

"I'm sorry," Boswhite interjects, "so there are actually two informants—your source and the guy who laid this out? Is that correct?"

Baranson frowns and nods.

"Alright, sir," Boswhite says, as he stands up, gesturing to Caldwell and Paulie to do likewise. "Then we needn't bother you any further."

Baranson rises with them.

"Just a minute. When will I be able to review the reports and the case file?"

"Very soon," Boswhite replies, as he leads the other two out the door.

"This is highly irregular, Boswhite!" Baranson's voice bellows as they walk away.

Boswhite says nothing as he leads Paulie and Tania to his office. He closes the door, sits down, and sighs.

"You know he's lying, Anton," Paulie says, looking his boss straight in the eyes. Tania nods her head in agreement.

"He doesn't know what we know and that's helpful," Boswhite replies. "I understand you have a tail on Lopez-Martinez. Pick him up and take him to the office in San Bernardino, not here. Do it now and call me when you get there. Don't waste any time."

They leave. Boswhite rises and goes to see his boss, Agent Natalie Orosco.

Agent Manuela Gomez, the team member assigned to scope Lopez-Martinez and Carla Guzman's house, informs Paulie and Caldwell that no one is home.

"Agent Sanchez," adds Agent Gomez over the radio, "is tailing Martinez, and she just informed me that he's on the way home now. How do you want to take him, Agent Andrews?"

"When he gets out of the truck, I'm going to badge and identify myself," Paulie replies. "Hopefully, he won't be a problem, so that neither you nor Agent Caldwell will have to be made. You'll be there as back-up."

"I'm going with you, Paul," Caldwell says, as she adjusts the weapon in her holster. He says nothing in reply. There's no arguing with her.

Paulie and Caldwell barely beat Lopez-Martinez to the house. Two minutes later, his old truck comes barreling down the street toward the small house he shares with Carla. He parks his truck on the opposite side of the street and lumbers out of the cab. He does a full-body stretch as Paulie approaches him, badge in hand.

"Señor Lopez-Martinez," says Paulie, flashing his badge, "I'm Agent Andrews of the Federal Bureau of—Jesus!"

Lopez-Martinez throws a haymaker that grazes the left side of Paulie's head. A boxer since a young age, Paulie instinctively side steps the main force of the blow and with his right fist delivers several rapid punches to the solar plexus of Lopez-Martinez. The Mexican lets out a gust of air and collapses. Paulie pins him to the ground with his knee, grabs his left hand, and cuffs him, even as the man continues to struggle. Caldwell appears with her weapon drawn, pointing it at Lopez-Martinez's head.

"Easy, Pancho, easy," she says.

They take him back to their car, cuff him to the ring on the floor of the vehicle, and drive toward San Bernardino. The several neighbors who've gathered feign disinterest.

On the way, Paulie looks at Caldwell.

"Pancho? Really?" he grins.

"It just came to me."

They both laugh. Lopez-Martinez finds it less amusing.

68

BY THE BOOK

Agent Anton Boswhite is at the San Bernardino office when Paulie and Tania arrive with their suspect. Boswhite motions for two burly FBI agents to take Lopez-Martinez to an interrogation room and then directs Paulie and Caldwell to follow him. He leads them to an office where they're surprised to find Supervising Agent Orosco sitting at the desk.

"Agents Caldwell and Andrews, sit down."

"Yes, ma'am."

"I, like some others, was surprised when Agent Baranson assigned you two to this case. I figured he had a strategy. But my concerns were appeased somewhat when he also assigned Agent Boswhite to help you. In retrospect, considering Baranson's potential collaboration with the Sinaloa Cartel, I find it odd he made that call. Regardless, you've done well."

"Thank you, ma'am," Caldwell says.

"You can cut the ma'am, crap. I'm only forty. Do I look so old to you?"

"No ma—sorry," says Caldwell, blushing.

"In any event, you leave Baranson to me. Understood? What's left for you to do is to bring this case home as quickly as possible, but *by the book*. You hear me, Andrews?"

"I got it," Paulie replies, his mind flitting back to Vincent.

"If I uncover anything from Baranson that can help you, I will you inform you. Any questions? No? Good. Then get to work."

Orosco leaves.

Boswhite picks up where Orosco left off. "Okay, you'll interrogate Lopez-Martinez. If he does not cooperate, we'll let him stew in an isolation cell until he does—let him know what's in store for him."

With legal pads at the ready, Paulie and Caldwell enter the chilly interrogation room where Juan Lopez-Martinez sits shackled.

"Mr. Lopez-Martinez, as you may recall, I'm Agent Paul Andrews, and this is my partner, Agent Caldwell. You are in the custody of the FBI. Before we begin, I am going to read you your rights."

As Paulie does so, Lopez-Martinez looks into space without emotion. It's not clear if he understands what Paulie is saying.

"Do you understand your rights, Mr. Lopez-Martinez?"

"I wanna lawyer," he says.

"It appears you do understand. Then we can proceed."

"I wanna lawyer."

"Do you have a lawyer? If so, we will call him for you. In any event, you are now under arrest."

"Por que?"

"Is Juan Lopez-Martinez your real name?"

"Pinche guero. I tol you I wanna abogado—lawyer."

"We heard you, sir. As I stated, if you do not have a lawyer, one will be appointed for you. Now, you will be taken downstairs to be processed. Once they are done, you will be given a phone call. Do you understand what I have told you?"

"Calmate."

Lopez-Martinez motions to his trouser pocket. "Mi, uh, billatera... Ah, wallet."

Caldwell reaches into a tray holding Lopez-Martinez's effects and plucks out the wallet.

"El nombre de mi abogado está ahí."

Caldwell opens the wallet. She holds up a business card of thick, expensive stock.

"This it?"

"Si."

"Bueno," Caldwell says. Then she signals to the agents outside, and they take Lopez-Martinez away.

"Well, that went just peachy," Caldwell says.

"You really didn't believe he'd say anything to us, did you?"

"No, Paul. But I really fucking wanted him to."

"Okay, let's go tell Anton."

They meet with Boswhite and update him about Lopez-Martinez. In turn, their boss informs them that the deputy U.S. Attorney's office is still processing the paperwork for the search warrants. Boswhite lets them know that a grand jury is being discussed and that the agents should remain on standby.

69

THE TROUBLES OF ALPHONSE

Vincent spends a few pleasant days making arrangements for his office. He delights in the minutiae of setting up phone lines, recording a message for his answering machine, ordering monogrammed stationery, and deciding what name he should put on his business cards and office door.

He's busy in other ways as well, soliciting work from nearby lawyers on LaSalle Street and checking in with other agencies for freelance assignments—in short, spreading the word that he's open for business. After reviewing his finances, he considers hiring a secretary. He's sure he'll love the auditioning process. But first, he'll need some more cash. He calls his mother at the salon.

"Ma, I need to borrow back the money you're holding for Papa Tony. I will pay it back the minute I can, but I need it for operating expenses right now."

"I'll have it for you this evening, honey."

He smiles as he puts down his phone. He regards the door to his outer office with satisfaction. A sign painter came in the morning to stencil "SCALISE INVESTIGATIONS" on it. He thinks about who else he should contact to drum up business, and Shoes pops into his head. So, he drives back to the Neighborhood, parks in front of the barber shop, and walks in.

He finds Shoes, wearing python boots, berating an employee. *So, what else is new?* Shoes spots Vincent and gestures for him to wait in the alley. Vincent walks out and sees Papa Tony on the sidewalk outside the grocery store. He nods to the old man. Tony says nothing and goes back into the store.

Moments later Shoes comes out and delivers a hearty handshake to Vincent.

"Congratulations, Vincent," he says. "So, you're in business now, huh?"

"I am."

"Good. Meet me here tomorrow afternoon, and we'll take a drive. We have some things that need taking care of. I'll tell you on the way."

Shoes then goes back inside. Vincent hears him yelling the moment the door closes.

We? Vincent thinks, as he walks down the alley to the grocery store. Vincent relates the conversation to Papa Tony, who just sits in silence, rubbing his forehead with a handkerchief.

"Do what he asks," is all Papa Tony says.

Vincent walks to the register and kisses Rina. She asks about Paulie, as usual.

"We talked last night. He's doing really well. You should be proud. Don't worry, I didn't say anything to Papa. But trust me, this will all work out in the end."

He studies her as they exchange more pleasantries. Vincent finds it immensely difficult not to ask about her health. *She seems herself,* he thinks. He cannot detect any signs of illness. But Vincent is no doctor.

After dinner with his mother, Vincent ventures out. He meets up with Mikey and Angelo and is surprised to see Alphonse with them.

"Hey, Alphonse, how are you buddy?"

"I'm doing great, Vincent. Thanks again to all of you for helping out."

"We've been talking this over," Mikey says, getting down to business. "Even though we've worked together before, we have never declared ourselves a crew. Now with Alphonse back, we should go on record with Johnny V, don't you think?"

But Vincent is doubtful.

"You guys need to leave Alphonse alone while he's on parole," he says. "Alphonse, you do not want to go back, trust me."

"I need to earn, Vincent," Alphonse replies. "And if we're careful, like we've always been, there's no need to worry."

At this, Vincent's eyebrow raises.

"Look what happened last time," Vincent says, thinking about Angelo and Mikey. Neither one of them has been pinched, and he wants to keep it that way. "I don't see why you can't just lay low for a while. Let me check with Johnny V and see if we can get you a city job. Of course, you will never have to show up, but you'll get a paycheck."

"If something comes up, I want in," Alphonse says.

"There's something else," Vincent says. "Now that I have my private detective's ticket, I need to get my business established. I'll probably involve you guys from time to time, but first things first. The three of you need to understand that this is what I want—and not a bunch of scores."

Angelo and Mikey grumble a bit, but all of them nod their heads in agreement.

"That's settled then. Alphonse, I will get on that job for you next week. I want to stay away from Johnny V for a few days."

"Sure thing, Vincent. Thanks again!" says a grateful-sounding Alphonse.

"Okay, I'm off to see Valerie," he says, leaving his crew for the evening.

He waits on Valerie's stoop for about fifteen minutes before he spots her coming back from work.

"What's up, handsome? You here to take me to dinner?" she asks, all smiles and hope in her eyes.

"Sure, and I have some things to tell you."

"What is it?" she replies, suddenly suspicious.

"Ha! Don't worry sweetheart. Nothing bad."

"Okay. Let me just change into something pretty."

"That's my girl."

They walk up to the apartment. When they reach the door, Valerie starts undressing and then invites Vincent to join her, unloosening his belt for him. She tugs at his buckle and leads him to her bed. It's quick and furious—they haven't seen each other in a while.

"Whew, Val," Vincent says, pushing her off of him. "Are you trying to kill me?"

Valerie punches him in the arm and goes into the bathroom. She steps into the shower, starts to run the hot water, then soon calls out to Vincent from behind the curtain, "Are you coming?" Vincent can't say no to an invitation like that. After another round, they towel off, get dressed, and head out for dinner.

"I've got most of the office set up, Val," Vincent says during the drive. "I think I'll need a secretary. Maybe one of your girlfriends would like the job, someone who you could trust."

"Why not me?" she asks, defiantly.

"Because I'm just getting started, sweetheart," he replies, "and I can't afford you yet. I want you to keep your medical insurance. Once I get rolling, I'll need you for other things."

She smiles.

"Anything you want, boss man."

"Yeah, those things," he grins, "but business things, too. Once I start making money, we can move up."

After dinner, they catch a movie. Then Vincent drops her off and drives home.

His mother is watching TV but shuts it off when she hears Vincent's car pull up. She goes to her bedroom and then returns holding an envelope full of cash—six grand. She hands it to Vincent as he walks in, kisses him goodnight, and then closes the bedroom door behind her.

70

THE RETURNED PRINCE

When Carmine Commaretta checks into the YMCA, he's surprised to learn that his assigned case worker is the daughter of a family from the Neighborhood. Gloria Genco, a young woman with dark black hair and bright eyes, warily greets Carmine.

"Hey, how you doing, Gloria? I remember you when you were little. Your father still working for the city? Is your mom still at the bakery? Tell me everything. I would love to see them."

"Yes, my dad's still with the city. He and my mother bought the bakery, so my mom is there most of the day. But we need to get down to business, if you don't mind."

Carmine nods as she outlines all that he's required to do. She tells him that he'll be able to use the facilities in one week but he needs to do a number of things first. He's allowed all the visits he wishes, within the rules and per visiting hours. After about a half an hour, she concludes the meeting, and they say their goodbyes. Another attendant takes Carmine to his room, which he'll share with three others also on supervised release.

He puts his meager belongings in his assigned locker. His roommates, having been forewarned of who he is, will keep to themselves. On his second day, Carmine starts receiving all kinds of food as well as money to buy necessities. The returning prince is home, and his crime family is showing him his due.

After a week, Carmine, having endured his waiting period, ventures to the handball courts where he's greeted by his friends and Outfit members. He is the heir apparent and may one day take over the leadership. But he has enemies he's unaware of, not only among the FBI and local law enforcement, but within the family as well. He plans his future, visiting secretly with some associates and openly with others. Eventually, he sends word to Papa Tony that he wants a meeting.

71

ALLEGIANCE

The following afternoon, Vincent goes to see Shoes. When he arrives at the barber shop, he hears Shoes in the back. He walks toward the noise when he's stopped by a large, sweaty palm attached to a big, round, greasy ball of fat with a comb-over.

"Whaddya want?" the fat-ball says.

Standing no more than five-foot seven, this guy must weigh at least 250 pounds, with a huge, protruding belly. Vincent stares at him but can't place him for anything. He's never seen this guy in the Neighborhood—ever.

Vincent is about to say, "Fuck you," when he hears the voice of Shoes bellowing, "Hey, Lenny, he's with me. He's the guy you need to talk to."

"Oh, sorry, pal," this Lenny says, as he backs away from Vincent.

"Let's go out back," Shoes says. "We can talk there."

Vincent follows Shoes into the alley, with Lenny waddling slowly behind.

"Vincent, this is Lenny Bluestein, an associate of mine. He runs an operation up in Skokie and he thinks he has a problem with past posting. He has about twelve guys who take bets, and one of them is making trouble for Lennie. I want you to find out who. I do not, and I repeat, I *do not* want you to do anything about it."

Vincent thinks back to the molested girl, Debra Morton.

"I just want you to catch this piece of shit, whoever he is," says Shoes. "He's costing me money."

"How do you want me to do that?" Vincent asks.

"How the fuck do I know, kid? You're the private eye—do private eye shit and find out. I've seen TV show about guys like you doing all kinds of electronic shit, so, maybe, you know, do *that*."

Vincent says nothing.

"Next week you go up and see Lenny," Shoes continues. "He'll give you the dope on his guys. Lenny, give him your address and phone number."

Lenny hands Vincent a piece of paper.

"See ya, pal," the fat-ball says, as he maneuvers his hulk past them.

"These guys are making me nuts," says Shoes, watching Lenny wobble toward his white Cadillac.

"Okay, but who is going to pay for all this?" Vincent says. The second he does, he knows it's gonna be a problem.

Shoes turns on him with a menacing look and deeply sighs. "You and I are going to take a ride," he says.

They walk to Shoes' black Oldsmobile. Shoes says nothing on the drive. They get on the expressway, heading west. *Probably Cicero*, Vincent thinks. When they exit on Austin Avenue, Vincent is sure.

Shoes parks the car a block away from the restaurant and walks so quickly toward it that Vincent has a hard time keeping up. Inside, Vincent sees Marco Angelini sitting at his table. Shoes tells Vincent to wait by the door and walks over to Angelini. He whispers something in Marco's ear. Marco looks directly at Vincent, then Shoes waves Vincent over.

"You deal with him," Shoes says within Vincent's earshot. Then he turns and leaves the restaurant, walks to his car, and drives away.

Marco gestures for Vincent to sit down next to him.

"Give me your hands," he says. Reluctantly, Vincent does as he's told. Marco grabs both hands, putting his own over Vincent's.

"We have been watching you for some time," Marco begins in a slow, deliberate, but potent manner.

"You showed Johnny V respect and you need to show Shoes that same respect. I don't know if you know this, but we all voted to let you get your license. And we got it for you, son, but you need to know how things work. When we ask you to do something, you do it. You don't worry about being paid. We will take care of you."

Marco squeezes Vincent's hands tighter. "Pay attention! I see your eyes drifting."

"Look, I want to be my own man," Vincent responds, with more force than he intends.

Marco puts more pressure on Vincent's hands, which are now throbbing.

"We are not going to interfere with your business, but you are with us now. You need to understand that."

Marco smiles, releases Vincent's hands, and sits back.

Vincent places his hands under the table and rubs some life back into them.

"They tell me that you're a tough kid," Marco continues. "They also tell me you're very smart." Marco raises an eyebrow. "We don't need the tough, we got plenty of the fucking tough. What we need is smart."

Marco lets this sink into Vincent's brain for a moment and then resumes. "There are lots of things you can do for us with all those smarts you have. If you don't want to, say it now. Nobody's going to force you to do anything. I would have thought that by your past actions you would have wanted to help us. As a matter of fact, I heard that is what you said yourself."

"Yes, I did, and I do. But I want to do it voluntarily. I don't need any bosses."

"Son, we *all* have bosses. We're all responsible to others—that's just the way it is—and you need to realize that now. We will protect you, and with you under our wing, you will have more power than you could ever imagine. But you need to make that choice. Papa Tony would tell you the same thing. I think he already did, didn't he? So, what's it gonna be? You with us or not?"

Vincent sits back, his mind racing. *Isn't this what you wanted all along?*

"Yes," Vincent replies, after a moment. "I'm absolutely with you."

"Good."

Marco gestures to someone standing in a shadow against the wall. Vincent hardly noticed the man, who now walks over to Marco and hands him a manila envelope. Marco takes it, and the guy withdraws back to the shadow.

Marco hands the envelope to Vincent.

"There's ten grand in there," he says. "Take it and use it to get things done. If you need more, come and see me, not Johnny V. He has a lot of heat on him right now, and I do not want him exposed. You and your crew stay away from the club until I tell you otherwise. Understand?"

"Yes"

"Sonny will drive you back."

Sonny Falco, the guy who gave Marco the envelope, materializes again. As they drive toward the city, Vincent thinks about what just happened, and what he will tell Papa Tony.

Falco drops Vincent off at the grocery store. When he tells Papa Tony, the old man sits down on a crate of tomatoes and shakes his head.

"I told you so," Papa Tony says, in pain and sorrow. "I told you they would own you, and now they do. But this is what you wanted, so now you must live with it. Just be honorable and keep your word. All I ask is that you keep my grandson out of all of this. Promise me."

Vincent stands statue-still, in awe of this outpouring.

"Papa Tony, Paulie is safe," Vincent replies, quickly composing himself. "He is far away in Los Angeles. He will never have to deal with any of this. Paulie is my brother, and I will never let anything hurt him, I promise."

"I kept him safe," Tony says, with tears welling in his eyes. "I did my best. But some things I can't protect him from, some things that will no doubt cause him grief."

"What, Papa, what?"

Tony just shakes his head and walks into his office, shutting the door behind him. *Rina,* Vincent assumes. He'll ask his mother again what is going on. He hopes she'll tell him, but it's not likely.

72

BIRTH CERTIFICATE

It takes weeks to get an appointment, but Rina and Tony finally sit in the waiting room of another specialist recommended by Dr. Alito.

"Rina," Tony says, in hushed tones, "Carmine sent word for me to see him. I'm going tomorrow."

Rina's eyes well with tears. She folds her arms across her chest and leans forward.

"Are you in pain?"

"No, I'm just worried," she replies. "Please be patient with him, I beg you. He'll want to see Paulie."

Tony takes out his handkerchief, wipes his forehead, and nods.

"I know, but when he learns what Paulie has become…" Papa Tony's voice falters, "he may not want to. To my knowledge, no one has said a word to him. They've followed orders. I don't think he knows yet, but we will see. I am going to see Marco first."

The nurse calls, and Rina goes into the examination room. Tony looks on with concern and worry.

The next day, Tony calls ahead, and then leaves for Cicero. Marco is waiting for him in the restaurant.

"Hey, Tony. You look troubled."

"Carmine sent word that he wants to see me," Tony answers, "and I thought that I better talk to you first."

Marco frowns.

"You know we have stayed out of all this because you asked, and Carmine seemed to go along. He did his time and is out now, so I'm not surprised."

"The agreement we made was that he would let me take custody of Paulie during those hard times," Tony says. "He and Rina agreed that it would be best for his son to have as normal a life as possible. I don't see how that's changed. But now he may want to meet his son, and that might be a problem."

"So, to your knowledge, Carmine has learned nothing about Paulie all this time? *Nothing*?"

"No, he has not interfered. But he is going to be very angry at me for keeping some particulars from him, I have no doubt."

"What do want from us?" Marco asks. "Paulie is his son, even though his name is not on the birth certificate, right?"

"Correct. It says 'father unknown'. Look I don't want you to interfere, but I wanted the family to know. I will go see Carmine and tell him everything. I hope he will be reasonable, but we shall see. I knew I would have to face this someday."

73

THE WORST FEAR

A few days after they grabbed Lopez-Martinez, Paulie and Caldwell are visited by Agent Boswhite at their cubicle.

"As of this morning," Boswhite says, "Baranson has taken a leave of absence for medical reasons." He waits for their reactions.

Paulie says nothing. He merely shakes his head slowly.

"What does this mean?" Caldwell asks.

"We proceed as planned. The search warrants have been issued and executed. More are in progress as we speak. Mendoza has been sent a target letter, and the grand jury is set to convene. We just have to wait to see what occurs."

"What about Lopez-Martinez?" asks Paulie.

"His real name is Hector Ramirez. He has a record under that name and is wanted for narcotics distribution in Arizona. He still won't cooperate. But that comes as no surprise. In the meantime, he's not going anywhere."

"So, we're still in standby mode," Caldwell says.

"Is there nothing we can do at this point?" asks Paulie.

"Aside from assisting the deputy U.S. Attorney, not yet," answers Boswhite. "I'm sure we can keep you both busy in the meantime. There's always more fish to fry, so you'll be assigned new cases soon. By the way, I'm recommending the both of you for commendations."

"Thank you, sir."

"Oh, and I think you might be interested: Mendoza's lawyers are already trying to bargain."

Caldwell and Paulie grin.

"Well, whaddya say? Lunch?" Paulie asks Tania, after Boswhite leaves.

"Paul, it's 10:30 in the morning."

"You heard the man—nothing else for us to do."

Caldwell's phone rings.

"Hey, mom, what's up? Accident? What? No, I'm fine! Wait, mom, calm down. Breathe, mom. Is it Tyler? What happened? Oh my god, I'm going to the school right now."

She hangs up and begins packing her things.

"I'm coming with you," Paulie says.

"Paul, this isn't your business."

"That doesn't matter."

Fifteen minutes later, Tania and Paulie barge into the office of Principal Hamlin, who is sitting at his desk. Their sudden appearance startles him, but before he can speak, Tania shouts, "Where is he?"

"Mrs. Caldwell," he says, "I'm sorry. Is there a problem?"

"My son, he's been taken."

Realization dawns on the principal. He stands up but decides it best to stay behind his desk.

"I don't know what to say. Your husband picked up Tyler at recess. He told the teacher that you had an accident at work, so she let him take your son. Tyler went with his father willingly—he even seemed happy to go, according to the teacher."

"Has she been fired?" Caldwell spits out, unable to hold in her fury. "Where is she?"

"Mrs. Caldwell, please calm down."

"Don't tell me to calm down!" Paulie wedges himself between Tania before she can move any closer to Hamlin. Holding Tania by the shoulders, he turns to Hamlin.

"Did you notify the police?"

"No, sir," Hamlin replies.

"Why the hell not?" Caldwell yells.

"Ma'am, please, I've asked you to calm down," Hamlin replies. Then, addressing Paulie, he continues. "We called Mrs. Caldwell's home to try to find out what was going on, and her mother, I believe, told us that she would contact you. We've heard nothing else."

"You gave my son to a criminal, you know that?"

"Excuse me? Aren't you an FBI agent? I would think that you of all people would understand the security protocols for your own son."

Paulie feels the tension in Caldwell's body, knowing she can barely restrain herself from attacking the smug principal.

"Okay," she says, her mind immediately turning to action, "Let's call his job. Maybe he showed up for work today—or if not, they should know where he's living. Can we use your fucking phone?"

"Ma'am, there's no need for that kind of..." Seeing the look in Caldwell's eyes, Hamlin prudently does not finish his statement. Instead, he points to the phone on his desk.

"Do you have a phone book?"

After rifling through the pages, Caldwell calls the scrap yard, remembering the company name from the paystub Edgar showed her. No one answers.

"I feel so helpless, I think I'm going to explode!" she cries.

"Let's go to your house."

"Alright. We're getting nothing accomplished with these useless people, anyway." She glares at Hamlin one more time before they exit his office.

Soon, they're sitting in Caldwell's living room, with her mother anxiously pacing about.

"Look," Paulie says, "do you remember any of the names of Edgar's friends?"

"I'm an idiot for not pressing him for details," Caldwell replies. "I just didn't want to know."

"Okay, what's the name of his old gang—where are they located? Maybe we can ask around."

"Paul, shut up. They'll eat you alive in that neighborhood."

"Let me try, Tania, please. Give me some information, and maybe I can convince some of his friends to give him up to me, or I can contact the local sheriff for help. It's better than just sitting here, don't you think?"

"Please, Paul."

The phone rings. Tania leaps to pick it up. She listens for a second and then screams into the receiver.

"Where are you! Why did you do this? Why?"

Paulie looks around for another phone. He finds one in Caldwell's bedroom and quietly picks up the receiver to listen in.

"I'm going to keep Tyler for a while," Paulie hears Edgar say, in an almost calm manner. "And I'll take him to school and pick him up. Don't worry, baby."

"Don't you tell me not to worry!"

"I have a job and I'm trying hard to make things right."

"I don't care if you're trying to make things right. You made them wrong."

"Baby, I'm so sorry for the past but now that I've seen Tyler, I realize that I need to change, and I will."

"Are you finished?"

"Yes."

"Let me talk to Tyler, now," she says, her voice regaining that eerie and unnerving calmness.

She hears the sound of the phone changing hands. Then her son's voice comes through clear.

"Hi Mommy," Tyler says. "I'm here with dad. We drove out to the aquarium and saw lots of fishes."

"Wow," she says, forcing her voice to sound joyful. "Did you have a good time? Did you eat?"

"Yep."

"Okay, I love you. Let me talk to your dad."

Edgar gets back on the line. "I told you everything was okay, Tan."

"What's your address, Edgar?"

"I'm not telling you that right now."

"Edgar, I'm not mad. Just tell me your address."

"Tania—"

"Okay, enough of this," she says matter-of-factly. "If you bring him back, right now, I will forgive this. If you don't, you definitely will never see him again, because I'm going to *kill* you."

"Tan, I borrowed a friend's car and gave it back. I have no way to bring him to you tonight. Let him stay with me overnight, and I will drop him off at school tomorrow before work. For good faith, I'll give you the number of where I'm at, and I'll make sure he calls you to say goodnight. Okay?"

"Okay Edgar, what's the number?" He gives it, and she writes it down.

"I promise it'll be fine, Tan. Give me a chance to prove myself, please," he says, and when she doesn't respond, he hangs up.

Paulie hangs up and walks to the living room. Tania is dialing another number.

"What are you doing?"

"I'm calling the Bureau. I'm gonna get a trace on that number."

"Hold on."

"What, Paul?"

"Think about Tyler. You don't want a whole bunch of agents coming down on that house while your boy is in there. Listen, do you think Edgar will hurt Tyler?"

She's quiet for a moment.

"No. He only wants to hurt me."

"We'll go to the school tomorrow to make sure Edgar does what he says. I will follow him from there."

"Okay, but I'm gonna get his address anyway. I won't tell people why."

"Do what you gotta do."

The night is filled with restless sleep. Tania learns that Edgar lives in a boarding house, and the number he gave her belongs to a public pay phone in the hallway on Edgar's floor. She cannot bear that her son has to spend a night in a place like that. *Is it better to trust?* she wonders, as she tosses fitfully. She'll be up at the crack of dawn, no matter what.

Caldwell arrives outside the school two hours before the opening bell. Paulie arrives about an hour after that. He takes a position on one side of the school gates, while Caldwell stands at the top of the stairs. Students stream in for class, but there's no sign of Tyler or Edgar. They wait for fifteen minutes after the first period bell. Tyler isn't coming. Paulie goes over to comfort her.

"He will fucking pay for this, Paul. And you will, too," she adds. "I can't believe I listened to you."

She slaps him across the face, then gets in her car and drives off.

Paulie crosses the street, goes to the pay phone, and dials the number for the boarding house. It rings ten times before a male voice answers.

"Hello?"

"Who is this, please?"

"Who're you?"

"Look, I'm trying to reach Edgar..." Paulie pauses, realizing he doesn't know Edgar's last name. "Is there an Edgar there?" he finally asks.

Silence on the other line. Then the man speaks.

"You da police? Cause if you be, you should already know."

"Know what?"

"He dead. He was shot leaving for work. Had dis little boy wid him. The boy wid the police now. You ain't the police?"

Paulie reels at the news.

"No, sir. I am a friend of the boy's mother. Do you know what police department has the boy?"

"It be the police, all I know. It terrible what da boy saw. You call the police and they gonna tell you."

Click. The man hangs up.

Paulie speeds to the Compton precinct of the LAPD. He rushes inside and immediately sees Tyler sitting in the lobby. He's been given some toys to play with. Paulie approaches two police officers standing near the boy.

"Agent Andrews, FBI," Paulie says, taking out his badge. He explains that the boy is his partner's son, and that he needs to use their phone.

"Hello?" Caldwell answers on the first ring.

"Tania, it's me. I'm with Tyler. He's safe." He gives her the address of the station and hangs up. Then Paulie walks over and introduces himself to the boy.

Tania arrives shortly afterwards. Tyler hugs his mother and starts to cry. A woman from child protective services asks to speak with Tania, so Paulie waits with Tyler. No one asks the detectives about Edgar. They will find out later.

"Tania, I—" Paulie says, as she carries Tyler out of the station.

"It's not your fault, Paul," she says, cutting him off. "But you need to leave me and my family alone."

74

DEAD EYES

Papa Tony rises early, as he always does. He shaves, puts on some nice clothes, and gets ready to see Carmine. He slept fitfully, uneasy about the meeting to come.

At the YMCA, he walks up the stairs to the office and is met by Gloria Genco. He recognizes her from the Neighborhood. He knows her parents, who own the bakery that supplies the grocery store, but he didn't know she worked here.

"My goodness, how you have grown!" says Papa Tony. "Give my love to your parents."

"I will, Tony," Gloria says. "I have set up a room with some privacy for you and Carmine. This way."

"Thank you, Gloria."

She leads him down a hallway and opens a door to let him in. There sits Carmine, all smiles.

"Tony," he says, standing and embracing Tony. "You're still an ugly Sicilian, but it's great to see you."

Tony tentatively embraces Carmine, then he stands back and looks into his eyes. What he sees is a confident man. It appears that, in jail, Carmine has not lost his strength and indeed, he seems filled with resolve. Tony settles himself in a chair opposite Carmine. He's come to bring Carmine the truth, no matter what the outcome.

"Carmine, there are things I must tell you. Please try to stay calm and let me finish. Then I will answer all your questions."

Carmine's smile disappears. He has waited many years for this moment, anticipating some good news. But now…

"Okay, Tony. Tell me."

"First, you should be very proud of your son. He is an honorable man—kind, considerate, and loved by—"

"Tony, cut the shit and just fucking tell me."

Tony sighs. He wanted to ease into his disclosure, but Carmine has given him no choice.

"Carmine, Paulie is an agent…for the FBI."

Carmine stares in silence.

Tony sits up in his chair awaiting the onslaught. His eyes begin to tear, and he takes out his handkerchief. With cold, dead eyes Carmine fixes his gaze at the old man, the father of the woman he still loves and the grandfather of his only child. He pushes his chair back, the metal legs screeching against the tiled floor, and stands up, startling Tony, who sits still, waiting for the attack. Then it comes.

"You waited all these fucking years to tell me this?" Carmine explodes. "My son is a fucking FBI agent!"

Tony cringes and waits for more. Carmine walks over to the window and looks out.

"How in the world could this happen?" Carmine continues. "Did someone brainwash him? Tell me, Tony, how could this happen?"

Tony tries to explain the unexplainable, something even he doesn't understand.

"Ever since he was a kid, Paulie has always been looking out for the underdog, always taking on bullies. And as he grew up, he talked about nothing but working for law enforcement. At first, he said he wanted to be a police officer, but before long, he set his sights on the FBI. In high school, he graduated at the top of his class, then did just as well in college, which I paid for. I hoped by the time he graduated, he would have changed his mind, maybe decide to become a lawyer or..." Tony stops, not sure whether to continue. But Carmine says nothing.

"And then he entered the FBI Academy," he says. "No one believed Paulie would ever follow through—not me, not Rina, not his closest friend Vincent, *no one*. We were always proud of his accomplishments, his devotion to his studies, but we always thought he would change his mind and follow a different path. We all tried to talk some sense into him. But he pursued the Bureau with the same intensity as anything else. Rina and I were so torn. He made us so proud of his dedication to his mother, to school, to..."

Tony stops. "But he also broke my heart, Carmine," he adds. "He changed his last name. He's no longer my Paulo Andriano."

"What the fuck, Tony!" This new revelation is almost as disturbing to Carmine as anything else Tony has said.

The old man nods. "We have not spoken since he made that decision. He is now FBI agent Paul *Andrews*, and he's working out in Los Angeles."

Carmine sits back down hard, his mind racing. It is all he can do to contain his rage. He leans back and looks out into space.

Tony delivers one last admission. "He does not know you are his father, Carmine. Rina and I kept that from him."

Carmine looks at him. If looks could kill, Tony would lie dead on the floor.

"I want to talk to Rina, and if you try to stop me—"

"Rina is ill, Carmine," Tony interrupts. "I ask that you please take that into consideration before you act."

"Get the fuck out!" Carmine says, seething.

Tony gets up and approaches Carmine, who turns his back on him. Tony leaves heavy-hearted.

When Tony arrives at the grocery store, he asks Rina to come to his office. Frowning with dread, she follows her father. In the office, she sits down, folds her arms across her chest, and leans forward.

"Tell me."

"He is upset, and I don't blame him. I do not know what to do next or what he will do."

Rina shifts in her chair.

"I want to see him," she says, "but I don't want anyone to know. How can we get that done?"

"I don't know. At first, he said he wanted to see you, but when I left…" Tony shrugs his shoulders. "I will ask, but don't be surprised if he changed his mind. Don't be surprised if he rejects you."

She stiffens in her chair and sits up. "He won't reject me, Papa. I know that."

A few days later, Carmine calls a few of his people in and sits them down.

"I've been hearing about this young kid in the Neighborhood named Vincent Scalise. Find him and tell him I want to see him. Do it now and do it quietly. Bring him to me."

After they leave, Carmine stares out the window. Things are shifting within the Outfit. He feels his power growing, and he will take the measures needed to make that so. He also feels the presence of an enemy, one whose identity is not yet known to him.

75

THE ALLURE OF JEWELS

Vincent sits in his office contemplating how he'll pursue his project for Shoes. In order to be the best private eye, he'll need to procure state of the art of equipment—electronic wiretaps and other bugging devices. He's seen the effectiveness of these from his experience in the Army. That's why, a few days prior, he reached out to a firm based in Virginia, headed by an ex-military intelligence officer, Lieutenant Colonel Allan D. Bell, Jr. Bell invited Vincent to visit the following week, and he counts the days before his trip, excited at the prospect of acquiring new knowledge.

Vincent is leaving his office when his crew calls him. He tells them to meet him at his house in an hour. When he arrives, Angelo, Mikey, and Alphonse are waiting in Mikey's car.

"We have a score we're working on," Mikey says. "And we wanted to run it by you and see if you are interested."

"I told you guys that I'm not interested in scores right now." When he sees the crestfallen looks on their faces, he adds, "But go on."

"Alphonse found this score," Mikey continues. "It's a jewelry store with limited security. The tipster is the nephew of the owner."

"Another nephew? That fact alone turns me off," Vincent replies. "Alphonse, do you have a death wish or what? I got you a job, so what's the problem?"

Alphonse's face turns red, but then he gets a grip on himself. "I didn't want to trouble you with this," Alphonse says. "But I feel like you should know. My mother has been diagnosed with a liver disorder—and she has no insurance."

"Fuck. What can I do?"

"Nothing," Alphonse replies, "just don't get in my way for now. I know you have the best intentions, but I have no choice."

Vincent slowly shakes his head.

"Alright, I'm not gonna actively participate, but I will help in every way I can. Give me all the specifics in massive detail."

They talk for over an hour until Vincent knows enough to come up with a game plan. They will move tonight, no use wasting time. Angelo promises to report to Vincent first thing in the morning with the results of their score. When the crew leaves, Vincent goes back to planning his trip to Virginia.

At ten the next morning, Vincent hasn't heard from anyone. He's about to walk out onto Taylor Street to look for the crew when the phone rings.

"Hello?"

"'Cenzo, it's Angelo. Meet me at Mama Schiavone's at noon." Then he hangs up.

An hour later, Vincent shows up at Mama Schiavone's. He spots Angelo sitting alone at the back of the dining area of the family-style restaurant, a Neighborhood landmark.

"Angelo, what happened? Everything go okay?"

Angelo frowns.

"Yeah, we're okay but there was a problem," he says, in a quiet voice. "The old fart who owns the store surprised us—at four in the fucking morning! We were packing up and just about to leave when he came in. He sees us and starts yelling. Mikey grabbed him and as they struggled, the old man pulled Mikey's ski mask off. Mikey beat him unconscious, but the old man got a good look at him."

Angelo sits back in his chair and looks around to make sure no one is paying attention to their conversation.

"I checked the old man's pulse," he continues, "and he was breathing. We had the air, so we listened for a few minutes, but no cops came around. So, we left. I just hope the old man didn't croak."

Vincent sighs. He's involved now. He has no choice—these are his guys. Very calmly, he asks, "Where is everybody?"

"Mikey has the take. He will call us later. I think he drove out to Indiana or somewhere, where his aunt lives. My wife said he hasn't called yet, so I called you. Alphonse just went home."

Vincent sums up their position: "So, if the old man lives, he could identify Mikey, which is bad enough. But if he *dies*, then we have a major league problem."

Vincent gives the matter some thought. He doesn't have a solution yet, but Angelo doesn't need to know that.

"Okay, here's what you do. Go home and wait to see if Mikey calls. I will drop by Alphonse's and keep him calm. Whatever you do, do *not* discuss this with anyone else. And don't panic, Angelo. You got that?"

"Yeah, okay Vincent, but I'm worried about Mikey. I don't know what he's gonna do." Angelo is visibly shaken.

"Okay, give me the address of the score, and I will see what I can find out. Now go home. And most of all: Don't. Fucking. Panic."

Angelo gives Vincent the store address and then leaves. Vincent sits for a few moments and then gets into his car. He needs to assess the situation firsthand and determine the fallout. And to do that, Vincent must be careful. He cannot just walk up to the jewelry store and ask for information. That would arouse suspicion. Though he's got his private detective's license, he hasn't received his ID card yet, which he might be able to flash. Instead, he may have to rely solely on his gagging skills.

Vincent parks a couple of blocks from the store. Outside on the street, he finds a pay phone and calls Bill Faraday, his connection in the local police department. Faraday doesn't answer. Vincent will have to scope out the situation himself. He walks up the street, strolling by the store, which he's amazed to find open. There's even a young couple inside looking at wedding rings. For a moment, he wonders if he's at the right place. He crosses the street to a grocery store that stands directly across from the jewelers. He makes a beeline to the elderly lady at the cash register.

"Excuse me, Ma'am," Vincent says, pulling a gag line from his old days. "My name is James Fredricks. I'm an insurance accident investigator."

"Hi dear, I'm Lily."

"Pleasure to make your acquaintance, Lily. I was wondering if you saw the car crash across the street this morning?"

"I didn't see any accident," she replies. "The only thing I know is that the owner of the jewelry store had a stroke."

"No, poor thing."

"I know!" She leans in, as if to tell him a secret. "Apparently, the owner's daughter found him on the floor when she got in this morning, and the safe had been broken into."

"Oh, dear," Vincent says, feigning concern.

"Anyway, I think everyone's fine now, thank Christ. The daughter called for an ambulance, and they took him to the hospital. I saw them leave. I was sitting right here."

"I'm sorry but, how do you know all of this?"

"My daughter, Sarah—she's single, you know—is friends with Cora, Sam Bernstein's daughter, you know—the owner. She came by this morning."

"I'm surprised the store is open now. Surely they must have called the police?"

"You know, I don't know! It seems a little fishy if you ask me. But they definitely didn't. I haven't seen any police there, and I've been here since eight."

Vincent's mind is churning. He cannot believe what he's hearing. But he stays cool. He thanks the old busybody and leaves the store, thinking *What the fuck!*

Next, Vincent returns to the pay phone and calls Angelo. He tells him to meet up at Ali Baba's in an hour. Then he drives to Alphonse's house. When he gets there, he finds Alphonse and Ralphie cleaning out their car.

"Alphonse, we need to talk."

"Here?"

"Let's take a walk," Vincent says. "Ralphie, we'll be back in an hour."

As they walk toward the beef stand, Vincent scans for more busy bodies. He sees none.

"Okay, tell me."

"Just bad luck, Vincent," Alphonse says, before proceeding to confirm Angelo's story.

"So, you don't know what you guys took?"

"No, not really. Like I said, we were just shoving things in the bag when the door opened."

When they get to Baba's, they sit on the bench outside and wait. Soon, Angelo drives up, and gestures for them to get in the car.

"Mikey called," Angelo says, as they drive away. "He's at his Aunt Ginny's house in Flossmoor, near the Indiana border. She lives there alone after her husband died. Anyway, Mikey did the right thing. He ditched the work car and called Fat Louie's guy to tell them where it was. They'll pick it up."

Then Vincent shares what he's learned. Their reaction is the same: *What the fuck?*

"There must be a reason the daughter didn't call the police, and I'm guessing the answer was in that safe. We need to find out what," Vincent says. "Did Mikey look in the bags to see what you guys got?"

"No, he stashed them in his aunt's garage as soon as he got there."

"We need to know why this jeweler came in at four in the morning. Maybe he was going to retrieve what was in the safe, and maybe that's why he got so worked up."

"Who knows?" Alphonse says.

"Okay, Ange, drive me to my house," Vincent says. "I want to pick up some things up before we go down there."

At home, Vincent is immediately confronted by his mother.

"Tony called. He says you have to go see Marco at nine tomorrow morning. He says you know where to go."

"Okay, tell Papa Tony that I'll be there first thing."

Then, looking out the window at Angelo's car, Teri adds, "Where are you off to?"

"Southside.

Vincent rushes to his bedroom, grabs his wallet and some cash and stuffs them in his pocket. He kisses his mother's cheek on his way out the door.

76

FLOSSMOOR

As they drive out to see Mikey, Vincent's mind spins. as he thinks of everything he has to do. First, he wonders what Marco wants. Maybe it has something to do with things going up in Skokie and the bookies for Shoes. Then he wonders if his Virginia trip will still work out. But he must focus on the task at hand.

An hour later, they're in Flossmoor. At first, they wonder if they've found the right house. It's beautiful and so green, right on the golf club fairways. They stand in awe. They know it's the right one when Mikey comes out to greet them. Like a lonely dog, he's been looking out the window waiting for them to arrive.

Mikey's Aunt Ginny is puttering in the garden under the front windows of her house, and Mikey introduces them. She's sweet and generous.

"I'll go inside and bring you boys some of my famous lemonade," she says. "I make it from my own trees out back."

Mikey follows her in, waving to the guys to join him. "Auntie," Mikey asks, "can we use Uncle Matt's office to talk? We have some things to discuss."

"Sure, Mikey. I'll bring the lemonade to you there."

Mikey shows them into an ornate office lined with books, many of them leather-bound. They all sit down in leather chairs, eyeing everything around them.

"Wow, will you look at all this?" says Alphonse. "What did your uncle do, Mikey?"

"He was a lawyer, then a judge."

"But where'd all this money come from?" Alphonse asks.

"It's no different down here," Mikey grins, "if you know what I mean. He had lots of the right friends up in Chicago."

"Where is everything?" Vincent interrupts, all business.

"My uncle loved his Buick and kept it pristine," Mikey continues in a ponderous tone. "The three-car garage is so clean you'd think someone lived in it. All of my uncle's woodworking tools are hanging up in there. Did you see those bird houses out there? He made them all."

"Mikey, let's get a move on," Vincent says, anxious to take action.

"Yeah, so, I don't know why, but I put everything in the trunk of the Buick. It has a tarp over it, so no one's the wiser. No one drives it, anyway. My aunt has her own car and mostly parks it in the driveway. Anyway, that's where everything is. Angelo told me not to open the bags, so I didn't. What's going on?"

Vincent relates the situation, leaving Mikey as confused and stunned as the rest of them.

"We need to find out what's in the bags," Vincent says. "Mikey, bring the bags in here."

"Let's wait until my aunt leaves, okay?" Mikey says. "She has bridge club, so she'll be going out in a half hour or so, anyway."

There's a knock on the door. Angelo opens it. There's Aunt Ginny with a huge platter of cookies, glasses, and a pitcher of lemonade on a rolling cart. Angelo helps her wheel it inside.

"Now, you boys enjoy yourselves. I made these cookies this morning," she says, with a wide-mouth smile, seeming to glow with all the attention she's getting. "I have to go out in a few minutes. Will you boys be okay?"

They all smile and compliment her. She beams and leaves, closing the door behind her. Their smiles fade. They review every step of the score again and again until Vincent is satisfied that they have all the facts. They're not conscious of the passing of time. It seems like just a few minutes have passed when they hear Ginny shout as she walks out the front door.

"BBBBYYYE BBBOOOYYYSSS!"

Soon after she leaves, Mikey and Angelo bring back the two heavy bags from the garage.

They lay out the treasure on the desk. There are rubies, emeralds, opals, and lots of diamonds in trays wrapped in paper pouches. There's also watches and rings and other fine jewelry. There's even a solid gold Mezuzah, almost seven inches long, wrapped in a fine felt bag.

Finally, there's a heavy package, wrapped in duct tape. Mikey reaches for it when Vincent instantly stops him.

"That must be what this is all about," Vincent says. "Wipe your fingerprints off the tape, Mikey, and let's leave that alone for now. Get a bag to put it in."

Mikey walks off to do Vincent's bidding.

"What are you thinking?" asks Alphonse.

"I don't know," Vincent replies, shaking his head. "But I have a bad feeling about this. Let's pack all of this back in the bags. Mikey, I think this is as good a place as any to hide the stuff, so put it all back in the trunk of your uncle's car until I learn more, okay?"

"Why can't we divvy up the rest and leave the package for later?" Alphonse asks. "I need the money now. My mother needs medical care as soon as possible."

"I understand, Alphonse" Vincent replies. "But it won't take long to find out what's what. Be patient."

77

A NEW ASSIGNMENT

The grand jury in the case of *United States v. Mendoza* convenes a few days after the incident with Edgar. The jury issues a multicount indictment against Mendoza. The accusations against the young supermarket kingpin make the front page of newspapers across the country. Mendoza's legal team calls the charges unfounded and argues that their client has been targeted because of his race. Citing the fairy tale story of his life, they say the case is un-American.

When Mendoza is arrested, his lawyers ensure that a gaggle of reporters are on hand to watch FBI agents place him in handcuffs. Mendoza is in custody for the better part of a morning, but is quickly released on $2,000,000 bail. His ample holdings more than sufficiently cover the amount.

The day Mendoza is released, Paulie is called in to Agent Boswhite's office. This time no coffee is offered.

"Here are your new orders and assignment, Agent Andrews," Boswhite says. "You are to be transferred to the Chicago Bureau, where, I've learned, you will be assigned to Organized Crime."

Paulie looks at Anton in shock. "Why?" he asks.

"I truly do not know," Boswhite replies. "If I had to guess, I would say it might have something to do with your background."

Paulie ignores this.

"This is a real promotion, Andrews. You should be proud, as this is one of our original Bureaus. In any event, your appointment is effective immediately. You report to Chicago one month from today."

"What about the Mendoza case?" Paulie asks, irritably. "Am I off that?"

"You know as well as I that there's nothing left to do."

"Is this about Baranson?"

"I'm sorry, but I can't comment on that."

"What about Tania?" Paulie asks, then quickly adds, "Agent Caldwell?"

"She will remain here," Boswhite says, with finality. "That is all. Good luck in Chicago. Your Supervising Agent—your *boss*—will be Agent Leonard Phillips. I think you will like him. I believe he's Italian as well."

Agent Anton Boswhite holds out his hand. Though it pains him, Paulie shakes it. He's dismissed.

Back at his apartment, Paulie cannot stop looking at his phone. There are many calls to make but he cannot bring himself to pick up the receiver. He wants to call Papa Tony, but that's out of the question. He could call Vincent, but he's not ready to tell him the news. He knows how upset he'll be. Carolyn has been distant whenever she answers his calls, which is not often. And then there's Tania, the most difficult call for Paulie to make.

Instead, he busies himself with packing. He arranges for all his belongings to be shipped to Chicago. He thinks about driving there, so he'll need to have the car checked out to see if it's in shape for the trip.

Then he thinks about where he's going to live. Probably downtown. He cannot move back in with his mother and grandfather. Indeed, he won't be able to go back to the Neighborhood at all. He shudders at the thought. He'll have no peace if he goes back there—the first FBI agent from the Neighborhood. When he goes back home, it'll be like moving to a new city.

He's packing when the phone rings. It's Carolyn.

"Hi, what a nice surprise. I'm glad you called. I was just thinking about you."

Carolyn is silent on the other end.

"Paul, I met someone," she says, when she finally speaks. "I'm going home to see my parents this weekend and introduce them to him."

All the words Paulie wants to say just stick in his throat. She continues.

"He's a law student with me here at Georgetown. I wanted to do this in person, but we never did see each other, did we?"

"You don't love me anymore?" he asks, his voice surprisingly firm. There's another silence on the line.

"I...no, I don't think I do. Not anymore. Please take care of yourself, Paul. Goodbye." She hangs up.

Paulie sits down, surrounded by the packing boxes, trying to process the phone call. He's in a state of shock, but not quite surprised. *Things sure are going just great,* he thinks. *If it wasn't for bad luck, I'd have no luck at all.* He stands up again and continues to pack. He thinks about Tania.

Later that day, Paulie drives all the way down to the Santa Monica pier. He parks and walks on the beach to Venice. There, feeling hungry, he walks up to the shops. He's waved over by a young blonde woman behind a sign that reads, "Psychic."

"You look like you need a reading," she tells him. "Twenty dollars for a half hour."

Paulie sits down. He hands her a twenty-dollar bill and looks into her eyes.

"I have to tell you that I do not believe in this hocus-pocus," he says, "but have at it."

She smiles and pulls out her Tarot cards and lays them down in front of her. Then she looks concerned. *Very dramatic*, Paulie thinks, smiling smugly. *She's probably an actress.*

The fortune teller says that he will be making a serious change in his career, and that his family and friends will oppose his decision. Paulie stops smiling. Then she says that he's being tested, that he has doubts about his career. She goes on. His most recent romantic engagement was never meant to be, she asserts, and he should focus on his future.

"How do I do that?" he asks, almost pleading. She shushes him and keeps reading. A look of confidence crosses her face.

"You'll meet someone soon who will dramatically change the course of your life."

"What does that mean? Is it good, or bad?"

"I can't tell."

She waits for a response. When she gets none, she asks him if he has any other questions. He smiles weakly, as if to say no, and then rises, walking away confused and unsettled. The noise, the smell, and the people along the boardwalk begin to irritate him, so he turns around and walks back to his car, all the while thinking about what the psychic told him.

He thinks about what it might mean when he returns to Chicago. *Can I arrest people from my own neighborhood?* The thought fills him with distaste. *Is the Bureau testing me to see if I'm truly dedicated to this life I've chosen? It has to be.* He tries to shrug it off, chastising himself for being so self-centered. *I'm just being reassigned. That's that. It's not the end of the world.*

When Paulie returns home, he picks up the phone and makes what he thought was the most difficult call on his list. After several rings, someone finally answers.

"Hello?" says Tania. In the aftermath of Edgar's death, Agent Caldwell requested time off to spend with her son and mother. She and Tyler have enjoyed a few days of peaceful isolation, free of intrusive busybodies, her mother notwithstanding.

"Hey, how are you?" Paulie says, trying to sound cheerful.

When she recognizes his voice, she considers hanging up. She doesn't, but replies icily, "I'm fine, Paul. How are you?"

"I just wanted to tell you. I've received orders. I'm being transferred to the Chicago office. I'll be working on Organized Crime."

Caldwell is stunned. "What? Why?"

"I don't know."

"Is there anything I can do?" she says, her anger at him slipping away.

"I don't know what you could do. I'll miss you." There's silence on the phone. Caldwell breaks it.

"So, I don't know if you were following this, but Edgar was shot by one of his own gang members. Apparently, he told them he was through with the life—*again*—but they weren't willing to let him make that decision. I don't know if there is any truth to that. I spoke to the detectives, and to be honest, they didn't really seem to care. Just another gang-banger shooting."

"Yeah, I heard. Are you happy he's gone?"

"I think so. Maybe. For myself, anyway. I'm not so sure what this will mean for Tyler, though."

"How is he doing?"

"The social worker who saw him at the precinct comes over, and that's helping, I think. He's just been lying in bed, and my mother's doting over him. He'll come through."

"He's strong, like his mom."

"I can't believe you're being reassigned."

"Listen," Paulie says. "I've been thinking, or rather, hoping—do you have time to get dinner? Or just lunch is fine, too."

"Sure," she replies. "When?"

"Tomorrow?"

"Okay, dinner. Pick me up at 5:30."

"I'll be there."

Paulie hangs up. Tania is his only friend here. Sure, he had met lots of people in and out of the Bureau, but no one like Tania. Then a thought crosses his mind: *Vincent would've made lots of friends. He'd be a star out here.* Thinking of Vincent triggers another thought he hadn't considered before: *What if I went into the private eye business?* Then the miserable thought of going back to Chicago hits him again, and his gloom returns.

At dinner, Paulie and Tania rely on small talk to get through their meal. The conversation is awkward for both of them. Despite how much he cares about her, he cannot bring himself to tell her how he feels. When they finish eating, he wants to ask her back to his place or suggest they go for a walk along Venice beach—anything to prolong the evening. Instead, he drives her home. He steps out of the car before she can stop him. They briefly hug goodbye. Paulie wants to kiss her, but the distant look in Tania's eyes prevents him from doing so. On his drive home, Paulie berates himself for not sharing his feelings to Tania, wondering if he'll ever again get the chance.

78

NOT YET

While Paulie gets his affairs in order for his return, his mother is contemplating her own future. Rina calls Teri at the salon.

"I have to speak with you," Rina says.

"Okay," Teri replies, hearing the stress in her voice. "Come over in an hour."

When Teri opens the door, Rina falls into her friend's arms, weeping. Teri senses what this is all about. She knows everything in the Neighborhood, including the fact that Carmine is walking free. They talk for hours.

The phone rings. It's Paulie on the line, asking for Vincent. He's finally built up the courage to share his news. Teri abruptly tells him that Vincent is not home. She turns to Rina, pointing to the phone and mouths, *It's Paulie*. Rina shakes her head, *No*.

"So, I'll have him call you, honey. Everything okay?"

"Yeah, thanks, Teri. I'm gonna call my mother now. Take care." He hangs up.

"He said he was going to call you. Why didn't you want to talk to him?"

"He knows me," Rina replies. "He'd sense something was wrong. I've got to see his father before I speak with Paulie."

They continue to discuss Rina's problem. About an hour later, there's a knock on the door. Teri opens the door to two guys she thinks she recognizes.

"Sorry to bother you, Teri. Is Vincent home?"

"Who are you and what do you want?" she replies.

"We're friends of Tony's. He sent us here to see you and talk to your son."

"My son is not home now," Teri says warily. "Give me your phone number, and I will have him call you."

They look at each other.

"We'll come back tomorrow," one says. "Please, do us a favor, and call Tony. He'll tell you we're okay, okay?"

They turn and leave. Rina looks out the window at the two walking down the steps. She recognizes one of them as Peter Pazienza, a friend of Carmine's.

"I haven't seen him in a long time," Rina says. "He moved out of the Neighborhood years ago. I wonder what he wants from Vincent."

"Who knows?" Teri replies. "But I'll have Vincent call Tony tomorrow and find out. My son has now got himself ensnared. I think he'll get lots of visits in the future."

79

CLOUSEAU

Vincent wakes at seven the next morning and looks up at the ceiling. When he got in last night, his mother told him about the visit from Tony's "friends," as she put it. So, he has to talk to Tony, but also see Marco at nine for another issue he knows nothing about.

After showering, he goes to the kitchen for breakfast. He kisses his mother and tells her he only wants a glass of Ovaltine. He doesn't look well rested.

"Vincent, what's on your mind?" she asks.

"Lots," he says, humorlessly.

Back in his room, he notices the mail his mother left on his dresser. He must have missed it the night before. It's a large envelope from the state. Inside are his credentials and paperwork authorizing him to engage in private investigation, along with a certificate. He'll hang that in his new office. He shows all of this to his mother, who smiles and gives her son a congratulatory kiss.

"I'm so proud," she says. "Now go share the good news with Papa Tony."

As Vincent is leaving his house, Mikey, Angelo, and Alphonse are sitting at a table in front of The Patio, drinking coffee and mulling over everything that Vincent has told them. Mikey lights his fourth cigarette of the day.

"Why don't you just cut out your lungs with a spoon for Christ's sake, Mikey," Angelo says. "I hate the smell of those Camels. No wonder Jessica won't let you smoke in our house."

Alphonse just bats the smoke from in front of his face with a disgusted look.

"Quit ragging on me. I've cut down," Mikey says, almost seriously.

"Okay, we do what Vincent says for now," Angelo says with finality, moving away from the smoke. "I don't want to wait, but I trust Vincent's judgment. He has never been wrong before, right?"

They all nod in agreement and continue to drink their coffees.

Instead of going through the front door, Vincent cuts down the alley to the loading dock. He doesn't want to see Rina just yet. Before he reaches the loading dock, he hears Shoes call out his name.

"You're going to see Marco this morning, right?"

"Yeah, and I'm close to solving that problem with the guy in Skokie."

"Yeah, okay, but we have another matter to discuss—Cassini in Melrose Park was pinched, along with some other of our guys, so we strongly need you to look into that."

Vincent suppresses a sigh.

"Sure thing. But can I get the details from you later? I have to see Papa Tony right now, okay?"

"Yeah, okay. Go see Tony and check in with me on Monday."

Vincent nods and walks to the loading area. Tony is speaking to a driver and Peter Dante.

"You have a moment, Papa?"

Tony nods and they go into his office to talk. But, before they go inside, Tony stops and turns around. He takes Vincent by the arm and walks him back out to the alley.

"Your mother told me about yesterday's visit," Tony says. "Rina was there, too. Those guys are part of Carmine's crew. He has twenty guys now. When they come, they will tell you what's up, I can just guess. Do not resist—just find out what they want. Now go see Marco."

"You know about this?"

"Yes, I know. I don't know what it's about, but you better get used to being called upon all the time. Get used to it—this is the life you've chosen."

Vincent nods. He decides to tell Tony about the certificate later. He walks back home and gets his car. He has time, so on his way to Marco, he drives past the jewelry store and sees that it's open. He even catches a glimpse of an older man talking to some customers. Down the block, he pulls a U-turn and drives past the store again. If the old guy is the same one that Mikey knocked out, then he must be okay.

On the way to Cicero, Vincent is deep in thought. All these things are happening at the same time, and he hasn't even had a chance to get his business started. He sighs. *Maybe this is just the way it's gonna be for a while.*

In Cicero, he parks his car down the street from the restaurant. He walks past the window and sees Marco and two members of his crew sitting inside. As he walks in, another one of Marco's crew takes him by the arm to another table. While he waits until Marco's meeting is over, a waitress asks him if he wants anything. He orders a Pepsi.

Marco's conversation is very animated. He looks angry, though Vincent cannot hear what they're saying. After about fifteen minutes, the two guys get up and walk out. Marco sits for another moment before looking over at Vincent. He nods to his guy, who gives Vincent the go ahead.

"You wanted to see me, sir?"

"Stop with the sir shit, Inspector Clouseau." Marco smiles at his joke. "Clouseau," he says again, savoring the name. "From now on, that's our code name for you: Clouseau."

Vincent frowns. Marco gets serious.

"Do not be offended. We don't want your real name to spread around. You never know who's listening, you get it?"

"Yes, I get it. And I'm here."

Marco looks a little peeved at Vincent's response, but continues.

"The other night a crew knocked down a jewelry store that we protect, and they took something that belongs to us. Nobody knows who did the score, so I need you to find out who and give me their names. That's your first major assignment, Clouseau."

Vincent shows no outward signs of distress. But inside he's reeling, and his head throbs. He sits in silence for a moment, which produces a confused look on Marco's face. Marco's sometime uncanny perception is right again. Vincent looks into Marco's eyes and quickly makes the decision.

"I already know who took down the score."

Marco abruptly leans back in his seat—surprised, but not quite astonished.

"Before I give up this information, can I be assured that the guys involved will not be harmed or harassed?"

"Are you fucking kidding me? Whoever they are, they're in trouble. They did not get the okay to pull a fucking score in Chicago."

"Then you need to blame me," offers Vincent. "You told me to stay away from Johnny V, who I was going to get permission from. You told me not to see him, so I made the decision for my guys to go ahead. Once the score was successful, I planned to respectfully bring this to everyone's attention, as I did with Johnny V on previous occasions. So, the fault is mine, not theirs. I helped them plan the score but did not otherwise participate. If you're going to be mad at someone, that someone is me, not my guys. I already gave you my allegiance, and so there it is."

Vincent then exhales.

His admission is delivered with so much conviction that it takes Marco a moment to absorb what he's just heard. He leans forward and looks into Vincent's eyes. The kid shows no signs of fear whatsoever.

"Okay," Marco says, slowly. "You can *never* do this again without permission. In the future, come to me first. Is that understood?"

"Yes."

"Okay, you do not have to give me the names of your crew, because this is now on you, and you alone. So where is the stuff your guys took? Did you look at the take?"

"Yes, a bunch of stones, gold, and other things. And a duct-taped package, which we did not open. Nothing is missing, I give you my word."

"This is gonna be a shitstorm. Okay, go and get the duct-taped package and bring it to me today. Then inventory the rest and give that inventory to me. You can take your time on the inventory, but the package needs to be in my hands today. You got that?"

"Yes, but can I ask for one more day? The package is stored somewhere distant. I can promise you will have it tomorrow. Is that okay?"

Marco grunts, not a good sign. "You got a pencil, Clouseau?"

Vincent shakes his head. Marco shouts out to the waitress, "Sheila, bring me a pencil and a piece of paper, will you please?" Then he turns to Vincent and adds, "What kind of a private eye are you? You have nothing to write on and no pencil? Wise up."

Vincent shrugs.

Sheila brings over a pencil and paper.

"Okay, you call this number tomorrow when you are ready to bring the package, and you will be told what to do. Say nothing more than 'I'm ready.' Not another word, and you will get the instructions. Next week I will send for you and you can bring me the inventory then. Got it?"

"Yes."

"You're gonna be a handful, I can already tell," Marco says, shaking his head slowly. "But we like you. Don't fuck up again because if you do, it will not end well, not well at all. Now get out of here."

Then two guys enter the restaurant. They nod at Marco, who frowns.

"Okay, Clouseau, go with these guys. You're gonna meet a close friend of mine."

"Vincent, give me your car keys," Peter Pazienza says. "You're gonna ride with Nicky here, and I'll follow in your car."

80

THE NEW REALITY

At the YMCA, Carmine gestures for Vincent to sit, and with a motion of his head towards the door signals his two guys to leave. They shut the door behind them.

"Vincent, do you know who I am?"

"I guess I do. You're Carmine Commaretta."

Carmine nods and sits back in his chair. He studies Vincent. "I hear that you are very close to Paulie Andriano. Is that true?"

"I don't mean to be disrespectful," Vincent replies, his head still throbbing, "but why am I here? What's Paulie to you"

Carmine's face shows disapproval. But then he stands up, walks over to Vincent, leans over his shoulder, and whispers into Vincent's ear.

"Paulie is my son."

Vincent looks up at him, his mouth agape. He swallows and shakes his head from side to side, absorbing what he's just heard.

"Only Tony and Rina know this, Vincent," Carmine continues. "And maybe your mom," he adds as an afterthought. "I want to keep it that way. Do you understand me?"

Vincent slowly shakes his head and says nothing.

"Yesterday, I met with Tony and he told me all about Paulie," Carmine says, "*every* thing." He moves toward the window, hands clasped behind his back, like an actor embarking on a grand soliloquy. But this is no play, and Carmine isn't acting.

"They told me that Paulie does not know I'm his father. And they kept the fact that he wanted to be an FBI agent from me. At first it made me angry—and I mean *really*, *fucking* angry—that they waited this long to share such news. I wanted to pound Tony's fucking head into the ground when he told me. But, after I had time to think about it, I reconsidered."

Carmine pauses, still staring out the window.

"I wanted to see Paulie as soon as I got out. But knowing that he is an FBI agent really fucking changes things. Just a few days ago, Rina sent word to me that she wants to see me. I want to do that right away as well, but my head is still swimming. I have the FBI up my ass, and now this? Fuck!"

Throughout Carmine's speech, Vincent sits still. His loyalty is to Paulie, no doubt, but he's puzzled. Carmine sounds so sincere.

"They tell me that you are like Paulie's brother, thick as thieves," Carmines says, turning to face Vincent. "If you *are* like his brother, and you two are that close, then I need you to help me through this, Vincent. Are you willing to do that?"

"I love Paulie," Vincent says. "He is my brother, and I will do anything I can to keep him from harm. But I have to tell you, I have no idea what he'll do if he learns the truth, I really don't. If this is a surprise to me, can you imagine the shock to him?"

At that, Carmine puts his head into his hands, shaking it from side to side. For Vincent, it's actually sad to see this gangster—this feared mob boss—so perplexed and confused.

"Why did you all keep this secret from Paulie in the first place?" Vincent asks.

Carmine tells Vincent everything.

81

THE TALE OF CARMINE COMMARETTA

"When I was twenty-five years old," Carmine begins, "Rina Andriano was eighteen. I was her first love. I was the first and only man that she made love to. And only once," Carmine notes wistfully.

"When the FBI started pursuing me, I didn't know she was pregnant. They were on my ass trying to prove that I'd murdered a government witness who was about to testify against the Outfit. They had no real evidence of this, but it didn't matter. Knowing I was the FBI's main target, the Outfit bosses decided that I should go on the run and avoid the investigation for as long as I could. I was preparing to leave when I found out Rina was with child. I argued with the bosses, I pleaded with them to let me stay. But the Outfit needed me out of sight and ordered me to leave, so I had no choice.

"The night before I left, Tony Andriano sat down with me and urged—no, *begged*—me not to contact Rina. Nor was I ever to acknowledge that Rina's baby was mine.

"I knew Tony well. I knew he was fond of me. I knew his deceased father and his family in Sicily, as they were from my father's home town.

"From nothing, my father became a boss here in Chicago. After he died here, my mother and sister went back to Sicily. But I stayed. I never wanted to leave. This was home. When Tony asked me to promise to never contact Rina or see my unborn child, it was the hardest decision I ever made. But I did so, not knowing what the future held for me. I escaped to Sicily, where I was protected and hidden.

"The Feds indicted me a few years later on circumstantial evidence, presented by an informant, a rat named Bobby Valedomo. But back in the homeland, I gained stature. I was in contact with the bosses in Chicago the whole time, and they kept me apprised on all matters. They told me that Valedomo further dishonored himself by revealing my whereabouts in Sicily.

"So, after years of pursuit, I was apprehended, and with the help of the Italian government, I was extradited and brought back here to Chicago. I did not fight the extradition. I thought that matters would be resolved in my favor, that the bosses had worked something out."

Carmine pauses briefly for effect.

"But I was wrong. I was locked up with no bail. But I stood my ground, never cooperating with the Feds. Finally, after three years in purgatory, I had my day in court. The only *witness*, Bobby "Fucking" Valedomo, testified. The lowlife lied his way through the testimony, but the government propped him up on all of his inconsistent statements.

"My lawyers argued that the evidence was purely circumstantial and relied on a single witness, and an unreliable one at that. After several days of hearings, the prosecutors agreed to reduce my charges to aggravated manslaughter. I suppose I should have been grateful that I wasn't convicted on first degree murder. Ultimately, I decided, along with the bosses, not to fight it any longer. I was sentenced to fifteen years.

"But the fact remained: I was innocent. I never killed that fucking government witness. But that didn't matter. I would not rat. Meanwhile, Valedomo was quickly placed in the Witness Protection Program to be secreted away. They needed him gone.

"In prison, my feelings toward Rina only grew stronger. I was at peace with the fact that my son was going to live a normal life. Maybe I thought he would know in his blood who he was. Throughout it all, I sincerely felt that after everything I went through, one day, I would be reunited with him and my Rina. Now I doubt any of that can happen."

Vincent gets up and paces. It's his turn to speak. He tells Paulie's father all about his son. All throughout Vincent's recitation, Carmine seems enraptured, listening intently.

"I think you should meet with Rina," Vincent says, as he finishes speaking. "You say you love her, so prove it. I will help you in any way I can—any way as long as it does not hurt Paulie. You have my word that I will definitely try."

Carmine gets up and embraces Vincent with a bearlike hug, holding him tight.

"I'm so happy," Carmine says, almost teary-eyed, "that Paulie has such a loyal friend, one who cares so much about him."

Then he pushes Vincent away and looks in his eyes.

"So, tell me about yourself," he says. "I hear you have brains."

"I've given my allegiance."

Carmine embraces Vincent one last time. He's reluctant to let him leave, but he does.

Vincent walks to his car, his head swimming more than it ever has before, and thinks, *What a fucking day!*

82

A MADE-UP MIND

Vincent goes home and immediately calls Angelo and tells him to call Mikey about the package. A few minutes later, Angelo calls back with the confirmation.

"Hey, Mikey is on his way with the package and will be back around five, like you asked. Do you want to meet then?"

"Yeah, I will explain everything to you. There is nothing to worry about as long as you do everything I say, so calm everybody down."

Vincent hangs up and then calls Valerie at work. He tells her that something has come up, so they won't be able to meet later. She's disappointed, but she takes it in stride—he disappoints her often.

His mother walks in as he hangs up. All she has to do is look at him to know something is up.

"Ma, can you call Rina and ask her to come over?"

"Why? What's going on?"

"Trust me, Ma, you'll know everything when she gets here, and I need you to be here with her. Please call her and ask her to come over now."

Teri frowns, but calls Rina at the store. Rina promises to come over soon. In the meantime, Teri goes into the kitchen, sits down with a cup of coffee, and waits with Vincent.

About twenty minutes later, Rina knocks on the door. Papa Tony stands behind her. Vincent is dismayed at the sight of the old man. *This is gonna be harder than I thought.*

"What is this all about?" Tony asks.

"Hey, Papa Tony, I wasn't expecting you, but now that you're here, it's probably just as well. Can you and Rina take a seat?"

Vincent paces while they take their places on the couch.

"Okay," Vincent begins, "From the top: I was just called in to see Carmine. He asked for my help because of my closeness to Paulie. Anyway, he told me everything."

At this, Rina's eyes open wide and Papa Tony releases a heavy sigh.

"Yeah, I was shocked, as you can imagine," says Vincent.

"You," he says to Tony and Rina, "never told me any of this and it would have been helpful if you did, but so be it—only *now* it's become a major problem. Carmine doesn't want anyone else to know that Paulie is his son, and more importantly, he does not want anyone to know that his son is an FBI agent. I don't know how we'll be able to keep it a secret, but no one in the Outfit can learn about this. It would be a huge problem for Carmine and maybe cause a war within the Outfit."

Tony looks crestfallen. Rina begins to weep. All this because they chose to deny Paulie his right to know who his father was. Now it is all coming back to haunt them.

"I've made up my mind to see Carmine," Rina says, looking directly at her father.

Tony starts to speak, but she interrupts.

"He needs to know everything. I want this to be resolved."

"Good," says Vincent, giving Rina a hug, "because he wants to see you. This is not going away, believe me, so we need to figure out how to protect Paulie."

"We'll find a way," Tony says.

Vincent nods. "I believe Carmine won't do anything that might hurt his son. I really believe that. If you could have seen him, you would believe that, too. It's a good thing that Paulie is in Los Angeles playing his FBI game out there."

The phone rings. Teri goes to answer it in the kitchen. "It's that girl," she says, calling to Vincent.

"Not now, Ma," Vincent replies.

"She says it's important!" Teri shoots back.

"Ma!" Vincent rejoins, walking into the kitchen.

"Take it in my room," she says firmly. "Do what I say."

Vincent looks at his mother, confused. He goes to her bedroom and closes the door. He picks up the phone.

"I got it, Ma!" He puts the phone to his ear and hears a click.

"Hello?"

"It's me, dummy. I overheard your mother say it's that girl, what the fuck?"

"Paulie?"

83

PERFECT TIMING

"Yeah, it's me," Paulie says wondering what all that was about.

"What's up, G-Man? Did you guys get that grocery guy? I hope he beats the rap and embarrasses all you boy scouts."

"Yeah, fuck you." Paulie replies, his voice subdued. "Listen. I got some news and it's problematic. Fuck, it's a nightmare, Vin."

"Just spit it out."

Vincent hears his friend draw a deep breath.

"Vincent," Paulie says, "You're not going to fucking believe this. I've been reassigned to the Chicago Organized Crime unit, effective in two weeks."

Vincent nearly drops the phone. The silence is deafening.

"Vin, you there? Did you hear me? I'm coming back to Chicago."

"I heard you," Vincent says, almost whispering.

"I know this is going to be a pain in the ass, but I have no say in the matter. I go where I'm told to, like it or not."

Vincent glances at the bedroom door.

"Paulie, let me get back to you in a little while. My mother has some company over. Can I call you later?"

"Yeah, as soon as you can, though, okay? I'm gonna need your help to sort this all out. And I need a place to stay. Obviously, I can't stay in the Neighborhood."

"Yeah, boy scout, we will have to pitch a tent for you somewhere in the forest," Vincent says. "You gonna be home in a couple of hours?"

"Yeah. Find me someplace nice, will ya?" jokes Paulie before hanging up.

Vincent puts the phone down, incredulous. *He's worried about a fucking apartment? If only he knew.* He looks at the door again and thinks about what he's facing on the other side. *Things just keep getting worse.*

He opens the door and goes back into the living room. Rina is still weepy-eyed while Tony acts like he's in a trance.

"Rina, go see Carmine," says Teri when Vincent joins them. "Maybe things won't be so bad." Then, to Vincent, she says, "Don't you think so, honey? I'm really happy that Carmine has put his trust in you."

"Yeah, terrific," says Vincent.

The phone rings again. Vincent answers. "Hey, what's up Angelo? Yeah, I'll meet you guys in a half hour at Ali Baba's."

Tony gets up, tries to say goodbye, but the words fail him. He waits for Rina at the door. Rina and Teri hug and Vincent joins them. Rina looks into his eyes, searching for reassurance.

"We'll work this out, Rina," Vincent says. "I promise I will find a way."

Rina pats his arm a couple of times and then walks out with Tony. After shutting the door, Vincent goes to his room for the piece of paper Marco gave to him and then kisses his mother goodbye. He'll drive over to the beef stand and pick up the guys.

84

DELIVERY

Vincent picks up the guys at Ali Baba's. After he drives some distance from the Neighborhood, he pulls over to the side of the road. He lays out everything related to the score.

Alphonse is the first to speak.

"Fuck me! So, what happens to the rest of the score? Do we need to give that up or what? I'm fucking against that. I need that money for my *mother*, Vincent."

"Calm down, Alphonse. If they wanted it back, they would have said so already. Now, give me the package, Ange."

Angelo hands over the duct-taped package.

"None of you have looked in here, right?

They all shake their heads no.

"That's one good thing, at least," a relieved Vincent says. "I don't give a fuck what's in here, but if they found out we'd looked inside, I don't know what would have happened, but nothing fucking good, I can tell you that. I'm just super happy that Marco gave us a pass."

"Okay, so now what?" Mikey asks.

"I'm going to bring this package in, and you guys need to do a complete inventory of what's left. And I mean *every*thing, because we do not know what they know, and there is no way we are going to fucking lie. Not now, not ever!"

"I wonder why they want an inventory," Angelo says, "and not tell us to just bring everything back."

"There may be something going on with the jeweler that we do not know about. I'm sure Marco said nothing to him about who pulled the score—at least I can't think of a reason why he would. Let's see what happens. I think we are going to come out okay."

Vincent drives them all back to the Neighborhood. When he's alone, he goes to a pay phone and calls the number on the piece of paper Marco handed him.

"I'm ready," is all he says. He waits for the response, writes down an address, and immediately drives to the location.

The address is a two flat in Berwyn, a town adjoining Cicero. He parks the car outside of the address. Two guys he has never met before come down from the house. They look at him, and one guy puts out his hand. Vincent hands over the package. The guy turns the package over in his hands, inspecting it. He nods okay to the other guy and they leave Vincent standing there. He goes back to his car and drives home.

85

WHERE YOU STAND

With the Paulie dilemma now most foremost on his mind, Vincent arrives home. His mother approaches him with a serious hug.

"This is a nightmare, honey."

"You don't know the half of it, Ma," Vincent sighs. He's about to say more but thinks better of it. He needs to confer with Paulie. *So much fucking deception.* He hates being in the middle and having all this knowledge swirling in his head. But Paulie is his brother, and he cannot fucking avoid it. He has to find a solution somehow. First, he needs to call Paulie, but not from home.

He gives Valerie a ring, tells her he'll be over shortly. When he arrives, Valerie welcomes Vincent with a warm embrace, but she senses his tension.

"I need to make a call, sweetheart. Can I have a little privacy, please?" he says. "I really need to have this conversation in absolute private."

Valerie sees the sincere look on Vincent's face, so she retreats to her bedroom, shuts the door, and turns on the TV.

"Paulie," he says, once he gets him on the phone. He's careful not to say too much. Valerie might be listening. "Is there any way you can fight this transfer?"

"I don't know, maybe. But why should I?"

"There is a lot going on here, and you're better off not being anywhere near it, Paulie. Trust me."

"Vincent, like it or not, I am an FBI agent and I follow their orders, not yours."

"Just try to fight the fucking transfer, Paulie!" Vincent screams into the receiver.

"Have you gone over to the dark side completely?" Paulie responds, incensed. "Do you know what you are asking of me? I'm surprised. And I'm honestly fucking disappointed, too. All the jokes aside, Vincent, I always thought you'd back me up. You know what? Now I know where you stand. Fuck you." He hangs up.

Vincent slams the receiver down.

Yeah Paulie, my brother, you think you know where I stand, but you have no fucking idea. Deep in shit is where I stand. I wish you could stand here with me. But you can't. You don't know what it's about to be—an FBI son against Outfit father. And it breaks my fucking heart.

Vincent leans back in the chair and moans so loudly that Valerie peeks out of the door. She sees him holding his head rocking back and forth.

"Vincent, what's wrong?"

Vincent stops rocking and looks up at Valerie.

"Something I have dreaded all my life just came to pass, and I don't have a fucking clue what to do about it."

She walks over and kneels before him. Her hands go to his fly.

"Not now," he says. "Jesus."

86

DESIRE

The next morning, Teri gets word to Carmine that Rina will come to see him, but she insists that he must protect her and not allow anyone to bother her.

Around noon, Rina dresses very modestly, though she does apply a little makeup. She decides to walk the entire way to the YMCA. Once there, she's met by Gloria Genco, who has been told that Rina is bringing a message from Tony. Gloria is a bright girl, and curious, but she's from the Neighborhood and will not question nor gossip.

She leads Rina to the room where Carmine is patiently waiting. They just look at each other, neither knowing what to do or say, almost transfixed. Timidly, Rina takes a seat and waits for Carmine to speak.

"Rina, you have not changed a bit. You are still the most beautiful woman in the world."

She smiles.

"You look pretty good yourself, Carm. How is your health?"

He approaches and takes a knee in front of her.

"I have thought about you every single day," Carmine says, full of emotion. "You have never, ever left my mind. I wish that I could change the past, but I have never stopped loving you, Rina, *never.*"

Rina begins to weep.

"What are we going to do about our son, Carmine? I don't want him hurt. We did our best—wrongly or rightly—to make sure that he would have a normal, happy life, and he does. Believe me!"

"I know," says Carmine.

"Despite what either of us may think about his choices," she adds. "Papa Tony and I—we never thought, never imagined," Rina continues, searching for words, "that he was truly set on becoming an FBI agent. At first, Papa and I laughed. We couldn't take it seriously. None of us could understand it. The only one who stood up for Paulie was Vincent. He hated the idea from the very beginning, even when they were little kids, but Vincent was also devoted to our boy."

Carmine puts his arm around her and holds her like they've never been apart. She welcomes his embrace, but then withdraws.

"I met Vincent," Carmine says after a moment. "He seems like a good kid, a smart kid, and he loves Paulie, and I love him for that. I asked for his help, Rina. Did I do the right thing?"

"Carmine," she nods vigorously, "they are like brothers in all manners. Vincent is agonizing over all of this. You can trust that he will do all he can. Thank god Paulie is in Los Angeles, so we have time to work this out."

They talk for over an hour before Rina gets up to leave. "I know you have a lot on your mind right now, Carmine, but please put Paulie first. Talk to Vincent."

They embrace and she leaves. Carmine stands there with a heavy heart, watching the empty doorway, wishing things could be resolved, that he could change the past. But how, he has no idea.

87

TWO HANDSHAKES

Vincent wakes the next morning sick to his stomach. He doesn't want to get up. After his conversation with Paulie, he feels nothing but grief. He needs to see Carmine as soon as possible. He learns from his mother that Rina will be there today at noon, and that he should wait until after she's left.

Angelo calls while he waits.

"We're all set, Vin. We've got the inventory down to a single stone. Alphonse has got a figure. We all just want to get this over with."

"Meet me at The Patio in an hour," Vincent tells him.

"Got it."

At The Patio, Alphonse hands Vincent the carefully documented list of items, along with the figure that he calculated. Vincent tells them he'll have an answer for them no later than tomorrow.

Vincent goes back home and tells his mother to get word to

Carmine that he'll see him later in the afternoon. Then he gets in his car and drives to Cicero. He doesn't know how Marco will react when he shows up without notice, but he has too many other things on his mind to worry about it. So, he just makes the decision to go.

At the restaurant, he's relieved to see Marco through the window at his usual table. He's sitting with Lonnie DeMeo. Vincent walks in and is stopped at the door by one of Marco's crew. Marco frowns but waves him over.

"Vincent, sit," he says. "You want something to eat?"

"No, thank you."

Marco shrugs his shoulders as if to say, "What?"

"May I speak freely?" Vincent says, looking at Lonnie.

"Of course."

"I have the full inventory and an estimate. I have a lot of other things on my plate, so I'd like to get this out of the way as quickly as possible—if I can," he hastens to add.

Marco starts to look annoyed, but he sees Vincent's expression.

"I know we've loaded you up, son," Marco admits. "Cassini is the most important thing to get resolved, so the Skokie thing can wait a little longer if that helps. Let's see what you got, kid."

Vincent places the inventory face down in front of Marco, who turns it over. A surprised look crosses his face.

"*All* of this?"

"Yes, stone by stone. Everything as you asked."

Marco looks over to Lonnie and shows him the inventory.

Lonnie whistles. "No wonder that bastard wanted to keep this from us," Lonnie says. "This cannot be his goods alone, Marco. No fucking way!"

Lonnie looks at Vincent. "Did your crew know what was there before they got there?"

Vincent thinks about his answer before he speaks. "No, not really. We got a tip."

"Who tipped you?" Marco asks.

"I really don't know," Vincent responds quickly. "God's honest truth."

Marco frowns and looks at Vincent, who shows no fear nor discomfort. Then Marco looks over to Lonnie, who shrugs and says, "Do we care? If it was not one of us, who cares, right?"

Marco nods slowly, still not certain.

"Okay," Marco says to Vincent, sternly. "We're gonna think about this and let you know what we will do."

"So where does this leave my guys?" Vincent responds.

Marco looks annoyed and turns to Lonnie.

"What these kids did is a big help to us," Lonnie offers.

Marco slowly nods in agreement.

"We'll take care of your guys, Vincent. They will get a solid end. The good thing is that we got back something that was ours, something very important to us. If some other crew had gotten hold of it, the old man would have gone fucking ape shit! You were respectful, you did not lie. So, your guys will get a solid end, I promise."

Vincent's face does not hide his displeasure with that answer. This time, Marco laughs and gently pats Vincent's cheek.

"They will be happy! I promise you. Did you guys come up with a figure?"

Vincent tells him. Marco nods his head in assent.

"Okay kid, we will reach out in a day or two."

Vincent gets up and shakes Marco's outstretched hand. He's surprised that Lonnie also offers his hand.

"Maybe you won't be such a handful after all, kid," Marco says, with a wry smile.

Vincent leaves them sitting there smiling. He himself has nothing to smile about, however, as gets in his car and goes back to the Neighborhood. Next stop: Carmine.

But actually, he goes home first to check in with his mother.

She sees the look on his face. "That bad?"

"Worse, Ma. I need to tell Carmine the news first—I want to see how he reacts. After that, I'll tell you, then Rina and Tony. I'll be back home the minute I'm through with Carmine."

Vincent gets into his car and stops at Baba's because he sees Mikey there. He calls him over.

"Everything is fine," Vincent says. "Maybe even very good. I'll know in a few days, so tell the guys to be patient. I've got to run now but I'll see you all later."

Nothing else to do now. Vincent pulls into the YMCA parking lot. He stands outside for a few moments, looking up at the building. He's in no hurry to go in.

88

THE ORIGINS OF DECEPTION

At the top of the stairs, Vincent is met by Gloria Genco. She seems nervous.

"You okay?" Vincent asks.

"Yeah, but the rest of the staff is getting really nosy. I think that I'll either get fired or moved to another location."

"Sorry for your troubles, but I think it will work out. I'll speak to Carmine."

"This way, please."

She leaves him in front of Carmine's door. Vincent walks in, and Carmine immediately embraces him.

"You know," Vincent says. "Gloria is afraid she may lose her job."

"That will never fucking happen." He says it with such force that it takes Vincent aback.

"I have worse news," Vincent says, sitting down. Carmine pulls up a chair, turns it around, and sits directly in front of Vincent, looking deep into his eyes.

"Tell me."

"There is no way easy way to say this," Vincent plunges in, "so, I'll just spit it out. Paulie has been reassigned. He's coming back to Chicago to work in the Organized Crime unit here. He just found out. I thought I would tell you first—before Rina or Tony."

A sad, wry, smile forms on Carmine's face. Then he gets up, walks to the window and looks out at the street. He rotates his neck and stretches out his arms, as if trying to allay his inner turmoil. There's no doubt that this news is horrific for him. But he pulls himself together and sits down next to Vincent again.

"Vincent, each of us make choices in life—you, me, Rina, Paulie—all of us," Carmine says, his voice calm, almost serene. "Paulie chose a life for himself," Carmine says, "and this is the life I chose. But I don't want him coming back and worrying. I don't want him to ever think he's made the wrong choice—no matter how much it displeases any of us. Talk to Paulie and reassure him that he should just do his job and not fucking worry about anything else."

He stops, but Vincent senses he's not finished.

"We will deal with this," Carmine continues, his voice rising. "And he will not be harmed, touched, or threatened. But we need to keep a close eye on him for his own protection. That may mean that you will have to deceive him from time to time, but that is better than allowing the worst to happen. Are you willing to do that?"

Vincent sighs. "I have lied to my brother only once, and that was because of all this," he says. "Now you are putting me in the position of deceiving him again." He drops his head in his hands and sighs again.

"There is no alternative," Carmine replies. "Things are moving at a fast pace now, so we need to keep strong. I don't think the G knows he's my son, or it would be evident, and they would try to use that against us—and him. Maybe they're using him as a pawn—I cannot tell—or maybe they will in the future. But I learned to play chess in the joint, and I even got good at it. This is a game of chess, Vincent, and we are white pieces, so we move first."

"Okay, but what about Tony, Rina, and my mom?"

"Tell them the truth. Tell them that I know and that we need to continue to keep it a secret that Paulie is my son. Tell them everything I told you. As for Rina, tell her she must stay away for now. We will find a way to communicate, either through you or Tony."

Carmine sees the look on Vincent's face.

"Don't worry, Vincent. I know that this troubles you, but we will win in the end, believe me. You just need to watch out for your brother and let me—*and me alone*—know if there is anything to worry about, okay?"

Vincent believes him, believes his sincerity if nothing else. He's becoming very fond of Carmine, and it seems to be mutual.

89

THE LITTLE GIRL UNDER THE UMBRELLA

After Vincent leaves, he thinks about what he'll say to Paulie. But he's not going to wait until tonight to call him. He goes home. The house is empty. His mother is at work. Vincent picks up the phone, sighs, and dials Paulie's number.

"Hello?"

"Hey, boy scout. So, what's the plan? When are you coming home?"

"Nothing's changed. Are you still going to give me shit?"

"No, I thought about it and it's best that you do as you're ordered," Vincent says. "You may be the fucking enemy, but you'll always be my brother. It'll all work out. Just do your job, so you can earn your merit badges. As for the Neighborhood, we're all big boys. We shave and everything. It's our life and it'll continue on with or without you digging into our business."

"Okay, Cenzo," Paulie replies. "I'm gonna call my mother now and tell her, and then I'll call Papa."

"Why don't you let me tell them? I promise to do it as gently as possible, without lying to them."

"Okay, Vin. You know, I never said this to anyone, but I'm feeling pretty conflicted."

Vincent wants to say, *Then don't do it*, but he holds back. Instead, he assures his friend. "Trust me, it will all work out. I will find a way. You just do your fucking job, G-Man."

"I still have to find a place to live, Vin. Can I count on you to help me?"

"Paulie how could you even think that I would not? I will always be there for you. I already set up a tent for you in the fucking woods, so you will not feel left out. I'll even build the campfire. I have a flame thrower."

They both laugh but know things will change for them. There's no denying that.

After he hangs up with Paulie, Vincent goes to his room, undresses, and lies down on his bed. He props a pillow up against the wall, sits back, and thinks about what he'll tell Rina and Tony. He'll do it tomorrow, come what may. For the first time in years, he thinks of the small picture his mother hung in his room when he was a little boy: A little girl stands under an umbrella in the pouring rain, and the caption underneath reads, "Come what may." Every night when he went to sleep, he saw it, and every morning when he awakened, it was there to greet him—irrevocably ingrained and cherished…forever.

He glances up at the wall over his dresser, and there it is. "Come what may," he whispers. And then, exhausted, Vincent Joseph Scalise falls into a deep sleep.

ABOUT THE AUTHOR

ANTHONY PELLICANO was born in Chicago, Illinois in 1944. His career as a detective began in his home town of Chicago in 1969. He relocated to Los Angeles in 1982, where his reputation attracted high-profile clients in the business and entertainment industries. Pellicano's achievements earned him numerous sobriquets including "Investigator to the Stars," "The Hollywood Sineater," and "The Hollywood Fixer." "Call the Pellican," was the advice given to many celebrities and others who had benefitted from his work and respected his dedication and discretion. The hit Showtime series *Ray Donovan* was based on his exploits.

In 2002, Pellicano was convicted by the Federal government for unlawful acts committed in the service of his numerous celebrity clients, and as a result he served a lengthy prison sentence, forgoing many offers from the government to divulge information about his clients.

Pellicano was released from prison in 2019, on his 75th birthday. He now devotes his time to writing, producing podcasts, and advising clients in negotiations across a broad range of business activities.